The Last Fair Deal Going Down

The
Last
Fair Deal
Going
Down

...

DAVID RHODES

milkweed
editions

The characters and events in this book are fictitious. Any similarity to real persons, living or dead, is coincidental and not intended by the author.

Published 2010 by Milkweed Editions
Printed in Canada by Friesens Corporation
Cover design by Betsy Donovan
Photographs by Luther Sledge
Translated from the Braille by the Author
Interior design by Wendy Holdman
The text of this book is set in Chaparral Pro.
10 11 12 13 14   5 4 3 2 1
First Paperback Edition

ISBN: 978-1-57131-076-7

Please turn to the back of this book for a list of the sustaining funders of Milkweed Editions.

The Library of Congress has cataloged the previous edition as follows:

Rhodes, David, 1946–
The last fair deal going down.

"An Atlantic Monthly Press book."
I. Title
PZ4.R4755Las[PS3568.H55]813'.5'472-1125
ISBN 0-316-74233-3

This book is printed on acid-free paper.

For Nellie

The Last Fair Deal Going Down

Chapter I

...

I

WAS BORN IN IOWA — ONE HUNDRED AND SIXTY MILES WEST of the Mississippi River, and by looking at a map the middle of the country. My brother John Charles, whom I never knew, was hanged that night somewhere in Missouri and my sister, Nellie, not blind then, named me Reuben; and I was the seventh child born to Luke Sledge. I am Reuben. My mother, Andrea, died three days later from what I have come to believe was an internal hemorrhage. This is my book, written as a chronicle of myself hidden within the grayness of a story of the people and the City itself.

This book will allow you to see me through my own eyes. To reach where I am now you must read it. I must write it in order to go on. That is to say I must write it in order to survive. I will assemble those things that have happened to me, to us, leaving nothing out — nothing important. I will set it down, set it free and have done with it.

This country, Iowa. I can tell you about it. It is so much of me that sometimes I am confused: sometimes I believe it is more important — that it is the land and the city, Des Moines, that speak through me, using me the way I imagine I am using them. The earth itself is wet black and you can shove a spade down into it up to the handle without hitting a rock. A tin can will grow here. The fields and lots are filled with cattle, hogs, chickens, turkeys, sheep, ducks, and horses. Pheasants, raccoons, grasshoppers, mink, and crickets run teeming through the cornfields. They cannot eat it all. Trees continue coming back after they have been cut down — starting as weeds, thousands of them, so many that the animals and the farmers cannot wipe them away — some clutch hold of the ground with their iron fingers and explode upwards. The farmers come out then with axes and chainsaws, chop them up, burn them or build more houses with them, and wait and watch for it to begin again. Then the trees, pushed to the side, rise up along the fence rows, inching back out into the fields with their huge root-tendons. The farmer, jamming with his plow into these, curses and drives on.

The farmer, I know about him. I have no memory so long that he is not in it. I have always known him — his demonic love of Iowa. I have watched the sky cloud with rainbows of dust from his incessant machines. He is so filled with the earth that he is not capable of inactivity. Plowing, disking, cultivating, harvesting, picking, planting, harrowing, building fences, cutting trees, moving boulders, digging ponds, damming creeks, selling, buying, digging up weeds, spraying, trapping raccoons, resenting that he must sleep, ashamed that he does, procreating in order that his sons can help work the fields and daughters can seal the fruit in jars with melted paraffin and tend the gardens — miniature farms. Like a madman he weathers through the terrible winters, pacing through his house that he never pictures himself living in, looking out at the snow. Sometimes he will walk through the cold and out into one of his many sheds, where he stands looking at his frozen tractors. Like a war.

But now the end is in sight. Just over there the war will end and the farmer will win; all that will be left will be the doing, not the action, the motion, not the movement. The ground will give up. The farmer's children will be sick, will look at the old barn and the grain bins, at the scythes and rusting buggy wheels, the electric dishwasher and the cider press. They will look and look till their eyes turn inward. They will be sick and the City will send out and lead them in. But that is not now.

Luke Sledge was not a farmer. He had never been one. He was old before he even came into Iowa — old in the kind of way that made farming impossible. Carrying his age around him like a yoke, he had driven into Iowa in a wagon with a horse possibly as old as himself, a Black and Tan, one hundred fifteen dollars in silver, and my mother. He had come from Wisconsin, near the Mississippi. He told me this.

Of his family I know practically nothing, only small, unrelated incidents that he has told me and I have remembered . . . dates that I have tried to fit together. All of my attempts to locate the members of his family have been futile. They have either died or the steamboats carried them away to the East. The name, Sledge, is unknown to the people where they supposedly were to have lived at least until the time of Father's departure, and the only mention I have found of this name is in an autobiographical novel written between 1921 and 1924 by Henry Jimson, called *And God Was There*, the story of his youth, marriage, and declining years in Wisconsin. In chapter nine, entitled "Hard Luck," and covering that period of his life between the years eighteen and twenty-two (which I have placed somewhere between 1891 and 1895), he writes: ". . . seeking the solemnity and peace of the forest, and wanting a chance to think out these troubling questions, I went for a walk into the woods. During this walk I met a Mr. Sledge, who had burst upon me from the heavy foliage, followed by a large work animal, a Percheron, I believe. This man told me that he and his family lived fifteen miles away in a cabin he had fashioned with his own hands. I could see from his ruddy complexion and attire that he was indeed a man of the forest, his ancestry probably going back to the very founders of the country. But there was also something . . ." (page 217). This last word or words had been ripped out, as had the rest of the page, by some fumbling file boy in the Library of Congress and I was unable even through the author's relatives to locate another copy of the book. That was Grandfather.

For two years (Father never told me this, but from my study of his 1916 diary written several years later — the way his words tended to form small, definite patterns of despair, a kind of thinking solipsism, the way his paragraphs are sprung always from the omnipresent "I," and by carefully ordering the dates and memories he has told me — I know) he was held prisoner by his brothers in a cabin hidden in the woods. He remained there until he agreed to leave Wisconsin. As compensation (or settlement) he was given one hundred fifteen dollars in silver, a wagon, a Clydesdale named Amos, and a Black and Tan.

That cabin was of dried mud and split logs, perhaps rails, with a cement floor. Every week one of his two brothers would carry him food, dried meat, roasted potatoes, carrots, apples, corn, and water. At first he would bellow at them, demanding to be set free. He would throw the food back out the chute: "Bastards." And each week they, one of them, would tell him that he must agree to leave, to go away from their home on the river and their trading post. And each week he would refuse. After awhile he no longer shouted at them and no longer shoved the sack of food back out of the cabin; but still he would not agree. Each week became longer. He spent a winter in the cabin: that must have broken his spirit . . . because of the snow and the quiet. Every rustle of wind would startle him. Perhaps he pleaded with them — promised that he would not try to burn down the trading post again; that is to say he would not drink, which always prompted him to try to burn down the trading post that his brothers had built after his father had died sitting on their new secondhand front porch watching the steamboats. Their mother had refused to come out of the house after that, although Luke always maintained that she was a full-blooded American Indian and up until that time had never slept inside but in a lean-to to the side of the house.

It was then, in the winter, when he met my mother. In that terrible silence he must have heard a crunching sound of frozen leaves and twigs. And somehow with his confused mind that had nothing to think about but itself he was able to know that it was not an ordinary sound . . . and later that it was a walking sound, not of a deer or a bear. From a crack in the east wall where he had dug out the dried mud between two logs, he saw her. Pressing his fear to the bottom of his stomach, he called out to her; and she, though afraid of his voice that the endless months had tortured and hammered into a shape not resembling a communicative form, had come up to the cabin.

Unable to name what he feared he wanted from her, his freedom, he stood whimpering inside the cabin, looking out at the two eyes that were looking in through the crack in the wall stained with the blood from beneath his fingernails. "Give me . . . Give me . . ." He could not say it because by then he had been there too long — so long that he had given up to his own isolation, and even madness.

She, being what she was, could not have let him out even had he asked, because of her fear of his brothers, who had become quite influential during the past several years. She was, however, able to give him the thing he most wanted and every Saturday afternoon shoved him in through the latched feeding chute a bottle of grain alcohol, which he kept hidden under the blankets of his bed and which she picked up every Thursday morning to refill in order that the cabin would not become cluttered with the containers.

The alcohol and, yes, the occasional presence of my mother gave Luke Sledge a stability that enabled him to last another full year, through another winter, before giving in and agreeing to leave. His determination might have been broken before that without her help and so she must have thought to herself many times that she was actually harming him despite her good intentions. She must have thought of this very carefully before reaching a decision — she did! And she continued to make that same kind of decision about him.

Father was let out of the cabin. He took the money, the wagon, the horse, and the dog, drove to the Andover farm, loaded Andrea's few possessions, set her beside him on the seat, took a ferry across the river, and drove into Iowa.

They went on slowly. The horse was old and Luke stopped along the streams and unharnessed him, letting him wander up and down the creek banks drinking water and chewing on moss and waterweeds. Luke would sit with his back against a wagon wheel while Andrea walked in the water and talked to him about bugs and trees and how her father had laughed so hard when he saw the goose chasing her little brother around the yard, Luke looked at the water; and Bull Frog, the Black and Tan, lay down.

The sun clawed into Father's milky face. His shoulders turned red and dead skin peeled off in huge patches; the reins wore blisters into his hands that filled with water and burst. In a small town not far from Clinton they bought an ax, a razor, flour, needles, thread, denim, ribbon, beef, and blankets. Father shaved the beard from his face and the sun began to dig into his neck. His muscles ached and they went slowly on, the dust barely rising above the ground under the horse, and Bull Frog running in large circles around them, making a pattern like a writing exercise with two lines drawn through it. At night they slept under the wagon.

"Is it going to rain?" she asked.

"I don't know yet," answered Luke, looking out from under the wagon. "I'll tell you, though, when I do. See, if the wind shifts to the north then it will rain."

"You'll tell me then, if it does. Even if I'm asleep. Wake me and tell me if it will rain."

"Why do you want to know?"

"Just because . . . just because I like to know if it's going to rain. So I can wait for it."

"Do you want to know how you can tell?"

"Yes."

"Well, you can see that there must be a lot of clouds over there," and he pointed, "because you can't see any stars. You can tell it's colder too because . . ." But Andrea was asleep. Luke lay still until her body slowed down and her breathing was even. He carefully crawled out from under the covers, circled the wagon several times, located Amos, gave Bull Frog a piece of beef, and returned to under the wagon where he lay listening to Andrea breathing and watching for signs of rain.

They drove on toward Des Moines. Luke Sledge saw a railroad track and he saw a train full of people moving along it. He followed the track and found where it stopped to let people on or off. Andrea and Luke sat on the wagon seat and watched as people came out of the little wooden and brick building called Des Moines Depot carrying leather bags and paper sacks and magazines — the steam wafting up and across the wooden platform, around yapping dogs. Father looked at the engineers as they paraded along beside the trains inspecting the workers unloading the baggage and freight, the signal men and switch operators. Bull Frog lay down in the shade of the horse and went to sleep. Andrea yawned and rested her head against Luke. He watched the people coming off the trains, stretching their legs, surveying the layout of the station against the sky. Mothers careened down the platform pursuing their children gone ecstatic over the motion and noise of the trains. Pigeons clattered up out of their way and settled on the roof. An old man with whiskers and a seaman's knit hat walked out of the depot with a large push broom and began sweeping the cigar and cigarette butts off onto the crushed rock below. The signal men waved and the switch operators pulled at the long iron levers. A wino, though Father wouldn't have called him that, walked down the platform and settled onto a bench, where he kept a weary lookout for lucrative situations. The train schedule was nailed onto the outside wall under the overhanging roof; eight trains in and eight trains out every day, three passenger and five freight, two to the north, two to the south, two to the east, and two to the west. Once a week the Rock Island Express came through headed toward Chicago, but it did not stop. Father had seen three trains. The telegraph room was in the back of the station. John Tickie was the operator.

"Mr. Tickie," Father said, reading the sign on the man's desk through the wire mesh window.

"Schedule's posted on the front of the station. Buy your ticket on the train. The 8:27 will be fourteen minutes late this evening," said Tickie, not bothering to turn around.

"I don't want a ticket," said Father. "I'm looking for a job." Tickie turned around, lifted his spectacles to his forehead and squinted through the wire.

"Work," Tickie said with no emphasis at all, like someone might say "blanket" or "street clothes." Father nodded his head slightly, capturing the same enthusiasm.

"Come inside," offered Tickie, opening the door that also held the wire mesh window. "Care for a cup of coffee?"

"No thanks," said Father and stared down easily into Tickie's eyes.

"You want a job on the railroad. What do you know about railroads? You aren't an engineer, are you; we need one of those. No, you don't look like an engineer." He poured himself a cup of coffee from a metal thermos.

"No. I don't want a job *on* the railroad. I want a job here. I want to look over this station — watch."

"Watch. Well, to be honest with you, there's nothing like that here. I'm in charge of this depot and can do what I want, of course." He took a drink of coffee. "But I was thinking about bringing someone in. The company doesn't like to have to make all that change on the trains. To tell you the truth, though, I already had someone in mind. . . . Where you from?"

"Wisconsin."

"Staying here long?"

"I think so."

"No, I think I've got someone else in mind."

"Test me."

"Test you?"

"Before you hire a man to chop wood you watch how he manages an ax. Before you hire a man to fix your wagon you watch how he handles his tools, and if I were a coal stoker you'd hand me a shovel. But I want to be the caretaker of this 'depot' so test what I can see."

He talked slowly, knowing his words were still rough.

John Tickie stood up. "I've been working here for five years and I've been able to do a lot of watching in five years. We'll go outside for exactly one-half hour, sit on the same bench and look around the station yard. If you can tell me one thing, *one thing*, about this depot or the trains coming in here that I don't already know, you can have the job."

John Tickie carefully placed a straw hat on his head, rolled up the sleeves of his faded blue shirt around his stubby forearms, and marched out the telegraph door in front of Father. They chose the bench nearest the center of the platform and Father, in the position of challenger, nodded for Tickie to choose where he wished to sit on the bench. He, Tickie, looked at his pocketwatch and sat down directly on the middle of the bench. Father sat to his right, folded his arms, and they began. At exactly 8:20 Tickie put his watch back into his pocket and they went inside the depot, closing the door behind them. Tickie brought out a bottle of whiskey and two glasses, set them down on a round wooden table, and sat down. Father sat opposite him and drank a mouthful.

"Go ahead," said Tickie, "ask a question."

"What color is the cat?"

"Gray and white, with a spot of brown near the tail."

"How does it get inside the depot?"

"Through the hole in the wall where there used to be a vent pipe."

"Male or female?"

"Female."

"Which way does the platform slope?"

"West."

"How many cables hold up the telegraph pole?"

"Three."

"Where is the rain coming from tonight?"

"There won't be any."

"What creaks on the side of the station when the wind shifts from south to west?"

"The drain pipe."

"Who does the Black and Tan belong to?"

"You."

"What is peculiar about the sweeper?"

"He wears three rings on his left hand."

"Is the engineer, the one with the red badge, right-handed?"

"No."

"Why not?"

"Only four fingers on his right hand." They were drinking and Father was coming into his own.

"What should the woman in the green dress do?"

"Stay in bed a couple of days to get rid of her cold."

"Who did the kid with the short hair belong to?"

"Mrs. Johnson."

"What did she have on?"

"Pink and white checked dress, black shoes, and a wrist watch."

"What did the boy keep saying?"

"The boy was a girl and 'she' kept yelling, 'Stop wheel.'"

"What troubled the man with the brown leather suitcase?"

"Someone had taken his seat."

"Who?"

"A young blond man."

"Did he get it back?"

"No."

"Why not?"

"He was ashamed to ask for it."

"What did he finally do?"

"Went back to the next car."

"Who left the candy wrapper?"

"A woman with a blue hat on."

"Why did the man in new overalls leave hurriedly?"

"Because he was irritated that whoever he was waiting for didn't come."

"Why should he be careful in driving home?"

"Because his left rear wheel is falling off."

"What disturbed the woman with the green hat?"

"That she wasn't as young as the woman with the leather handbag."

"Who did the old man hope to get money from?"

"The young man who met the woman with the leather handbag."

"Why did he think he could get it?"

"Because he was nervous."

"Why?"

"You tell me."

"Because she was married to someone else, who isn't too far away."

"You've won. I missed one."

Father took his last drink of whiskey. "Four," he said. "The cat is a male, the man with the leather suitcase finally came and got his seat back, and it will rain tonight — coming from the east."

"That's not about the railroad," said Tickie.

"It will be," said Father.

"We start here at nine o'clock . . . six days a week. Forty dollars a month. If you and your wife will check with a Mr. Nelson he may be able to fix you up with a house."

"Good afternoon," said Father, rising.

"Good afternoon," returned Tickie and rolled down his sleeves. "Sledge," he called before Father had reached the door, "because you're not from around here I think I better tell you something about Des Moines . . . something that most people here take for granted . . . something they've lived with so long that they don't notice and assume everyone else knows . . . something that after you learn may change your mind about staying." And it should have.

Father turned around and stood waiting for him to continue: the reality of the cabin, he feared, had marked his face, and Tickie, able to see the marks, was about to tell him something — something about the world — that because of his isolation he could not understand. But he did, and with a profound indifference that he managed to pass on to me (though it was not his intent), and that has destroyed the rest of our family, even him.

"There is a City here," said Tickie. "Not a city like Des Moines itself, but an inner City of Des Moines . . . or a lower City. It is at the bottom of this gigantic hole in the ground. At the base — the beginning of the City — is a ghastly, stone, concrete wall surrounding the City, looming some twenty-five feet in the air. It encircles the City and is believed to be over two miles in diameter. Higher than this, along the wall, are seven monuments — giant monuments of awful creatures. These monuments, if you approach them from the outside, will open up and move back into the wall, letting you walk inside. Then they close. No one has ever gotten out of the City . . . the monuments will not reopen. No one knows what the inside looks like . . . except those who have gone in, I suppose, if they can see: the wet heavy air — fog — has over the years collected in the hole and the sun does not go more than a hundred feet into it. The children are afraid of this place. There are many stories about it. Occasionally teachers from the college talk about it, but to the rest of us it is neither evil nor godly. We ignore it."

"Is that all?" asked Father.

"Yes," Tickie answered.

Mr. Nelson took Father to the house. He (Nelson) wore a green, ill-fitting suit that looked to Father as though it might be slick to the touch, as though even water might slide off it. The house was not in good condition and Nelson knew that it would be difficult to sell — that it had to be sold.

Father was not listening. He looked at the house. It was built from oak trees, cut and gouged out by hand, nailed together as though *the square* was the only construction pattern and design that the builders knew; worn by the rain and sun, unpainted, fastened together with baling wire and pieces of corrugated steel tacked over the joints and corners that had been eaten away by insects and stagnant rainwater. A windmill to the side of the house pumped water into a wooden storage tank, and due to the weight of the water on itself a bathroom upstairs and a sink in the kitchen worked (as long as the water level was higher than the faucets, of course). The furnace burned coal. Electricity, none — though after World War II Father bought a generator that ran on diesel fuel from an orange tank.

Mr. Nelson told Father where to go to obtain a loan to finance the purchase of the house. Father did this and they, Nelson, Father, and a man at the bank, signed papers and handed them back and forth. Afterwards, they shook hands and Nelson told Father what a good house he had bought. Father asked the banker if the house was his now and the banker said that it was unless he stopped sending money in — in which case it would be the bank's. Mr. Nelson shook Father's hand again and Father told him to never come to his house, to never even walk by it if he could help it. Nelson was offended. The banker hurried back into a sectioned-off office, smiling.

Luke and Andrea drove home then. She was pregnant but did not know it. Neither did he. They were anxious to explore their new home. They arrived. Andrea went inside and said that the house had a "good feel." Luke found some old tools in the basement and felt — though he knew it wasn't so — that he had swindled Nelson. He looked at the furnace and opened all the doors he could find, looking in and poking around with the wooden handled screwdriver. His wife called him and he went upstairs. Unfamiliar with the house and the way sound moved through its rooms, he wandered for a short time before he found her on the back porch. He came out and stood beside her; she pointed down away from them. "What's that?" she asked. When he looked (and it was not right away because the porch seemed to Luke a likely place for someone to leave tools behind) he saw a large — very large — cavity, perhaps two-and-a-half miles across, that began in less space than forty feet from the porch steps where the grass ended and the dark sides of the hole began. (I can remember thinking when I was small that a volcano had once lived there and then had sunk down into the ground, leaving the ground around it level.) They walked to the edge and looked down. It was not so steep as it had looked from the porch — not so steep that someone couldn't walk down; but they were unable to see farther into it than twenty-five feet because of the heavy fog. Luke looked out across the pit. A faint putrid smell seemed to be down there. The same road that passed by the front of his house wound in a circle around the hole. Other houses stood beside the road. The buildings of Des Moines spread out in all directions from them; it was a clear, hot day and he could see all the way around the cavity. At seven places streets, macadam and brick, fled off down into the hole and disappeared in the fog.

"That's the City," said Luke.

"The City?"

"There's a City down there," he said, and up from the fog came a long sound like a giant boulder dropping several feet into a grass-lined pocket of earth.

"What's that?" asked Andrea.

"One of the monuments closing," he said and went back inside to look for more tools.

Chapter II

...

JOHN CHARLES WAS THE OLDEST. THE PATH THE REST OF US walked to the Independent Public School #4 he had made. The letters SLEDGE had been carved into the wooden desk tops and filled with ink before any of the rest of us had come. What we did as children John C. had done first; not differently, but first. And Mrs. Candlewine had seen us all. She had sat behind her desk and called the name *John C. Sledge* from a sheet of paper, had looked out across the room and had seen a hand rise, had looked into a pair of dark brown eyes half closed from want of sleep and thought to herself, "Bring the children unto me." Then she more straightened her wirelike body, tucked a loose fold of dress up under her thigh, caught a glimpse of a strand of once blond, virgin hair, and read *Richard L. Stephens.* She had seen all of us — John Charles, Mary, Nellie, Walter, Will, Paul, and myself — walk through the first-grade door and raise our hands after our names had been read. She had walked beside us while we stood in line along the cinder-block hall waiting to be let outside, punished us for throwing erasers, and even once had gone in front of the town council screaming, "The children . . . The children . . . What you do to the children," for us.

Mrs. Candlewine drove to our house one afternoon after school, parked her car next to the windmill (which is not important in itself), and walked around to the back porch, conscious that by doing so she was admitting, assuming, a familiarity with our family. John Charles, then eight, answered the door and pushed it aside for her to enter.

"Hello, John," she said. "Is your mother or father at home?"

"No," he answered, still holding the door, waiting for her to come in.

"Do they know you are playing with your father's pocket-knife?"

"It's mine," he answered.

"Do you know when they will be back?"

"Dad's at work and he'll be home in a couple hours."

"Where is your mother?"

"She'll be back, I think, in a little while."

"Where's your sister, John? Is she sick?"

"I don't know." John Charles had slowly closed the screen door, reasonably content that Mrs. Candlewine had no intention of coming inside.

"How is school going for you?"

"O.K."

Andrea Sledge came walking up onto the backyard out of the fog. She was five-and-a-half months pregnant. "Here's Mom," said John C. Mrs. Candlewine turned to face her and began talking before she had completed the steps up the porch.

"Hello, Mrs. Sledge. I'm Mrs. Candlewine, Mary's teacher at school, and Mary hasn't been to school this last week, so I thought I'd come out and see if there was any trouble and if I could help in any way. I've brought some work for her to do here at home so she won't be so far behind when she comes back. She's such a lovely girl, Mrs. Sledge."

Andrea sat down on the upper step and put her hands to her head as though to rub something away. "She's gone . . . Mary's gone."

"Gone?" asked Mrs. Candlewine, wondering not so much about Andrea's choice of word but of what the word had to do with Mary. John Charles had gone back into some farther room in the house.

"Yes," Mother answered, staring out away from the house. "Into the City. The City has taken my baby." And she began to cry. Mrs. Candlewine rested a minute against the side of the house and sat down beside Andrea. She did not know what to say but felt guilty just watching, the way it is funny to see someone fall down on the ice and break a leg — but not funny when they are watching you laughing.

"Mrs. Sledge, you're mistaken. She's probably just wandered away — to a friend's house or something. You know how children are."

"Not Mary, she'd never do that," Andrea said, still crying. "She was such a good baby . . . I wish I had never come here. I wish I had never left Wisconsin."

"Now, Mrs. Sledge, be strong. When was the last time you saw Mary?"

"Sunday afternoon. She was out here in the yard. I wasn't paying too close attention to her — but watching her just the same. She was playing some kind of game, chasing those little yellow butterflies, trying to get near enough to blow on them. . . . I hate this wretched place." When she had said this last thing she was not crying.

"Now where might she have gone, Mrs. Sledge? To a friend's house maybe. Have you checked with her playmates?"

"I've been a good mother, Mrs. Candlewine."

"I know, Mrs. Sledge, but . . ."

"No you don't. You don't think that at all. You think it's my fault that my baby's gone into the City — that I didn't whip her, or make her help with the washing, or do her Sunday School lessons. But she was always good . . . never unhappy." Her eyes were dry now and she pointed down into the fog. "It's That . . . that."

Mrs. Candlewine went inside the house and told John Charles to stay with his mother while she went away, and to stop playing with his pocketknife. She drove to the police station, the highway patrol, the homes of the other children in Mary's class, to the amusement park, and to the zoo. Late in the evening she returned to the Sledges', where she found Luke and Andrea sitting on the back porch. The afterdark had come.

"Mrs. Candlewine, this is my husband," said Andrea.

"Hello," said Mrs. Candlewine.

"Mrs. Candlewine was Mary's teacher," Andrea told her husband, who acknowledged the fact by lowering his eyes.

"I've checked with Mary's friends and none of them have seen her. I'm sure that if we have patience and pray, she will turn up. Children have been known to wander off into the woods and be gone for weeks."

"Mary's in the City, Mrs. Candlewine. Somehow she walked down there and a monument opened and she went in. It is an insult to tell ourselves lies."

"No," said Mrs. Candlewine, her whole body quivering but her voice steady and flat. "She is not in the City. She is not. God protects the innocent. He would never let such a thing happen. Were I to believe that I'd walk in there myself and find her."

"No you wouldn't, Mrs. Candlewine — just like you won't now. Just like I won't."

"She's not in the City," said Luke, being careful to talk to neither woman in particular. "Even she wasn't that stupid. But she'll never come back either — someone has killed her — perhaps by accident, in an automobile, was afraid and sank her in the river . . . or perhaps intentionally; there are such people."

"I'm sorry for you," said Mrs. Candlewine, "the way you think," and went home and waited. She waited for a week, then two, and then three. Once she stopped John Charles in the hall and asked if his sister had returned home yet. "No," he answered and she never asked again. She waited, and continued to wait. She read the names *Nellie Sledge, Walter Sledge,* waiting —*Will Sledge, Paul Sledge.* Then she quit waiting and told me once while I fumbled with sticks of colored paraffin to fill up the hollow spaces between the outline of distant characters in my coloring book: "I knew your sister, Mary, before she got on the train that took her away." I wanted Mrs. Candlewine to help me with the crayons because the colors kept running over the lines and leaving blotches inside the hollow spaces but she said I was doing fine and walked on down the row of desks to watch another colorer, of whose style I was envious.

When John Charles was twenty he was in love with a girl whose name I did not know for a long time because Nellie and Walt and Father had forgotten it. The idea of being in love excited him. That would have been in 1933 when the railroad was only running one train a week through to Chicago and that one didn't stop. The farmers had weathered the depression well and we had made out by what John C. and Father could steal and what was given to us out of conscience. He was in love with a girl who lived on the western side of Des Moines. They went to Missouri because he had been indirectly offered a job with a stone quarry by Tommy Robinson, a man from St. Louis he had met playing horseshoes. She was excited and a little afraid because John C. had told her St. Louis was a tough town.

He wrote home once, two years later, and Nellie had kept the letter and showed it to me. The paper had turned yellow and was dissolving the ink: "Doing fine. Read in the paper the other day that the railroad is starting up again. Life is hard out here and you have to be tough to stay alive, but I'm doing fine. Hope to be home for a visit soon." On December 22, 1939, Father met him at the station. Two railroad hands lifted the box out of the freight car and set it on the platform. Tickie unfastened the letter held by three achromatic thumbtacks from the lid and gave it to Father.

L. Sledge, Mang.
Des Moines Depot
Des Moines, Iowa

Dear Sir:
     We regret to inform you that on November 19, 1939, John Charles Sledge was found guilty of Section 31 of

Chapter 18 of the Missouri Penal Code, Judge Garnold
presiding. Executed at 5:10 A.M., December 21, 1939,
Missouri State Penitentiary and pronounced dead by
State Coronor Bill Mallory.
   (Casket and shipping charges paid by the State of
Missouri)

   Elliot Winfield
   Public Relations Dir.
   St. Louis, Missouri.

Father and Tickie carried John Charles inside the depot and
Father took him home in the pickup after work. He showed
Andrea the letter and she read it. Nellie cried while she held me
against her in the rocking chair. From her bed Mother looked
at Luke and then he went into the living room. Walt and Will
were not at home yet and Paul played his guitar until Father
told him that if he wanted to play it to go out on the porch.
Then Paul began to cry.
   Many years later Nellie told me all she could remember
about John Charles; the rest I have learned from the people
who knew and remembered him from Des Moines and from St.
Louis, back issues of the *St. Louis Daily,* and finally what I was
led to believe must have happened — those magicless, empty
(re)constructions of real people, real things, and real movement — thin lines that can never even hope to approximate
the color they are to represent.
   John Charles and Hermie Huber drove to Missouri in a blue
Plymouth. It took John C. two months to steal enough gasoline
for the trip, which he stored in five-gallon milk cans and put in
the trunk. Hermie had fourteen dollars and John had six. Just
into Missouri they broke down because of the fan blade cutting
into the radiator. John C. purchased the parts from a junkyard
and repaired the car. This made them nervous because they
hadn't counted on it and also because it was bad.

In St. Louis John Charles located Tommy Robinson, who oddly enough was there and helped him obtain a job at the quarry. This was a sign, a good omen. John C. and Hermie rented a trailer house in Eastown Court. Things had worked out. John C. sold the Plymouth to a "fish" living next to him. They bought a new car. They had done the things that they had planned in Des Moines to do — reached the goal they had imagined for themselves in the several months before and sat now, in their imagined blue trailer house, looking at each other and trying to be gentle. Perhaps that was it, limited expectations, that caused what later happened; but things are never that simple, and you must see for yourself.

John Charles worked for a little under three years as a dynamiter at the Rocky Edge Quarry. There was satisfaction in this. He learned quickly and an offhand manner soon characterized his work, which some of the men there called "dangerous." But the beginning novelty of his work drained away and he found himself left with the remains of a noisy boredom — his job. The safety regulations were obscure and as he had long ago discovered, no one really even cared about those. No, he was too much to be confined in such a way. He had expected more than this. After thirty months he quit his job at the quarry and became a bartender at the D & D Bar.

The new position was better — more than he could have hoped it to be. Missouri was a dry state then and only beer could be purchased and consumed in a public building. John Charles was inspired. He worked hard. He was a good bartender and the customers enjoyed his manner and conversation. He bought half interest in the bar and renamed it Dirty John's. Twice a month he drove over the state line into Iowa and bought thirty quarts of good bourbon and drove back to St. Louis. He never kept more than four or five bottles behind the counter and in the case of a raid would throw them out the window he kept open in the back, overlooking a steep hill which was used as a garbage dump by the people in the neighborhood.

Mr. Meadon, characteristically a regular, said that John Charles did a good business and was looked up to by the young boys in the area. And the only complaint he mentioned was with John C.'s "lack of discretion: There was nothing he liked better than to pull out a bottle of booze and set it on the counter in front of a new customer, and while his eyes bulged out of his head say, 'What can I do for you?' like it was an everyday thing to see booze for sale in public. It made the rest of us uneasy."

John Charles carried a small nickel-plated revolver in a special pocket he had fashioned for himself from a description in one of his paperbacks about the old West — *Two Gun Lust* (1929, J. Fellows) — where Lance turns to face the sheriff after emptying both his Peacemakers into the sheriff's deputies, who clutter the saloon floor below and around him, and silently takes a derringer from the pocket that kept it pressed against the small of his back, saying, "Sheriff, there ain't no man alive can arrest me." The sheriff answers, "You're looking at him, Lance. Your days are through." Lance fires the derringer from his hip and the sheriff falls dead across the doorway. "Sucker," mumbles Lance to himself as he steps over the sheriff's body and walks outside (page 123).*

John Charles was an exciting bartender because he was able to transpose these episodes into real events acted out by many of his friends in Texas and Wyoming. His voice was dynamic and during the climax of a story he would whip out his pistol (learned from many hours of practicing in front of the bedroom mirror at home, with the help of Hermie, who sat on the bed and commented on the dramatic impact of each draw), and from a semicrouching position deliver the end of the tale and replace the revolver in its secret pocket. In a special sling

---

*This section was likely not original; in fact, the use of secret holsters has been common in novels since 1847, when Sir Lucas Van Wheelen used one in his famous trilogy *Young, Wild,* and *Easy.*

around his arm he kept what he called a "stiletto," a knife he had paid over fifteen dollars for at a pawnshop owned by a man considering himself to be a shrewd judge of character, and when you pushed the button on its side a six-inch blade was ejected straight out the front end. He would take the knife out while no one was watching (he was never quite as good with his knife drawing) and shove it into the ribs of his victim, saying, "You're dead, pal," then pull the knife out in front of him and push the button, sending the blade zinging out into the open air.

For Hermie, St. Louis was not a particularly rough town. She grew tired of living in a trailer and so they moved into a large house closer to the tavern. John C. was sure it had been an old "hothouse." Hermie also grew tired of having nothing more to order than some fifteen pieces of furniture and three meals a day, two or three of which she ate by herself; so instead of simply waiting for her child to be born she sectioned off the upstairs rooms and took in boarders.

John Charles was quick to notice the change in his house and was even pleased. He returned home earlier in the evenings and sat in his living room with his boarders and told stories of what had happened at Dirty John's that night — the fights, the gambling, the raids, and the women. Many times he would follow an interested boarder to his room after the rest had gone to bed and stay up the entire night telling stories and drinking whiskey . . . or until Hermie came, demanding that he come to bed. But John Charles was more than this.

Alice Van Hooser had lived in St. Louis ten years and was a secretary for Eponic Business Forms, Inc. She was thirty-five, slightly heavy, with natural brown hair, a remarkable Indiana accent, and an image of herself that had become ever since high school increasingly fantastic. Together with a friend of hers of roughly the same potential, she decided to tempt the wheel of fortune and chance a beer at a bar they had heard about called Dirty John's.

The bar was very dark when they entered and everyone had stopped talking. But as soon as they had shut the door behind them the talking resumed and several lights were turned on. They shuffled toward the bar, casually. John C. waited for them. Looking at a bottle of bourbon sitting on the bar before her, Alice ordered a beer. John Charles filled a glass from a wooden keg and sat it before her. "Say, Baby," he whispered, "how about ditching that friend of yours and us getting together a little later on?" Alice's girl friend, taking the hint, not from the words, which she didn't hear, but from the tone that characterized the mumbling, immediately announced her departure, stating that she could be reached at any hour to provide a ride home. Alice took her beer to a table and sat down with it. John Charles closed the bar at ten P.M. and he and Alice listened to country Western music from the jukebox while John C. told of his experiences with the law in Texas and Arizona, where he had been a deputy sheriff, and showed her newspaper clippings of famous contemporary crimes committed by old friends.

Alice Van Hooser was a woman who had lived thirty-five reasonable years. She lived with her mother. Any advancement from this station was in some way going to be a concession, something given up momentarily before returning to normal. She gave in to being known around Dirty John's as "Lil," spending evenings in a motel, wearing black stockings, and sitting quietly at a back table watching John Charles behind the bar and knowing from his face that his wife would be coming in that night. To all this she gave in, but she was more than these things. She kept some to herself.

Hermie had a baby girl while John Charles took Lil with him on a "run" into Iowa to pick up another load of bourbon. She lay in the hospital as quietly as an unexploded charge of dynamite: that is, she might have thought many things but mostly she was a wife who had heard so many plans and schemes and adventures and happenings and stories and tales from her husband and about him that she failed to care whether they corresponded to things that actually had happened or if they had happened, when. Furthermore, because she never knew what was true and what wasn't concerning the actions of her husband, she either decided that everything was unreal or that at least everything was irrelevant to her situation, which included John Charles, the man. She thought this was the way she felt. Yet she could not account for the anxiety. What she did not know was that John Charles, the man, was very much connected with those everythings that were unreal and irrelevant.

John Charles told Hermie about numerous fights he had taken part in at Dirty John's. He recounted them in a very matter-of-fact manner though each presentation lasted over a quarter of an hour.* Once, listening, struggling with the baby, she had said that she didn't care. This ended the story. John C. had bolted from the room, thinking that not caring was the same as not believing, which was more important.

One night while Alice Van Hooser waited at her table for Mrs. Sledge to leave, two heavyset insurance salesmen walked into the bar. They had been drinking earlier in the evening and shouted at John C. to bring drinks. John C. brought them drinks and went back to sit next to his wife at the counter. Hermie, who didn't like being at the bar at all, offered a statement establishing a relationship between these two men and the quality of the overall atmosphere of Dirty John's. John Charles looked at the men for several minutes and got up from his stool to give them another drink. He secured himself

---

*I am unable to discover if these stories were in fact true at the time in which John C. talked about them. That he was involved in several fights in his own bar has been substantiated by several people and by clippings from the *St. Louis Daily*; but whether these fights occurred before he told Hermie about them is unresolved. I am inclined to doubt it but not without reservation. With further information this footnote may later be deleted.

a standing position between the two men. They were having difficulty standing up during those intervals when a high degree of gesticulation was necessary to the conversation. One of these physical explanations glanced off the shoulder of John Charles and he pivoted on his left foot and hit the man square on the jaw with his right hand, which mysteriously concealed a roll of nickels from the cash register. Before the other man could turn around John C. was in a low, semicrouching position with the stiletto blade extending from his left hand. "Come on, big man," he shouted, "let's see how tough you really are." The man busted the top of a beer glass off on the counter and made a slow lunge at John Charles who easily stepped aside, cutting his arm as he passed. The man he had originally hit was picking himself off the floor and John C. stopped his assault with a kick to the face. His opponent with the broken glass had dropped it and was standing in the middle of the barroom, holding his bleeding arm and swaying back and forth. John Charles put his open hand against the man's face and shoved him back onto an occupied table, sending glass, beer, bourbon, and cigarette butts flying around him. "Somebody patch up his arm," said John C. "then throw the bastards out. I don't want anybody dying in here and giving us a bad name." Several men laughed and John C. walked back over to Hermie and cleaned his knife with a napkin.

"Those bums will think twice before coming in here and starting trouble."

"So what!" Hermie said. "I'm going home. I hate this bar. It stinks in here and why do you want me to come anyway? Are you showing off? Well I don't care. I DON'T CARE." (She yelled this.) "You don't impress me and I've got to take the baby-sitter home."

"Baby-sitter!" John C. closed the knife and put it back in his arm holster.

"Yes, baby-sitter. It may have not occurred to you that that's what it's all about — baby-sitters and shopping and

getting by. . . . And don't wake the baby when you come in."
And she left.

John Charles watched her walk out, smiled warily at several
people sitting next to him, and went back to sit with Alice Van
Hooser. Alice arranged her hair around her head and smiled.
"How did I look?" he asked.

"When?"

"The fight."

"Fine," she answered. John took a drink out of Lil's glass
and sat swirling the beer around the bottom of the glass, forcing out the few remaining bubbles.

"The wife suspects something," he said.

"Did she say something?"

"Yes."

"What?"

"She's getting a private investigator to follow me. Somebody
around here must have been informing her."

"John . . ."

"Sure, Lil, I saw my lawyer yesterday and he said that the
divorce papers will go through in a month. But until then we
have to be careful" (he gestured), "because if we get caught by
this detective the divorce will be thrown out of court."

"Why?"

"Some legality."

"But John, a separation. Anyone can get a separation. My
cousin . . ."

"Right. I'm getting one. As a matter of fact I'm all packed.
The only thing that is left to do is decide about who takes the
kid."

"But she's only three months old, John."

"I know, but Hermie hates kids — always has. She wants me
to take her."

John Charles did not have to take the child. In fact he never
left home at all except for a week when Alice's mother went for

a visit to her sister's house in Illinois. John C. started a Friday-night poker table in Dirty John's and Alice began collecting her debts; she refused to come to the tavern when she knew Mrs. Sledge would be coming; she refused to stay overnight in a motel room, but went home to her mother; she said whiskey runs were too dangerous and refused to go along. John Charles bought her a diamond ring and complained that the divorce proceedings were being slowed down by false information brought in by the private detective, whom he had had a gun-fight with in Iowa after picking up a load of whiskey — but no one was hurt because John C. knew that if he shot him there would be a lot of very ticklish questions that were better un-asked because it was just the excuse the law needed to throw the book at him because they had been after him ever since he had come to St. Louis from Texas because of the reputation he had built for himself down there and that in order to keep one step ahead of the law he had to be smart — smarter than even his emotions. Alice had the ring appraised, and threw it away.

Perhaps Alice's new attitude had penetrated into John Charles's general understanding of the area in which he lived; or perhaps that understanding, responsive only to sharp varia-tions, had failed to contain Hermie; or perhaps it had slowly, finally, failed to contain anything that was not already defined by it. Somehow within this labyrinth of understanding one single action became necessary. *This action, by itself, is opaque and bleak, as if there had never been an infidelity charge against Hermie — never had been a desperate confusion in John C: just as though there had never been a Chief Black Hawk living on the Rock River, only someone who had built a huge monument resembling an Indian and called it that: just as though there had never been a world full of people thirty years ago. The stone remains and fantasy is the only way of memory.* John Charles called Alice Van Hooser on the telephone while she sat eating dinner with her mother, August 16, 1939.

"Hello," she said.

"Hello, Lil?"

"Yes."

"This is John."

"Where are you?" she asked. (This must have been unexpected. John C. had used the phone before, many times, to call Alice. Unusual, I believe it was, but not important enough to be exigent.)

"I'm in the hospital. Hermie has been seriously hurt. She got out of the car to shoot at a crow with my shotgun and it exploded. She is in critical condition and they don't know if she will live."

"What?!" And John Charles retold the story—his wife was dying from an injury she had received when an old shotgun she was firing exploded. Alice stayed home that day with her mother and talked again to John C. that afternoon. He said that there was no change in Hermie's condition and asked her to come to Dirty John's that evening. She did and John C. closed the bar early in order to visit his wife before visiting hours were closed.

The following afternoon Alice Van Hooser went into downtown St. Louis after work to buy a piece of material for her mother to make draperies with. From the front window of Woolworths she saw Hermie Sledge carrying her baby and walking toward the post office. She, Alice, changed a quarter and telephoned John C. at his home. He answered and he sounded tired. "She was in the intensive care ward and they wouldn't let me see her," said John Charles and added that the divorce proceedings were complete and that he only had to go to his lawyer's office and sign them. Alice was not able to find a suitable color of material and drove home. John Charles was in some way surprised by the phone call.

He bought a box of twelve-gauge shotgun shells—Nitro Long Range Express No. 4 Shot—and a stick of dynamite. He cut open one of the shells and poured the shot down the toilet in his basement. He placed the shotless shell in the firing chamber of a single-barrel gun and cut open the stick of dynamite. With a kitchen spoon he poured two and a half large spoonfuls of dynamite down the barrel of the gun and poked a piece of wadded paper after it with a cleaning rod. He carried the weapon outside and laid it on the floorboards of the back seat of his automobile.

Two days later he asked Hermie to bring the baby and come for a ride in the country. She consented and they drove out of St. Louis. After two hours of leaning over the steering wheel and looking up into the sky John Charles stopped the car and asked Hermie if she wanted to take a shot at a crow. Hermie at first couldn't see the crow, then she didn't want to shoot at it because the noise would frighten the child. John C. offered to take the child away, but by this time the crow was gone. They stopped at Dirty John's on the way home and went inside for a beer, though Hermie complained. John C. then wanted her to go outside and shoot bottles in the dump behind the tavern but she didn't want to. He asked her to come outside and throw bottles in the air for him while he shot, but she declined again and demanded to be taken home. Hugh Carson, the daytime bartender, said he'd throw some bottles up in the air for him, and John C., irritated, asked if he wouldn't rather shoot them himself. The baby was screaming at the top of her lungs by then and John Charles and Hermie and the baby went home.

He took the shotgun out of the car and put it in the basement, where he carried it from room to room, first putting it down and going upstairs, then coming down and moving it again, not sleeping well. Three days later he was sitting on the toilet in the basement and called upstairs to his wife. She came down and he pointed to the shotgun standing against the wall, indicating that there was something wrong with the firing pin, and asked Hermie to try it out. She did and the gun worked, decapitating Hermie and splattering huge pieces of her around on the basement walls, running blood on the floor.

John Charles got off the toilet and vomited. He ran upstairs and met a boarder, told him to call the hospital, that a gun his wife was shooting had exploded, and ran outside.

The police held an investigation and reporters took pictures of the room in which the calamity took place. The paper wrote "A HORRIBLE ACCIDENT." But John Charles was not out dancing in the streets. He was sitting in an uncleaned corner of Dirty John's drinking bourbon and raving internally. He wanted nothing but to go back to his basement and reconstruct the act again and again, and vomit till exhaustion came over him. But he was hiding from the reporters — it was all he could do to be coherent enough to telephone Alice and tell her what had happened, and that didn't take much.

But Hermie's death was not an accident of that kind, and it was a short time before the investigators noticed that no shot could be found in the walls, and that no Nitro Long Range Express No. 4 Shot known could blow holes in water pipes from six feet away, holes in concrete. More careful inspection showed the missing shot lying in the bottom of the toilet, its weight too heavy to be moved by the force of the water. The sheriff was notified and he brought John Charles to the St. Louis station house for questioning.

Thirty-six hours later, without sleep, the sheriff again reconstructed the supposed murder for John Charles who still sat in his chair saying: "No . . . No . . . That isn't true. . . . Give me a cigarette, you bums." But this time the sheriff brought in a blown-up picture of his wife after the explosion, severed fingers and eye-gell in perfect focus, and John C. gave up. He confessed putting the dynamite in the shotgun, getting his wife to shoot it, and wished he had died with her. The sheriff let him go back into a cell, where he fell asleep and slept for three hours, when he was awakened to retell the story to the County Attorney.

The stupidity of the shot in the toilet, of removing the shot at all, and the confession afterward were not grossness or even depravity. John Charles was not a killer by any estimation or in any extent except that he had killed his wife — an accident within his mind, a slight oversimplification that he might have avoided if he had only stayed in bed later one morning or had a little less to drink some afternoon. If only he hadn't thought about it, the killing. If only he hadn't killed Hermie. And I must remind myself again in order to get through this next part, he did kill Hermie.

On September 3, 1939, Howard Vendermarken, County Attorney for St. Louis County, filed the County Attorney's True Information statement at the State Court House, wording the charge as follows: "That John Charles Sledge, in the County and State aforesaid did on or about the twenty-second day of August, 1939, A.D., unlawfully, feloniously, and with the intent thereof, murder Mrs. Hermie Sledge, his wife." John Charles was brought into court and asked by Judge Garnold if he had legal representation; to this he answered no. Asked then if he wished legal representation; to this he answered yes. Asked if he had preference he answered no. Asked if Wayne B. Hanek met with his approval and he answered yes. Newspaper reporters asked Wayne B. Hanek if there was a special reason he had been chosen and he answered no, that it was not in his power to refuse to act as legal counsel when appointed to do so by the court. Asked to make further comments on the "dynamite murderer" and he declined.

Two days later John Charles was in court with his lawyer. He sat on a wooden chair, highly varnished, and listened to Howard Vendermarken's motion to change the wording of the County Attorney's True Information by inserting the words "willfully and deliberately." Wayne B. Hanek stated that the proposed wording established a degree of crime that was hitherto unsubstantiated by legal procedure. The Clerk wrote: "Comes now Howard Vendermarken, County Attorney of St. Louis County,

Missouri, and for and in behalf of the State moves the Court to permit him to file an amendment to the County Attorney's True Information filed here on September 3 so as to correct errors and omissions therein and he attaches hereto a copy of said proposed amendment. Then comes Wayne B. Hanek speaking for and in behalf of the defendant John Charles Sledge and opposes aforesaid amendment on the grounds that the newly proposed wording is not fully implied by previous evidence acquired by lawful procedure. Judge M. Garnold sets date of September 10, 1939, to decide on ruling."

On September 10, 1939, John Charles was again in court. The County Attorney, his first amendment being overruled, offered a new amendment to the County Attorney's True Information which included the words "specific intent to kill." Wayne B. Hanek objected to this amendment on the grounds that it established a degree of crime not yet substantiated by lawfully begotten evidence. Judge M. Garnold set the date September 11, 1939, to decide on the ruling. County Attorney Vendermarken then moved that a special assistant, Peter Lynch, be appointed to help compile evidence for the County of St. Louis. Wayne B. Hanek objected on the grounds of non-impartial treatment but was overruled.

"September 11, 1939. Comes now Howard Vendermarken, County Attorney of St. Louis County, Missouri, and for and in behalf of the State moves the court to permit him to file an amendment to the County Attorney's True Information filed here September 3 so as to correct errors and omissions therein, proposing that the words 'specific intent to kill' be inserted after the second 'with' in County Attorney's True Information, omitting the words 'intent' and 'thereof,' thus allowing the County Attorney's True Information to read: '... did on or about the twenty-second day of August, 1939, A.D., unlawfully, feloniously, and with the specific intent to kill, murder Mrs. Hermie Sledge, his wife.'" Wayne B. Hanek objected to this amendment on the grounds that it was not substantiated by legally begotten evidence and the objection was sustained.

All of this is necessary — important to see precisely how these men go about their living — how they do what they do.

"September 12, 1939. Comes now Howard Vendermarken, County Attorney of St. Louis County, Missouri, and for and in behalf of the State moves the court to permit him to file an amendment to the County Attorney's True Information filed here on September 3 so as to correct errors and other omissions therein, proposing the words 'designedly and with malice aforethought' and a comma (,) between the words 'designedly' and 'and' be inserted into the County Attorney's True Information, thus allowing the said statement to read: '. . . did on or about the twenty-second day of August, 1939, A.D., unlawfully, feloniously, designedly, and with malice aforethought and with the intent thereof, murder Mrs. Hermie Sledge, his wife.'" Wayne B. Hanek violently objected to the above amendment on the grounds that the particular wording was in no way a description of a crime as stated specifically by the Missouri Penal Code. Judge M. Garnold overruled this objection and passed the amendment, after which Hanek, reading from a piece of paper extracted from his briefcase, demanded (in behalf of his client, John Charles Sledge) that the County Attorney acting for and in behalf of the State of Missouri:

1. Show how the defendant did, on or about the twenty-second day of August, 1939, murder Mrs. Hermie Sledge, his wife.
2. Show how the defendant did murder feloniously.
3. Show how the defendant did murder with the intent thereof.
4. Show how the defendant did murder designedly.
5. Show how the defendant did murder with malice aforethought.
6. Show how the defendant did murder unlawfully.

7. Show how the defendant, if guilty of the above, has specifically committed an act in violation of the Missouri Penal Code.

Two days later John Charles stood before the court and in counsel with his lawyer asked to be allowed to stand on a demurrer. Judge Garnold denied this and asked John Charles for his plea. John C. again stood on a demurrer and was taken back to his cell under a bond of twenty-five thousand dollars. Asked by the press what this meant, Hanek answered: "Standing on a denied demurrer is essentially a plea of guilty, though not necessarily."

The trial was set for November 3, 1939. John Charles requested a guitar brought to his cell which he played and sang to himself. The *St. Louis Daily* was allowed an interview with him and he consented to pose with his guitar. "I've been in hard scrapes before," he said. John Charles seemed to be winning.

On October 15, 1939, "the defendant was served with a Notice of Additional Testimony in criminal case Number 1131 by the County Attorney, consisting of forty-three typewritten, single-spaced, legal-sized pages, covering the testimony of sixty-seven witnesses." Attorney Wayne B. Hanek appeared before the court and asked that the trial be postponed in order that he and his client might have time to go over the Notice of Additional Information. The County Attorney argued that the material was not unexpected and was even common in cases of this sort. That objection was overruled and due to the extremity of the case the trial was postponed twelve days.

On November 12, 13, and 14, while John Charles sat playing his guitar in his cell, Hanek sat in the courtroom with the County Attorney and his assistant, selecting members of the jury.

"Your name," the Judge would ask.

"Steve McMorgan."

"Occupation?"

"I run a gas station on lower Manchester."

"Have you formed any opinion whatsoever concerning the upcoming State vs. Sledge trial?"

"No, Sir."

"Are you for or against advocating the death penalty in cases of this nature?" And depending on the answer to this question one of the two attorneys would object and the proposed jury member would be eliminated. This continued until 10:32 A.M., November 14, when Judge M. Garnold informed Wayne B. Hanek that he had reached his limit of objections. Out of the next eighteen persons the County Attorney picked twelve. John Charles was allowed another interview with the press. Twelve character witnesses were subpoenaed by Wayne Hanek and waited outside the courtroom to be called: Ivan Norice, Richard Irwin, Lawrence Owens, Susan Pugh, Jack Ruimer, Dorothy Hammer, Chester Lutz, Mrs. Chester Lutz, Edwin Elder, Jr., Donna Erickson, Loren Burr, and Ken Butters.

John Charles's trial began with the presentation of three exhibits by the County Attorney; a shotgun with a damaged barrel, People's Exhibit A; a small handful of Number 4 shot, People's Exhibit B; and three enlarged pictures of Hermie Sledge, one before and two after the explosion, People's Exhibit C. Wayne B. Hanek objected to the pictures, calling them "pure sensationalism with no judicial value," but was overruled. The County Sheriff was called to the witness stand by Vendermarken and related John Charles's confession following the thirty-six-hour interrogation. Hanek, cross-examining, asked when a charge had actually been made against John Charles. To this he answered two days following the confession. Hanek moved that the evidence be stricken from the record or be labeled "circumstantial" on the grounds that the evidence had been obtained in such a way as to be a violation of legal procedure. The motion was overruled and the County Attorney called the State Coroner to the witness stand. He told of the dynamite burns on Hermie's body and further substantiated the confession. When cross-examined, the Coroner, in answer to the question of the mental condition of the defendant at the time of this confession, stated that he was told by John Charles Sledge himself that he was of "sound mind." The next witness, Bill Gordon, day bartender at Dirty John's, testified that John C. and Hermie had come into the bar on August nineteenth and John C. had asked Hermie to come outside and shoot bottles. Under cross-examination he told the court that John Charles had also offered to shoot the "dynamite gun" himself if someone else would throw bottles — and that John C. had even offered to let him, Bill Gordon, shoot it.

The following day Alice Van Hooser was called to the witness stand and testified that John Charles had telephoned her on August 16, 1939, and told her that Hermie Sledge had been injured while shooting an old shotgun, and was in critical condition. She further added that she had seen Hermie the following day in St. Louis and she had not appeared to be suffering from a shotgun exploding near her. This was taken from the record and the question withdrawn because Alice Van Hooser was discovered to be no true authority on physiology. She admitted a relationship between herself and the defendant and said that John Charles had told her that divorce papers had been drawn up and awaited his signature. John Charles's attorney asked Alice Van Hooser if she had any reason to believe that John C. would murder his wife but the question was rejected because it was discovered that Alice Van Hooser was not a qualified psychologist. Wayne Hanek asked for a recess and it was granted until the next morning.

"The Last Punch . . . Final Trick from Hanek's Bag of Tricks . . . Surprise Tactics used by Hanek," were what the papers wrote about that morning in the courtroom. Hanek's wizardry over legal rhetoric as exemplified by his brilliant objections to the County Attorney's evidence was superseded by this final act. The State rested its case against John Charles Sledge and Judge Garnold called out for the defense to offer its case. Wayne B. Hanek stood beside his client and a hush came over the courtroom. The Court Officer stood by the room where the witnesses waited to be called. They had not been allowed in the room. Hanek placed his fists down on the table in front of him and said, "The defense rests." Then he sat down. County Attorney Vendermarken, surprised and taken off guard, motioned that the court be recessed for thirty minutes while he prepared his closing speech to the jury. Wayne B. Hanek objected. Judge M. Garnold declared that the court be recessed for one-half hour. The County Attorney's closing speech was given by his assistant over the objections of Hanek and the jury left the courtroom. Fifteen minutes later they returned and every member in turn stood, and giving his name first said, "Guilty, and I advise the court to execute the death penalty." Wayne B. Hanek stood up then and said he would appeal the case before the State Supreme Court. Judge Garnold, before the five newsmen that had taken notes through the trial, stated that he would follow the recommendation of the jury unless prompted to do otherwise by the Governor of Missouri, which he evidently was not because on November 19, 1939, he declared to John Charles that he should be hanged by the neck until dead. Asked if he had anything to say and John C. said, "I did it and I guess I'll have to take what's coming to me." Judge Garnold leaned forward in his chair and folded his paper hands. "Perhaps it's only divine destiny that . . ." He was not allowed to finish.

"No," said John Charles, "it's not. I'm guilty. I've even convicted myself. I was just born mean, I reckon."

The appeal was granted and the Missouri Supreme Court read over the Official Transcript of the trial and upheld the finding of the lower court. John Charles played his guitar and was allowed another interview; then they came and moved him to the State Prison. He remained in "death row" twenty-five days and was allowed no interviews. No one came to visit him and the prison help was cordial to him — beer-can-like people to whom "shotgun killer," "dynamite murderer," and "Dirty John" meant nothing. Up to here is about all that I know. Isn't that really all anyone needs to know? So the following is not fact, but a condition I place on the past, to let John Charles keep ahead of himself — so that he did not wake up that morning covered with a sweet gray sweat growing out of his body, shaking and screaming, vomiting from half-dreamed visions of Hermie and an ugliness too horrible to realize with all the lights turned off by a master switch and his cell door opening and three figures coming toward him across the concrete — only one's supposed to be a priest but long ago he told them not to bring one because he despised the sniveling excuses of men — and retching green and blood-black vomit onto the bed — sick, they puffing him across his cell — fully aware of his own terror, thus pushing the terror still further and further, up the steps and tying his feet, his body crippling over with pain, unable to see now, and jerking his head up to the rope and the jeering from the throng of good people come to watch him die. Screaming and writhing. I invoke the past to let that not have happened, so that he rose from his bed and walked straight out of his cell, onto the platform waving to the hundreds of people that had come to honor him, knowing that he was not a real killer, and even kicked one of the henchmen down the stairs when he was not looking, saying: "Sucker." That crowd laughed and another henchman pulled the lever and John C. was dead. And the prisoners rioted because of the hanging and one of the guards was shot off the wall and another lost his hand. Let Fast Eddie inherit his cigarettes and guitar. After all, what does it matter?

And I remembered the child. It took me two full months of looking at dusty, disease-ridden records of long collapsed detention orphanages to find her name — Jennie — and another two months to find her. Alice Van Hooser had wanted to adopt her but was unable to because of her unworthiness revealed by herself during the trial. Alice's mother took out adoption papers for the girl but was also refused because of her association with her daughter. It had cost Alice five hundred dollars to get Jennie and they moved into Iowa with her mother and were living in Cedar Rapids when I found them.

"Yes?" Alice said. She had not opened the screen door. Her eyes were like light-bulb sockets, only expressionless, and any excess weight she may have had at one time was gone.

"My name is Sledge, Reuben Sledge. Are you Miss Van Hooser?"

"Yes."

"Is Jennie here?"

"What do you want with her?"

"I just want to talk to her. Clear some things up." A tall slim woman came up beside Alice. "This is Jennie," she said.

"Jennie, my name is Reuben Sledge. I suppose you were too young to remember your father." She looked at me through the screen door.

"What do you want, Mr. Sledge?" asked Alice.

"Well . . . do you remember your father or mother?"

"No," she said, still looking at me like a magazine salesman. I stood looking back at her and mumbled something about thank-you and I was your father's brother and your mother's mother lived not too far from me and left. I thought I heard Alice say something then as I walked away but I couldn't be sure what it was.

The Des Moines City Council learned of the execution of John Charles and acted immediately. Orders were sent out by the director of these affairs and Father learned that his son had been denied burial rites and sacred ground anywhere in Polk County and that similar action was being taken in the surrounding counties for fear that he would attempt to transport his son across the county line. So he went to the farmers and asked for a couple of yards of secluded land; but was unable to obtain anything because they felt that it would be illegal.

"Andrea," Father said.

Mother looked up from her bed and stared at him. "No," she said, "they wouldn't . . . anywhere else and they couldn't."

"They have," said Luke. "There is nothing left. I'll go tomorrow to the junkyard and . . ."

"No," said Andrea, "no . . . no . . . no. Burn him in the furnace — throw him in the river — bury him in the yard."

"But he's our son. Do you want him laying out in the yard for the rest of our lives?"

"Not *our* son. He was my son. I grew him in me — where were you then? — at the depot. I fed him and where were you? I told him to leave, from the time he was old enough to hear I begged him to leave — to go away and never come back. I begged him to leave the girl behind, to take nothing with him — nothing that could bring him back — and where were you? And he's come home, to me, to kill me with his deadness, scream at me from his tomb in the basement — the horror, the mockery. There is a curse on my body."

"No," said Luke. "The people have done this."

"A curse. Look at my hands, my face. I'm dying. I'm dying from something that was small when I was born and like ink has smeared through me. Look at my legs." And she threw back the covers, revealing her thin legs, lined with varicose veins. "Those are veins, black veins bulging with poison, tearing themselves out of my body."

Nellie had come to the door and stood holding me against her, and looked at Mother sitting on the bed rocking back and forth, her hands rubbing up and back, down her legs. Nellie carried me to the bed and held me out for Mother to take. She took me in her arms, clutched me hard against her breasts, and then turning her head aside thrust me away. Nellie gathered me from her and left the room. Luke caught the edge of the covers in his hands and raised them to cover Andrea. "Don't touch me," she screamed and grabbed at the blankets herself, pulling them around her and from under the mattress.

Father went to an auto salvage yard and bought a car, a Ford as Nellie tells it, and pulled it home with a chain. Walt and Father brought John Charles out of the basement and put him into the back seat. They carried Mother's body, wrapped in a sheet (because even though Father did not believe her talk of curses and poison he might not have been so sure and didn't want Paul to touch her), from her bed and laid her across the front seat. They pulled the car down Clinton and at First Avenue unloosed the chain. They pushed the Ford by hand around the corner and sent it off down into the fog. They stood on the rim and listened to the tires against the road. Below they heard the monument closing, like a huge boulder dropping several feet into a grass-lined pocket of earth — the perfect seal. . . . No other sound came up from the fog and they went home.

Chapter III

...

EACH MORNING ON HIS WAY TO THE DEPOT LUKE SLEDGE bought one pint of whiskey. On Saturday he bought two. He drank half a bottle in the morning and half in the afternoon and threw the empty into a trash barrel in the parking lot that was our front yard. He was not a drunk and I never saw my father without control of himself. However, he was mildly intoxicated constantly, and so appeared to have no vices . . . the cells of his body gulped whiskey like a tree drinking water out of the ground, pulling it up into its roots and sending it out into the farthest, highest leaves. Even the smell soaked into his brain and disappeared. Few people ever knew that he drank. There was only one way to know — the eyes. Father had told me that. "Look," he'd say. "Look at the eyes," and he'd point to his eyes. "There, Reuben, a thin layer of film, like glass — and that's the difference. Without it you can't see right." But I wasn't sure about that. "A dust storm, for example," he said. "Who can see a dust storm better, a man standing inside it or a man standing behind a window?"

Father had learned somewhere how to engrave. He sat behind his desk in the depot with his burins and copper plates and carved intricate designs — lines and curves that intersected and went parallel, tangents, parabolas, hyperbolas, squares, three-dimensional cones and hexagons. Paul once found an engraving of a dollar bill in a drawer cluttered with dirty paper and rusty bolts. The detail was perfect. But Father never printed any of his engravings. "The ink spoils it," he said. "The colors are never right and always smear and make the lines fuzzy. It's best to throw the plate away after you make it. As soon as you print it it becomes something not like it was.

And the lines in the plate get ruined." One summer Father attempted to teach me how to engrave, but I kept wanting to touch the plate with my fingers to feel the lines because it was difficult to see them at all unless you tipped the plate at just the right angle from the light. But Father was critical of this. "That leaves fingerprints and makes for a messy job," he would say, and finally gave up teaching me altogether after he apprehended me introducing different colored inks into our engraving studio.

Paul quit high school in his junior year and taught himself to become an auto mechanic. After a couple of years he had our front yard littered with the engines, frames, seats, and bumpers of dead automobiles that he meticulously resurrected and transplanted into living automobiles. At first, the people's resentment still being what it was after John Charles's death, he was unable to get work. But slowly, a few at a time — those who couldn't get a distributor or a transmission fixed anywhere else except by specialists in Chicago — they began to come, pulling their injured cars up in front of the house for Paul to fix. Father once told him that if he would start a garage away from home, business would be better. But Paul wouldn't do that. "If they want their cars fixed they have to come here . . . this is where I live," he said. And they did come, but only when there was no other choice, and then only apologetically. "I've got some trouble here with my car," they'd say, "I wouldn't come but Mac's Garage don't do work on fluid drives, and I need the car to get to the plant and back." Many of them wouldn't come to the door but sat in their automobiles in the front yard and honked until Paul came outside. "Those son-of-a-bitches," Walt would scream, "I'll go out there and shove their fuckin' heads down those horns." But Paul would get up and say that it was O.K. — that they only did that because they couldn't do nothing else. The money Paul made fixing cars he put in a cupboard in the kitchen and whenever anyone needed some money that's where he got it.

Will was like Father in one way: if you knew either of them well it was impossible to imagine him without a central understanding permeating your conception of him in such a way as to be inseparable from him — like trying to imagine life in Europe in 1943 without considering the war. Will was handsome. He stood over six feet two inches tall, had a face of long, well-balanced lines, high cheekbones, and hazel eyes. He walked like an athlete on the sides of the balls of his feet and spoke in a deep, rich voice that was not at all monotone. At a very young age he had artfully combined the experience of our ostracism with the late forties' and fifties' fascination with the idea of the tragic hero to his own advantage and there was no woman in Des Moines that he did not consider as his prey, and few that did not have a similar image of themselves reserved at least for those dark hours when their husbands had gone to sleep, and they, still unsatiated and restless, lay staring up to the ceiling, watching fantasies.

I can remember watching Will (then sixteen) gather his clothes about him late at night, slip out the door and make his way carefully between the wrecks in the front yard with long shadows lying under the tires and in the ditch, over to the bed of Mrs. Griffin who had a light showing in her attic that I could make out from the porch. Later then, only when the air was heavy, I could hear a long, winding, tiny screaming. Just as it was beginning to be light, I'd watch him leave through the front door and run back down the street and into the yard, running as though he knew someone were watching. But he couldn't have. Soon then he did not do it anymore.

Mr. Griffin came over to the house one night and knocked on the front door. He had returned from a sale, still in his suit. We were eating dinner together as we frequently still did and

Father told Paul it was probably for him. Paul walked across the room and opened the screen door. Mr. Griffin immediately jumped inside the kitchen and looked quickly over at Will, saying: "I've got some trouble with my car," the projection of his voice shaking around in the cupboards. "What seems to be the problem?" asked Paul as our visitor moved toward the center of the room, his progression looking like a thousand pages of drawings in the Looney Tune Production Studio flipped over by the thumb of a janitor. "It's my carburetor . . . my carburetor needs fixing." Walt coughed and Griffin turned toward the table. "And you keep that boy of yours away from my place," he yelled at Father. "Just what boy are you talking about, Mr. Griffin?" asked Father, putting a cigarette out in his coffee cup and fingering his fork with his other hand. "That one," said Griffin and pointed a large, hairy finger at Will. "Well, now," said Father, "that boy's only sixteen; doesn't seem to me that he could be doing you much harm." I could see Walt out of the corner of my eye sliding his chair back toward the shotgun leaning against the wall. Griffin's face turned the color of an October tomato, rotten, and he shook his fist at Father and said, "If I catch him anywhere near my house, I'll kill him." Then he bolted from the room. Walt began to laugh. "And so he was gone," he said.

"I don't want to see it happen again," said Father to Will. "You've got to stop this. You're too young anyway."

"Too young?" jeered Will. "You mean old man Griffin's too old, don't you?"

"If I'd meant that, I'd've said it. You can't understand anything yet — can't see behind the act. Of course you're old enough to grow a stiff prick and go around jabbing it into wherever it will fit; but too young to see behind that, behind where the ugly colors of emotions are. You're too young because you don't see that, and later, when you do, won't want it anyway."

"What's wrong with using what was given to you when you were born?"

"Nothing," yelled Father, "nothing was given to you. You just got what you have — nobody gave it to you. You just got it, and now that you've got it you're in the same boat as everyone else. The kind of life you're talking about will drive you mad; then you and Griffin can start a club."

"And you had seven kids."

"That's different. Marriage is different. It's why there is such a thing."

"Like John's."

"John Charles was an idiot. I knew it from when he was little. He was too stupid to see that everything he would do was damned before he did it."

"We aren't vegetables."

"No, and knowing that should teach you. Like a warning."

These arguments between Father and Will were frequent. Nellie always left the room as soon as she could see them starting, but I always stayed — stayed and listened and tried to understand why Father hated Will as much as he did.

Father never convinced Will, but maybe he wasn't trying to. By the time he was twenty Will had been three times ordered into court on charges of statutory rape and unlawful and lascivious actions, all of which were dismissed due to lack of substantiating evidence. Will was careful in that he never took advantage of anyone (except once), but would put himself in the position of being taken advantage of and ride along on the wave of emotion that he had festered until he grew tired of its personality and got off, leaving behind him empty accusations aimed at the ineffable part of Will that was empty itself, and there was never anything done to make that emptiness unlawful.

Father never argued with Walt. No one argued with Walt that knew him. In a half sentence of pointed words he was able to synthesize, capsulize, and ignoblize your premise, many times unknown to yourself, in such a way as to leave you nothing to do but walk away. (Only Nellie, she could laugh.) And any argument he couldn't reduce to an absurd axiom would invoke the single response, "So what?" which was more damaging than all the rest. The steel trap of his mind took in thousands of mutilated, twisted, jumbled words, and like a machine in a junkyard that takes bent cars and smashes them into small steel cubes, fed out motionless propositions laid bare by the removal of all extraneous and colored words.

Walt was understandably the best street fighter in Des Moines and was afraid of nothing. Many times I had seen him standing out in the street in front of a tavern meticulously tearing apart some man with quick jabs and stompings. His object was one-fold, never cluttered with anger, revenge, jealousy, or envy: he was out to win, to reduce his opponent to a lifeless form on the cement, and his hate was of such a general kind that it never obstructed his view of the quickest and easiest method of achieving this end. He was not malicious though he was seldom in fights that he hadn't provoked. Labor unions hired him during striking periods to stand in front of the factories and shops as a deterrent to scab labor, but his loyalty was never assured and he often fought with the picketers themselves. It was impossible to avoid Walt if he decided he wanted to fight with you because he had a way of looking at you and seeing just that part of you that was sensitive to the touch and then begin jabbing away at it. I do not mean to imply that this is difficult with most people because what is most suspect in them is usually surrounded by walls of protective clues standing out like street signs on the corner, and there are names for those things. But several are able to remain elusive to everyone — but Walt, who could dig up the most obscure, forgotten, seemingly insignificant characteristics, thus lighting a fire under his opponent. There was one way for the good people of Des Moines to protect themselves from Walt:

After dinner, Will and Paul and I were in the kitchen with Nellie when we heard shouts coming up the road in front. "What's that?" said Nellie, but no one answered because the rest of us knew what it was. Will and I carried two kitchen chairs outside and Paul picked up a towing chain by the side of the house. Walt was backing up the asphalt road, holding a tire iron in one hand and a metal barrel-rung in the other. Around him circled five or six men from the Rooster Tavern trying to find a knife-blade opening between the revolutions of the tire iron and Walt.

"Son-of-a-bitches," Walt was saying with as much emphasis as a long-distance operator at three o'clock in the morning. One of the men came too close, made a mistake and Walt caught him in the face with the barrel-rung and he fell screaming to the side of the road. "Son-of-a-bitches," Walt said. Will and I started jabbing at three of them with our chairs. Paul was swinging the tow chain around his head but he should have known that it was too awkward to control and one of the men caught it with an ax handle and Paul backed up against Walt when we heard Father's twelve gauge go off behind us. The five men turned around to see Nellie standing in the front yard with the gun leveled in front of her screaming that she would blow their heads off if they didn't leave. They picked up the man Walt had hit with the barrel-rung and walked back down toward town cursing Walt and all of us in general. "Son-of-a-bitches," said Walt and threw his weapons into the ditch. "Thanks," he said.

"That's the third time this year," said Paul.

"That many?" said Walt.

"What are you trying to prove? Someone else might have been hurt. Yourself, maybe."

"So what," said Walt, and Paul walked silently back to the house with us. Father was standing in the kitchen and told Walt that one of these days he would be killed.

"Everything I know, I learned from watching you," said Walt, and I knew he was right.

Walt was hired by a lobbying group to bomb a construction site at the edge of town in order that the city council's judgment concerning further road construction would be assured in favor of construction companies. Although this is the only bombing I knew Walt to be responsible for, he was responsible for many more. But he was never discovered and never would be discovered because without passion, abnormality, or perversion his actions left no messy red threads hanging about the ragged sweater of the explosion. Of them all Walt was the greatest threat to me when I was young. I loved him even more than Nellie. I followed him downtown and he'd take me in the bars with him and no one would say anything about me being too young. The blind hate I felt for the good people of Des Moines was glorified when I saw Walt backing up into the front yard swinging a piece of metal he had picked up somewhere and saying, "Son-of-a-bitches," which I picked up as a battle cry and ran screaming out of the house dragging Paul and Will with me to help.

Walt was offered a full scholarship from the Philosophy Department at the State University of Iowa after Nellie had painstakingly arranged a secret interview between the head of the department and unsuspecting Walt in the Rooster Tavern, where he, the department head, somehow discovered that Walt knew something about whatever it was that his department had to do with, though there must have been more to it than that. Walt wrote back:

Dear Sir(s):

Drop dead,
     regretfully,
     walter Sledge

When Will became so old as to begin worrying about reaching thirty he was different than before. He never laughed. His involvements became more elaborate and frequent; his attitude was no longer youthful: he looked tired and was taking some kind of a drug. He rarely looked at you in the eyes, and when he did you were forced to look away. Whenever he talked to one of us he seemed like he was trying to explain something that he didn't know anything about. The telephone rang all hours of the day and he was caught up in trying to regulate his doings so that he was leaving out the back door as a young (they were all young, then), frightened girl diffidently stepped up on the front steps to knock on the door.

"Is Will here?" asked a tiny voice.

"I'm sorry, but he's not here," said Paul. "Can I take a message?"

"He's not here?" she asked again.

"No. I'm sorry. Would you like to come in for a cup of coffee? Pretty cold out there."

"Oh . . . no . . . no . . ." (They never came in if Will wasn't home.) ". . . If he comes back . . . do you know where he went?"

"Well, no. He's kind of hard to keep track of," and Paul laughed. He was a horrible actor.

"Tell him Marsha was here . . . ," she said, looking around Paul into the kitchen, hoping to see Will — hoping that Paul had been lying.

"Sure . . . Okay. I'll tell him Marsha was here. Do you want him to call you?"

"No . . . I mean I want to see him — but to call me if he can't come. But I want to see him."

"Sure. Okay. I'll tell him." And she stayed standing on the steps.

"Sure you don't want to come in?" asked Paul.

"No . . . I'm going. Tell Will that Marsha was here." And she'd go away, walking out through the junkyard that was our front yard.

An hour later the phone would ring and Nellie, thinking of Paul, would answer it. "Hello."

"Is Will there?" a voice too demanding to be real would ask.

"No. He's not here right now."

"Who's this?"

"Nellie."

"Nellie who?"

"Nellie Sledge, his sister."

"Oh."

"Can I take a message?"

"Yes. Tell him Meg called and wants to see him."

"All right."

"Tell him to come over tonight if he can."

"All right."

"Do you know where he went?"

"No . . . sorry."

"Well, tell him Meg called."

"All right."

"Uh . . . do you know me . . . I mean has he mentioned me, or that I might call?"

"Well, he was in such a hurry that . . ."

"Tell him I called, will you?"

"Yes."

"Good-bye."

"Good-bye."

During these years Father was leaving early and staying late at the depot, working even on weekends, especially. When Will came home (usually with a nervous girl in modern clean clothes whose eyes you could never see clearly because she never took them away from Will), he'd shrug his shoulders and go into his bedroom.

One morning three cars drove into the front yard. Walt and Paul and Nellie and I could hear someone shouting: "Will . . . Will Sledge . . . Will Sledge," who as usual wasn't at home.

"Son-of-a-bitches," said Walt. Paul and I went outside. Walt came behind us and Nellie stood looking from the doorway out at Mr. Edgeway standing in the snow still shouting, "Will Sledge . . ." at the top of his lungs. The sheriff and a couple of city policemen were with him, along with a carload of neighborly reinforcements, because of Walt. Standing near the back fender of Edgeway's car was a young girl staring down at her feet that were shuffling along in the snow partially hidden from her eyes by a pregnancy. "Will Sledge . . . ," Edgeway kept yelling, and before he decided to address Paul, Paul had noticed the girl. Paul's expression passed through two extremes and finally came to rest in an attitude of indifference before he burst into laughter, gradually. "Where's Will?" yelled Edgeway, but Paul was laughing louder then and that laughter was ringing off the windshields and banging off the car doors in the front yard. And Paul kept laughing; I stood looking at him, not believing . . . and he kept laughing; even after Edgeway's face burned us all as witches and screamed, "Damn you . . . Damn you, Sledges," turned around, jerked his thumb toward the car and the girl got into the back seat still looking down at her feet, got in his car, and drove out of the yard, leaving his five neighbors and the two policemen and the sheriff to look at each other and listen to Paul's laughter and get in their cars and drive down the road. I couldn't understand that then — not from Paul — Will maybe, or Walt, but not Paul.

But during those chaotic times a plan was percolating within Will's mind, and as its design trickled down onto the surface of his originally instant consciousness Will took on a larger dimension, his life expanded into an area so immense that the colors of his most bizarre dreams could not fill it. And because he was unable to see to the extremities of his plan it became his dictator, holding the boundaries of him well within it, and the longer he kept his plan hidden in the conceptual stage (it was a long time) the more it twisted and coiled those boundaries closer to him, like constricting the mainspring of a stopwatch. This plan, he once told me, would save him and be like a personal monument. I had never heard Will talk like that before, was a little glad I hadn't, and because I was accustomed to not taking Will seriously (perhaps I should say this was a "practice" of mine) I continued along in my fool's paradise, not believing he was capable of more than the at best erratic moments of his life.

Will saw a woman stepping off a bus downtown and followed her to a department store where she bought a half-dozen silver plastic buttons. He thought her to be about twenty-seven, her body unusually firm and voice contemplative and rich. At a shoe repair shop she picked up a pair of fixed shoes, and waited for the 4:15 Middletown bus. Passing quickly by her and capturing a seat two sections back, Will noticed that her hair, which was held around close to her head with a white band, was healthy, showing no signs of color manipulations or extensive shaping processes. He got off the bus and slipped quietly into a small grocery store where he watched her enter a stone house, number 413 High Street, across from the Mercy Hospital, nearly. Under the pretense of compiling a "residential information survey" he learned from the owner of the store that she was Cedar Stern, twenty-eight years old, divorced now for four years, few if any friends, and an inhabitant of the number 413 stone house for four years — presently a saleswoman in Bridewell Greenery. He learned that Cedar Stern occasionally took in boarders — mostly medical students — who rented a small room on the second floor to the back of the house . . . with a private entrance and bathroom . . . and that the room was presently unoccupied, though it had been so for some time and the store owner thought that she had perhaps decided against renting it out. Will's happiness was difficult to contain and he quickly told the grocer that he was late for an important meeting, and buying a newspaper hurried out of the store.

Cedar Stern had not advertised the upstairs room, and Will needed it. None of the houses beside her or across from her were even remotely satisfactory. Somehow he needed to get the room — which was not advertised, perhaps not available — and he couldn't talk to Cedar Stern himself, or let her see him. It was too early for that. Will had no male friends and he couldn't ask one of his female friends to get the room for him because of the complications that might arise out of someone knowing where he lived; furthermore, the only people he knew Cedar Stern rented to were medical students, presumably male. On one hand she might refuse to rent to a woman and after denying one person find it easier to deny another, even a male: on the other hand she might agree to rent to a woman but then feel more inclined to pay personal calls to her roomer, so breaking the sanctity of the private entrance and bath arrangement. Both of these possibilities were of course unfavorable to Will.

"You want me to what?" I asked.

"To rent a room for me," Will said.

"Rent it yourself."

"I can't do that . . . I don't want anyone to know I live there."

"Get someone else. Get one of those girls that used to come over here all the time."

"I can't trust anyone but you. Besides you look sort of like you might be a medical student."

"What!" I said, feeling somehow insulted.

"Well, maybe not," he added, ingenuously, but still to my relief. "But more so than Walt or Paul—who wouldn't do it anyway."

"Get Nellie."

"I don't want a girl to do it. I told you that." He hadn't told me that, of course, but I felt that in a way he might have said it, or at least he thought he had, or maybe it had just slipped his mind.

"Why do you want this room?"

"I just want it. It's going to save my youth and stand as a personal monument to my stature."

"Bullshit!" I was sixteen then and not yet properly educated into accepting "bullshit" for something else.

"I want that room, Reuben. If you won't do it I'll get someone else." He was serious.

"Okay, where is it?"

"On High Street, now listen: she hasn't advertised this room . . ."

"She?"

"Never mind that. What you do . . ."

So that evening I walked up to Cedar Stern's house and knocked. I felt pretty ridiculous in the blue sport coat that Will had gotten somewhere because he thought medical students wore them when they weren't in white coats. I told him I didn't think they did but he was sure he knew more about medical students than I did and I didn't know enough one way or another to disagree with him — so I wore it.

"Yes," she said. I was momentarily paralyzed about the throat.

". . . Hello . . . I'm . . . Sorry to bother you . . . But . . . My name is . . ." The sound of my own voice finally caught up to me and as I listened to it I was able to organize what I was supposed to say into sentences. "My name is John Barnes. I'm a medical student at Drake University. This is my first year here and I have been given a job as an orderly in the Mercy Hospital as part of my tuition expenses. I don't have a car and I was told that you sometimes rent out a room. I really would appreciate it, Mrs. Stern."

"I thought that I wouldn't rent anymore because the last boys I had here were so noisy." I was staring at her, thinking about Will. ". . . parties and friends coming in at all hours." I was sure I had it by then. The rest was rhetorical — we both knew that.

"I'm not like that, Mrs. Stern. Not at all. You won't even know that I'm here."

"I don't know. The stove upstairs doesn't work too well and I don't have time to get anyone in to look at it . . ."

"I know a lot about stoves and mechanical things. My father used to be a do-it-yourself man around our neighborhood."

"It's not very warm in the winter. And there's no storm windows for that room."

"That won't bother me. I find most rooms too warm." A large dog with a motley nose was barking at the lower area of my legs, until he saw an orange cat hurry across the hallway. Cedar Stern, in pursuit of the two, called back over her shoulder between shouts of "no . . . Bad dog . . . Duchess, NO . . ." that I could have the room. She separated the animals by picking up the cat (Felix) and came back to accept twenty-five dollars for the first month. I told her that I would leave each month's rent in her mailbox and that I would be no bother at all — that in fact she wouldn't see me at all. And she didn't.

Will was overjoyed. I gave him the key and he drove to a root beer stand and bought me a root beer and a pork tenderloin with onion rings. He made me promise not to tell anyone about that room and I didn't tell anyone, except Nellie, and then not until two or three years later — when it didn't make any difference.

The following morning Will waited in the grocery store until Cedar Stern had locked her front door, walked down the sidewalk, and boarded a bus. He bought two large bags of food, three cartons of cigarettes, two cases of beer, and two boxes of various and curious items from the nearest hardware store.

There was a small yard in back of the house and a hedge of mulberry running around three sides, open to the sidewalk except for three lowgrowing maples, a small porch in front, and a larger one in back with a stairway to his room. He called the telephone company and had a telephone installed. With a putty knife he removed the putty and caulking compound from a basement window in back of the house. He took the glass out and put it carefully on the grass; then slid down into the basement, from where he gained approach to the entire house. With some fresh meat he made friends with the Great Dane and installed intricately hidden microphones in every room of the house, running the wires down into the basement, up between the walls, through tiny holes in the bathroom wall and into his amplifier equipment . . . complete with an individual, sure-tone channel for each microphone, a set of headphones, and a tape recorder. He disconnected the telephone in his room and wired it into the cable of the downstairs phone so that it acted like an extension, only didn't ring. Cedar Stern's bedroom and bathroom were both upstairs and separated from him by a single wall, through which he drilled two thin holes, one into her bathroom and the other into her bedroom . . . into these holes he placed hollow tubes on the ends of which were glass crystals cut in a pattern that revealed, when looked through, not a narrow tunnel of vision, but a view of the entire room. With the aid of several camera lenses he was able to see through these tubes by looking into a low-power telescope set on a tripod in front of the overstuffed chair next to the table. From this place he could also manipulate his amplifier and telephone.

Two and three times a week Will followed Cedar Stern to the Bridewell Greenery and spent the day in an adjacent public park. The customers were by and large ladies of fifty or sixty years wearing hats, with late model automobiles. Cedar occasionally ate lunch alone in the park, but always took the 4:30 bus and went home, except once a week, when she went to the grocery store. She seemed not overly friendly with either the owner of the nursery, Mrs. Bridewell, or the other saleslady, Mrs. Ondell. After a month, Will gave up going to the nursery altogether.

To Will's unexpected fascination he found a large stack of old letters and newspaper clippings in the bottom drawer of Cedar's bureau. With these, and the help of letters from and to her father and sister in Burlington, which he opened by holding above a boiling pan of water, reading and replacing back in the mail box, he was able to compose a skeletal outline of her past. This he arranged and wrote in a notebook. *Born, 1927, on a farm outside What Cheer, Iowa. 1933, pet robin died from an accidental overdose of table salt. 1939, spanked by father for negligence toward younger sister — afterwards it was decided that Cedar was too old. Starred in two high school plays;* The Cherry Orchard, *the other unknown. Broke high school track record in girl's 50 yard dash, time, 6.02 seconds. Enrolled in Iowa State Teachers' College, Mt. Vernon, Iowa, 1947, majoring in Botany. President of Audubon Club in 1948. Remained in college two years — grade point, 3.14. July 14, 1950, at age of twenty-two-and-a-half married an ex-Marine and insurance broker. They had no children (assumed by their doctors to be her husband's fault). Divorced, 1951, husband claimed mental cruelty, not verified. Charges of homosexuality withdrawn by Cedar. Ex-husband returned to Marines and was stationed in Korea. Moved to High Street and began collecting animals, fish, and plants. Mother died in 1952, cause of death attributed to unknown reasons. Younger sister married in 1953, presently with two children, living on a farm.*

Will traveled to What Cheer and searched for Cedar's childhood in the barns and fields and white house outlined with intricately carved panels of wood set along the porch and hanging from the roof: latticework. He imagined how these things would be to a child — how they would be even if they were not noticed. He sat in the rooms of the house and imagined how it must have been, with clocks and davenports and human smells. He smoked opium to help him imagine. In a high-school building — dormant then, a rezoning leftover — he surrounded himself with Cedar's class pictures, old photographs of her standing with her physical education instructor in the gymnasium; he visualized parking lots, gum wrappers, and small throngs of teenagers where buttonweeds and marijuana (left over from the rope industry of the War) grew. He tried to wedge together those fragments of recorded facts into a continuously coherent, rounded spiral . . . a feeling for the young Cedar Stern that was at once intelligible and self-contained — nothing untouched — no part of Cedar's youth would escape him. He experienced her high-school years, walked up the stairs to the bathroom with her, helped her comb her hair in the girls' room, read the messages written on the metal stalls surrounding the toilets, looked out into the parking lot from the typing room and wondered if Larry Murphy would ask her to the game, screamed obscenities at the enemy basketball players in the sweating gymnasium, accepted a trophy for record time in the one-hundred-yard dash, hated study halls and hall monitors, hesitantly tried on the masks of sentimentality, brutality, indifference, tolerance, rebellion, sainthood, and blind faith to see the effect they made on her environment — keeping those masks that were pleasurable and discarding the rest, riotously acclaiming her womanhood while secretly resenting it, finding her mother's religion finally inadequate and untrue, discovering that the adults around her were constantly telling her lies about the nature of the way things really were — believing that her generation would finally right the wrong and rock the world in a magnificent apocalypse in which she was to be the principal mover — bringing mankind once more into the divine order of nature. Will helped Cedar write poetry about young women with hair blowing in the winds, and running along lakes and in snowstorms, and of love; helped her buy clothes, lived on potato chips and soda in a land with no middle ground — everything was ecstatic or drab, waited in a car behind the liquor store while some old man from downtown that one of the boys had commissioned to buy sloe gin was signing away another section of his Blue Book for the price of a six-pack of beer, found that the ideas her teachers were occasionally talking about were fascinating and repugnant, was attracted to debauchery, unsure what it was but in every frantic action believing that she was moving toward it in some mystical, religious way . . . afraid of scorn from her friends, but desiring it secretly more than anything.

Will stayed in What Cheer for three weeks and then returned to Des Moines, satisfied. His image of Cedar Stern had a beginning. Safely, he could now begin his total construction of Cedar, complete to the last detail. Babyhood did not interest him. What came before the adolescence was irrelevant to Will because he was only concerned with Cedar as a woman, specifically with the kind of woman she was in contrast to the kind of woman she pictured herself to be; therefore, her earlier years — those spannings of time when her most frightening nightmares could at best only make generalizations about what insanity might be like — were of no concern to him. In his notebook he wrote:

Today I have seen the beginning of a pattern, a living obsession, a metaphysic. And like all patterns in their earlier stages it is impossible to know the precise nature of that pattern. I have before me (within me) a collection of seemingly unrelated symbols, like the numbers 3.14 that on first observation might appear sporadic or merely coincidental without the awareness that the series π is in actuality an infinitely repeating series just as definite as the series 3333. . . . I shall painstakingly continue to uncover the other numbers of the series until I arrive at the common repeating series 142857142857142857 . . . and so arrive at the simple fraction $^{22}/_7$. The mistake of the morons I have known is anticipated in their belief that the chaotic actions of a young girl (and a woman, though less pronounced) are indeed chaotic. They have failed to see that every woman is held together by a central series, an obsession or metaphysic that orders that chaos. There are no ambiguities in a woman. They are simple . . . prevented by their partial awareness of themselves and by the man-oriented world to contain any discrepancies. "Women are infinitely shallow." It is only our greedy acceptance of the unexplainable that renders them complex. It would be banal to attempt to possess a young girl in that her pattern, or obsession, has not been fully developed. They, the girls, will eventually grow out around any estimation of them because that estimation will always be incomplete. A young girl cannot conceive of what it means to be permanently deranged . . . is not aware that anything internal to herself stands between her and the good life. I will come to know Cedar Stern's obsession better than she does herself. I will possess her. She will cease to live but through me. My lungs will breathe air into her body. I will know love.

In the mornings Will was awakened by Cedar's alarm clock. He quietly got out of bed and watched her pull on her bathrobe through his vision-tube. (Will had given up the convenience of the telescope for the intense communion that the knowledge of less physical space between them gave to him.) She then went into the bathroom and Will followed her into his own and from his other vision-tube watched her urinate, defecate, and brush her teeth. Through his earphones he listened to her walk downstairs, greet the dog and cat, feed the fish from an orange box of dry fish food, expertly, never too much, open two cans of food for Felix and Duchess, put the food in plastic bowls, place the cat's dish at one end of the kitchen and the dog's at the other (Felix ate closer to the sink area), fill a metal pan with water and put it on the gas stove, turn on the fire under it and walk upstairs. Back at the vision-tube he watched as she remade the bed, took off her robe, placing it back in the bureau, removed her nightgown and hid it carefully under one of the pillows on the twin-size bed, and standing naked, combed her hair in front of the full-length mirror with short, inaccurate, almost casual strokes. She first put on a pair of underpants, always a little too large for her, and then a bra, never used more than three days without washing (unnecessarily, because she had eight bras and did laundry every week, on Saturday, although she never wore the bra with the heavy cords or the black one). The next item of apparel was a garter belt, stockings, then a full-length slip which she smoothed down and adjusted in front of the mirror before putting on a blouse and skirt (infrequently she wore a dress from her selection of nine). After choosing a pair of shoes, usually the brown, she went back downstairs to rescue the boiling water from the stove and make one cup of instant coffee, pouring the extra water down the sink, and causing Will's headphones to make a noise like *Pssssssssssss*. Felix and Duchess would be finished eating by then and would follow her with the cup of coffee into the living room, and while she sat on the sofa drinking the brew with short sipping sounds, would engage herself in a monologue with the animals. The topics of these conversations were sprung from either outstanding remarkable events of the day before — dog chases cat up lamp pole and lamp pole falls down — or expectations of the coming afternoon or weekend — taking animals for a long walk, going to the zoo, or a visit from her father or sister. Occasionally she would talk to them about matters that they had no interest in whatsoever. (These would become of special interest to Will and he listened to them over and over again during the day while Cedar was at work, but never without playing the entire tape of the morning and remembering her actions that he had recorded in a notebook and reread during the appropriate intervals for fear that he might draw a wrong conclusion by taking them out of context.) She took the empty cup into the kitchen and put it in the sink. Then, putting on a coat if the weather was even questionably chilly, would take the cat and dog out into the backyard while Will studied her face through his telescope, trying to lip-read. After ten minutes she would bring the animals back into the house, pick up her pocketbook and any letters she had written the night before from the dining room table, and lock the door behind her as she left.

This was a typical morning. The sequence of events rarely

varied during the week and was for the most part only elongated on the weekends. But sometimes Cedar Stern changed
her schedule — on certain days she would refuse to feed the
cat, or the dog, or both, or would let them out of the house to
vandalize the neighborhood for the rest of the day. These di-
gressions were crucial to Will, and because they were infrequent (only three or four times a month) it took him a half year
to pinpoint the causal relationship between those changes of
pattern and other changes of pattern during the morning or
preceding night, disregarding a certain randomness common
to everyone.

Will then remained the full day in his room listening to
the tape recorder, copying down her words in a notebook to
add more objectivity and distance to his thinking, recreating
her naked body before the mirror with his memory, circling
phrases and drawing arrows, looking at photographs, reading letters, writing out in longhand possible solutions, reading those solutions in light of previously written solutions as
a safeguard against oversimplification, and thinking. His last
entry under "Mornings" read:

The sound that Cedar Stern's alarm makes in the morning is precise and acute. She does not let it ring, but
slams down on the button with such force that I can
hear the shaking of the night table. This is one of the
many examples of her hatred of machinery: she has
no automobile, only the absolutely necessary electrical appliances, told Reuben that she had no time to
fix the stove, has several times thrown her key to the
floor when it refused to fit easily and immediately
into the front door lock, has a piece of leather that she
ties around the collar of Duchess instead of a simple
chain with a snap, refuses to clean the refrigerator
while keeping the rest of the house immaculate, does
not have a wristwatch, yells "shut up" when the phone

rings, has called in the television repairman twice when the dog accidentally brushed against the brightness control, turning the picture tube black, and threw her radio away after it started buzzing.

Cedar Stern is a moral woman; however, not without specific reservations. She feeds the animals before herself but not before she urinates and brushes her teeth, yet before she dresses. The fish feeding comes before the dog and cat for the reason that the responsibility of the fish is deeper because it is unaware of her coming downstairs — the dog and cat know they will be fed; therefore, they can wait. Cedar Stern not only must feed the fish, she must also remember to be conscious of the fish's hunger and remember to feed it.

When Cedar does not feed the dog and cat (or either one of them) it is because they have too overtly demanded to be fed. She is aware that the animals are *not* living in a natural state but are dependent on her for their lives and serve as instruments toward her pleasure. This situation is both necessary and repugnant to her — life-giving and god-playing. The fish, however, because of its complete sublimity can be always a small creature and a symbol for all of life; the glass bowl, the aerator and the manufactured fish food — because the fish is unaware of them — are not unnatural.

Cedar's motivation for leaving the animals to run loose around the neighborhood during the day is two-sided, two radically conflicting yet complementing desires are at work; first a desire for the animals to be free and unhindered in their movements; secondly a desire for their destruction from an automobile or an irate neighbor. These mornings usually follow a series of three or four days wherein Cedar suffers from ennui, thought-gazing. Her morning discussion with the animals during these four days becomes increasingly less specific, tending almost toward free association. In the last day, the very presence of the animals, their dumbness and spontaneous apathy, is irritating. She chases them out into the backyard, barricades the door behind them, but before leaving for work I can hear her pulling the kitchen curtains aside — only an inch, perhaps less, to see if they are still in the yard.

There is something special about a woman who in the morning looks into a mirror at her naked body. Many, perhaps most women, enjoy looking at themselves for even luxurious intervals at night or in the afternoon following a hot bath or shower and perform elaborate rituals with bathrobes and towels and underpants and changes of expressions. And Cedar is not an exception to these. But a woman who consciously pays attention to, looks at, and so admires her unclothed body in the morning is abnormal. She is aware that this communication between herself and her beautiful body is breaking a mystical norm and so brushes her hair with short, careless, choppy movements instead of long, steady, rhythmic, fondling strokes that characterize her night brushings. Despite the guilt she never relinquishes her morning encounter with her natural self and even turns around and looks over her shoulder at her rounded buttocks and soft thighs.

Cedar's insistence on putting on her underpants (always a little too large — they bunch up during the day and must be uncomfortable) before her bra is, like the short careless brushing of her hair, a reaction against her indulgence at the mirror and a check against any further indulgences. After she has put on her bra (I do not believe that Cedar was given the black bra — no, she bought it one day downtown after watching an exciting movie or prompted by a clerk she used to know from high school . . . or for some other reason and then

later, in the morning, was ashamed to wear it) her
reaction *against* her embarrassment brings her back
again to the mirror, where she smooths down her slip
around her hips. Her body now essentially hidden, the
rest of the dressing is business and the brown shoes
are chosen because they are older and more "common"
than the others and reinforce her belief that she has
nothing superficially to offer anyone—that her clothes
are the moat between the wonderful castle of herself
and the world, and that like the stone of the castle, its
ordinariness only serves to enhance the beauty and
magnificence inside. And with this secret she goes to
work. And because of this secret she is able to live in
the way that she does.

Will's apartment filled with flat, brown notebooks of character sketches, even short stories—fictional episodes that a
fictional Cedar Stern, endowed with the attributes of the real
Cedar Stern, was forced to encounter. In this manner Will was
able to imagine Cedar Stern in situations that were not available to his notice, and in many cases, her own. And so his understanding of her grew even larger than was possible within
the confines of the house.

In the beginning of this fiction-writing period, which only
lasted about three months, he was attentively narrow-minded
toward his character and material. His concerns were *thematic*
and determinedly held to the focus of single ideas; however,
by the end of this period his "stories" became groundless emotional statements of Cedar Stern, written in the first person
and entitled such things as "Thoughts before I go to Sleep"
and *"When Love Comes to Me."* (The ink on these pages was
smeared . . . sweating, I believe.)

Will soon gave up creative writing because of what he complained of in one of his notebooks as "emotional impurity—the
impossibility of keeping an idea or sensation simple and clean

while also attempting to warp that sensation or idea into a shape resembling a *form*." He found mechanical drawing to be more calming and his apartment began to look like an architect's basement. The control that was demanded in drawing straight lines added an amount of keenness to his mind and allowed his wondering thoughts to condense into concrete propositions and statements while his hands erected miniature towers and buildings with friezes.

Every so often, in the evening, Cedar Stern would masturbate. Will was particularly interested in this activity, more so than the animal conversations, the morning dressing, or the childhood picture albums. He learned to predict those sexual nights by Cedar's expression walking up the stairs: half-closed eyes, flushed color, quick breathing, and absentmindedness. He moved the microphone over to a bedpost in order to pick up the slightest vibration from the bed, or words that she might unconsciously speak (or consciously, for the excitement of hearing some particular word or words said out loud, even by herself).

Cedar Stern talked little while she masturbated. Occasionally she would mumble a group of words unintelligible to even Will's sensitive recording device, and infrequently she would pronounce groups of words resembling, "No . . . n . . . no . . . No, NO," or "Now . . . now . . . NOW," or "Stop . . . NO . . . stop." Will was disappointed. The words could obviously be nothing more than sexual words, easy to say, with long O sounds, or in the case of "stop," sibilancy. This probability — the immediate verbal pleasure that each of the words afforded — overrode any symbolic interpretation they might have had for her . . . and Will did not finally attempt to assign meanings allegorical or otherwise to the words because "no" and "now" and "stop" were in fact his own favorite words during his own monosexual experiences. The knowledge that Cedar's choice of words was indeed his own strengthened the growing intimacy between them, and to his almost uncontrollable delight Will managed to arrange several of his affairs with himself at a time corresponding to Cedar's; and with his headphones on his head he could listen to his beloved talking to him in his own language while he stroked toward his satisfaction under the mind's eye of Cedar mouthing those words.

After overcoming his initial excitement of secretly participating in Cedar's masturbating, Will became attentive to the circumstances that brought Cedar up the stairs with her eyes half closed and cheeks flushed. He was happy to notice that those circumstances were never so simple as a television program or a magazine article. Occasionally a novel would stimulate a smile not fully humorous and she would begin playing with the edges of her bedclothes; and Will wrote down the name of the book and the estimated page number to look up the following day. This is misleading: Cedar never bought books that were written for just that purpose, probably for fear that when she bought one the man at the paperback stand, after taking her money, would either find out her phone number and write it down in every telephone booth in town, or zip down his fly and expose himself in front of her in a knowing way. No, Cedar always bought good books, or at least books that sold relatively well, and was pleasantly affected when one of them turned out to be a "bad" book in disguise, or hidden among thousands of pages of sophisticated verbal zigzag puzzles was a scene that made her whole body go warm. One of these scenes was in a Des Moines best-seller named *Love's Carriage*, by Ruth Cartney. The story is about a young girl's life in California and her consequential suicide in the face of unimaginable forces:

> Teresa walked along the silent beach and felt the terrible force of the sea as though the very fact that she was there and alone was reason enough for the sea to reach out and carry her away. She pulled the light dress over her head and slipped out of her underpants and

bra. The wind from the ocean was moist and caressed her rich breasts and thighs with quiet fingers. Her hair blew back from her face and she walked out toward the water where the lapping waves pulled at her tiny feet and ankles, begging her to give herself up to the call of the sea, to return once again to the womb of all creation.

"Teresa, Teresa," a voice called from the house. She did not hear, but walked out still farther, her heart beating steadily now. The fear had passed and she was at one with the sea.

"Teresa . . . Teresa." The voice was frantic now and a figure ran out of the house and toward the beach, paused at Teresa's abandoned clothing and continued out toward the water.

"Teresa, Teresa," called the voice again, but Teresa did not hear. The dark figure ran along the water until he saw her silhouetted against the moon, the water running in golden rays around her body.

"Teresa, for God's sakes," screamed Tom. It was Tom. He had returned, come home once again. He dove into the water and with powerful strokes quickly reached her.

"Tom," sighed Teresa as she threw her arms around his neck. "Teresa," his eyes said softly back to her and he felt her nipples harden against his naked chest. Warm. "Take me, take me, Tom," she said and Tom loosened his pants and let them fall off into the water. She felt him stiffen against her stomach and thrust her tongue inside his mouth. Locked in each other's arms they walked inland until they could lie down. "I love you, Teresa," said Tom and they were at one with the sea, rhythmic in their satisfaction and eternal in their love. (Pages 278–281.)

This section was important, because unlike vaguely similar sections in other novels, it was kept by Cedar's bed in order to fully arouse her after one of the other novels had done so insignificantly. About this Will wrote:

My dear Cedar's sexual image of herself is inextricably involved with her underlying belief in the natural order and her own submission to it. Because of her preoccupations with guilt /morality it is necessary for her to fantasize a condition where her guilt would be alleviated — where her emotions and actions could be sanctified . . . humble in the eyes of God. This passage provides just such a fantasy, and is stimulating to Cedar because of the character Teresa's representative state of mind; furthermore, the way in which this state of mind is developed is so obviously fantastic that Cedar is in no way compelled to question its actuality, as monosexual experiences are satisfactory or unsatisfactory in direct relationship to how capable one is in excluding all reasonable, actual thoughts and drowning oneself in fantasy.

One afternoon at his drawing table Will realized that he had understood Cedar Stern and was able to predict emotional responses, etc. He wondered how long he had been able to do this before he realized it. The thought did not trouble him. The next element of plan required that he find an accomplice, someone in whom he could confide his design. He chose Walt, and the following conversation I heard through the walls of our house the night Will came to talk Walt into helping him:

". . . What I want you to do is spend some time with a not unattractive woman in a certain way for a certain reason." Will's intonation indicated something at least secretive. To Walt this meant possibly destructive and he continued to listen.

"... My plan is this ... I have spent the last nine months ... well, longer, understanding this woman, Cedar Stern ... studying her. Without details, I have located her metaphysic — what she lives by. I intend to remove that metaphysic, realign her dependence on it to myself. I need a catalyst. She has been insulated from men since an unsuccessful marriage, but because that was a long time ago it is possible that she may have forgotten her ugly experience — and is ready to think that all men are really not so bad after all. You are to reassure her that they are, so that when I come out of hiding and into her life she will be all the more prepared to give herself to me. In other words I will be more appealing because of your repugnance." Even without seeing Walt I could picture his forehead wrinkling and his jaw muscles twitching. He was thinking.

"What does she look like?" Walt asked. He was not finished thinking and needed more time.

"Nice. Very nice. Since when were you an aesthete anyway? Isn't it always the idea that counts? Purity of thought and all that bullshit."

"Why me?"

"Because of your age and looks and speech and because I can trust you like I couldn't trust anyone else to not get involved."

Walt's thoughts began to coagulate and solidify. He stood back and looked at them ... saw to the extremities of the plan, where Will could and would never see — beyond the idea and into the conception — looked toward the destruction, saw how he would contribute to that destruction, and accepted.

Will spent two days teaching Walt the proper attitude to take toward Cedar Stern; mannerism, phraseology, personality, interest, intonation, dress, humor, etc. His, Walt's, new name was Alex Cinder, and he was a used-car salesman. He borrowed one of Paul's automobiles (he, Walt, seldom drove anywhere; I don't know how he got to where he did or what he did when he got there; he never was without money but never worked anywhere that I could tell, and never had large amounts of cash) and drove out to the Bridewell Greenery in a light blue sport coat that Will was certain used-car men wore — and Walt didn't know enough about used-car men to say anything one way or the other, or just simply didn't care, and wore it. (I always trusted Will's judgment in everything colorless, but whenever a tone or a shade was involved with his memory, his ability to reason was immediately impaired, or at least suspect. Not that he wasn't colorful himself, but that it was difficult for him to believe that all colors were any more than extensions of his own colorful existence, and because blue was a repellent color to him, then used-car salesmen and medical students, who were also repellent to him, should of course wear blue sport coats. And how could you argue with that?)

Walt went into the greenhouse and identified Cedar Stern from the detailed description Will had given him, complete to the brown shoes with leather wrinkles and slanted heels worn to the outside. I have wondered what Walt felt then, but after a while I didn't wonder about it anymore. He asked her to show him some "flowers."

"What kind of flowers were you interested in?" asked Cedar. She was avoiding looking at Walt. . . . No, not avoiding. She was not looking at Walt.

"I don't care. Just some flowers . . . nice ones of course. I wouldn't want cheap flowers."

"There are no cheap flowers here. Perhaps if you told me what occasion you want the flowers for I could help you in your choice." Cedar had looked at Walt, had taken in the color combination of blue on green, his greasy hair and white-silver rings, and was now avoiding looking at him.

"Well, no occasion really. No occasion at all. It's my idea, see. What I intend to do is put some flowers around the showroom to make it seem more like the country, or like home."

"I guess I don't know what a showroom is."

"Ha . . . Ha . . . of course. No one would expect you to, Miss — ?" There was an ugly pause.

"Ha . . . Ha . . . A showroom is a room where you show cars. This is a showroom for flowers — just a plain showroom means a car showroom."

"We have plants in here too," Cedar mumbled.

"What?"

"Nothing. How about some tooth-of-the-lion flowers? They are the flowers over there."

"They'll do."

"How many would you like?"

"Sixteen or seventeen."

"Sixteen or seventeen."

"Yes. And I'd like to start an account here. Do you deliver flowers?"

"Yes; except Friday and Sunday."

"Could you have sixteen or seventeen of those lion flowers brought over to Mike's Chevrolet?"

"If you will write down the address I'll have someone bring them over — which day would you like them? We don't deliver on Friday or Sunday."

Walt was smiling rapidly then and in a friendly, congratulatory voice said that on second thought he would come and pick them up himself — that he really didn't see as much of greeneries as he knew he should. Cedar smiled back at him, but not much.

The next day Walt came back to the nursery and the day after that he asked Cedar to "accompany him" to a movie. The following day she accepted and that Saturday night they went to a rerun showing of *Libido in Paris,* a movie about the Nazi occupation of Berlin and two young women's defeated efforts to suppress their homosexual tendencies. The following week they went to the movie *Fast and Free,* a story of a young race-car driver, his affair with a nightclub singer and his diabolical mechanic who loosened his steering column and put sand in his gasoline. Afterwards Walt managed to be invited in Cedar's house and as Will listened he told Cedar of his plans to develop a special tachometer that could be set for speeds or distances and would print the elapsed time out in illuminated numbers.

During the next two weeks Cedar Stern accompanied Walt to movies, auto shows, stock-car races, and a lecture given in Tech High School Auditorium by Philip Trinket on industrial waste and the profession of a system analyst.

One evening in a crowded movie theater Walt put his arm around Cedar and asked in a loud voice if she "minded being kissed." Cedar was confused. She listened to the whispered laughter from the four rows in front and behind her. She implored her voice to say "yes" in a way to indicate that the entire horrible episode was a joke to both herself and Walt, a gay time, but she listened as a frantic, high-pitched "yes" screeched out across the theater, and her muscles were dancing. Later, in the parking lot Walt again put his arm around Cedar and asked if she would "enjoy being kissed." Cedar answered, "You can if you want to."

Walt kissed her very softly and then poked her in the stomach with his thumb. He started the car and began driving toward Cedar's house. On the corner of Sixth Avenue and High Street Will waited with a very old dog that he had bought from the dog pound and it was sitting on the curb next to the street. Driving fast, because of his elated mood, Walt approached the corner, saw Will and the dog, and swerved the car across and over the curb. The mongrel screamed but was unable to move out of the way. The front bumper struck her and she was thrown several yards up against the building where she lay yelping and biting her pain. Will was yelling obscenities and throwing glass bottles at the car. Walt drove on down the street laughing and telling Cedar of other, more exciting experiences he had had . . . and how once, when he was only twelve, he had killed a dog with a ball-point pen.

He parked the car in front of her house under the street-lamp and put his arm around her. Cedar tried to remove herself from Walt and the car, and managed to open the door before Walt jerked her back across the clear plastic seat, laughing and saying how "spunky" she was. She pushed at him with her hands and beat at him with her fists. Walt continued to laugh and said she needed to behave. He moved to the center of the car seat and pulled Cedar across his lap and began spanking her. She screamed with rage and kicked out with her feet — which opened the door still further. Her neighbors came to their windows and Walt pulled her dress up around her waist and directed his openhanded blows onto her white underpants. Some of the neighbors opened their windows or front doors in order to watch with no distortion. After a time Cedar was allowed up, and looking into the happy eyes of her neighbors (Cedar had always presented an austere image to the good people of Des Moines, mostly because of her beauty, and they were glad to see her put in her place) she began to cry and ran into her house, locking the door behind her. Walt called her once that evening, was hung up on, and never saw or spoke to Cedar again.

Will returned to his room and listened to Cedar's sobbing before she fell asleep. He waited several weeks for the experience to become both more detached and more concrete to her.

Then, one year and two months after he had seen Cedar get off a bus in Des Moines — dressed in a leather jacket, brown shoes and corduroy pants, he walked to the Bridewell Greenery.

It must be remembered that Will had never stood beside or spoken to Cedar Stern. The sound of her voice, her expressions, mannerisms, and actions he knew — they were almost as familiar to him as were his own. He fought to keep his body from shaking and prayed that his voice would not falter. He looked at her from across the greenery and she was lovely. He wanted to run over to her and put his arms around her and tell her to not be afraid, because he was like a child coming home, a father returning from the war, a husband recovering from a deadly disease. He wanted to tell her of what he knew, of the extent to which she already belonged to him, of how he would marry her. But Will was forced (he was still capable of forcing himself) to admit that Cedar Stern had in fact never seen him—that he would be simply a stranger in a leather coat to her.

"May I help you?"

"Do you have any Christmas cacti?"

"Only one, I think."

"With pink flowers?"

"Yes . . ." Her voice was preparing to tell Will that all Christmas cacti had pink flowers.

"No . . . really. I saw one with white flowers two years ago. It was just awful." He smiled and Cedar Stern smiled back at him. His intonations were exactly her own.

"White flowers," said Cedar, and her voice made cooing noises around inside Will's head. He had not been wrong. He had known it would happen.

Will, in a sense, slowly became acquainted with Cedar Stern; that is she became acquainted with him, or what he was then, which was what he was sure he had to be. They walked through the park during her lunch hour. They took her dog to the zoo on Saturdays and rode bicycles into the country. Will was ecstatic. Each difficulty he had predicted, and he solved each with the precision of a gyroscope-drawn circle. Her fear of irrational men he absolved by being obviously careful of small details. Her distrust he calmed by giving more attention to her than to himself. Her fear of exposing herself he corrected by being even more intensely withdrawn than she . . . and calling attention to the fact that he was. Will cleaned his room of all his detection devices and notebooks (which he gave to Nellie to keep for him, and she gave them to me to read, and I read them). Will's last entry in his notebooks was, "Triumph."

Because of the length of time Will had spent developing his own character approach to Cedar, the "real" Will Sledge, or the collage that was "Will Sledge" at times before, disappeared. He became what he had intended to pretend. By studying plant and animal forms he became genuinely interested in them; and because his increased sensitivity brought him pleasure in regard to its effect on Cedar, he became less reckless. . . . His plan had begun to enfold him, and the more overlappings it developed, blinding his self-consciousness, the more happy he became.

Cedar Stern was very much in love with my brother. She sang songs to herself during the day and told Felix and Duchess about him, and *them*. She slammed her door when returning home late at night and turned her new radio up loud enough to joyously intimidate her neighbors. She visited her father and sister less, and then smugly, because she had a secret worth protecting. She wore colorful clothes and her body was more beautiful than before. But did Will see these things? Could he extricate this woman from the image he had built of her during the last year?

"Do you want to play gin?" asked Will, after they had returned to her house from a walk along the Des Moines River where they had talked to the fishermen standing on Grand Avenue Bridge.

"Oh, Will," she laughed, "you're wonderful . . . a little old-fashioned maybe. I love you." She was laughing.

"What's old-fashioned about gin?" asked Will.

"Nothing. It's just sort of old-fashioned when you want to play it."

"Is that so?"

"Let's not play cards. Tell me about your family. You never talk about your family." She curled up under Will's arm.

"Well, my father was a professional wrestler that had no arms. He had polio when he was a child."

"That's awful, Will."

"No, not really; he used to fight with his head, and feet . . . he went barefoot in the ring . . ."

"Stop."

"Too horrible?"

"Too imaginary."

"You know what I'd like to do?"

"What?"

"See the ocean. Have you ever seen the ocean?"

"No."

"It must be wonderful. Those waves washing up on the shore — the serenity and timelessness of it."

"I've thought a lot about that too — just giving yourself to the rhythm of the waves, the sky, the rocks . . . and sand." Will began to caress her arms.

"To lose yourself like that . . . to be free."

"Yes," she said. They kissed each other, Will with passion and she with acceptance. He put his hand under her sweater, and with massaging motions found his way to her covered breasts. "No," she whispered, "Will, no," and rested her head against the sofa, putting gentle pressure against his chest with her hands. "I love you," said Will, kissing and biting her neck. He carefully uncovered one of her breasts from beneath the loose fitting bra and pulled at the nipple, feeling it become hard between his fingers. "No, Will . . . please, no," she said and let her body sink lower on the couch. "Shhhhh," he kept whispering, periodically. His hand dropped easily down from under her sweater and he slid his fingers down and around the hem of her skirt where he could feel the soft skin above her knees. "No . . . Stop," whispered Cedar, her eyes shut now and both her hands locked into Will's long hair. "Stop." But Will did not stop and pulled her panties down about her knees. He rubbed gently yet firmly around the outside of her vagina until he felt his fingers warm with Cedar's love syrup, and then thrust two of his fingers inside her. "NO, Will . . . No." She was almost talking then, her entire body rigid. "Shhhhh," he whispered, and left her vagina to begin taking her clothes off — being careful not to break the communion that had captured both of them.

After what seemed to Will a dangerously long time, they

were both naked and lying on the sofa, he between her opened thighs caressing her vagina with one hand, her hip with the other, and sucking on her second nipple. "No, Will . . . please stop," she was whimpering and he thrust his I-beam penis inside her. She began to moan and her love screaming filled the room. "I love you," said Will, and felt a rushing building up in his groin. Cedar's legs came up around him and she became almost quiet, whispering, "No . . . no . . . no . . ." while her vagina began pulsating slowly. His entire body felt possessed and his sperm jumped out of him and into Cedar. "Will you marry me, Cedar?" he asked, or maybe thought he asked, and was smiling wonderfully in his mind's eye. "No . . . no," whimpered Cedar. He lay quietly on top of her. "Will you marry me?" he whispered.

"Will, no," she murmured. Then the silence of the room was like a tomb. "Cedar," he said, "lovely Cedar, my Cedar. Will you marry me?"

"No," she said, and there was no mistake, no passion. It was not a whisper. Will thought his body must be shaking. His face was hot and the light from the table lamp was blinding him. "Cedar," he cried. "No," she said, "You've given me so much. I've missed so much. You've shown me that. I'm young again."

Will got out, got up, and got dressed. He exchanged all the words he could bear and left the house. It was cold outside, but not cold enough, he thought. He was burning; his mind raced with him and he feared he was going insane. A throbbing in the base of his skull was splitting him open. He walked down toward the City, down toward the darkness and the stench. The fog enveloped him. He walked down and heard a monument open — no, he didn't hear it, he knew it. But he did not go on. He did not go in. He stood and knew what he must do. Go back — back to the room in back of Cedar's house . . . go back and find where he had gone wrong — what he had failed to see. Watch her again, follow her wherever she went, for as long as need be, until he could find the key. And then possess her for his own. He turned and walked back up away from the City and heard a sound behind him like a huge boulder dropping several feet into a grass-lined pocket of earth . . . the perfect seal.

Nellie gave all of those old notebooks to me to read and I read them, though I did not understand them then or for a long time afterwards. And I never saw Will again for him to explain them to me. Nellie once said that Jealousy had turned on him, had consumed him. I said it was the Idea, but she said: "How could an idea do that?"

Walt stayed at home most of the time after Will had come to reclaim his recording equipment from Nellie. This made us uneasy. I had heard Will say to him that he "couldn't understand." But he, Walt, did not reply. He had not walked away, he had just not said anything. Will left, and Walt stayed in the house most of the time after that. Too long, I think. He had nothing to do. He began casting about and Father and he stayed up one night playing poker and drinking beer. Walt was a rotten card player and had lost most of his pile of poker chips to Father.

"You lose because you don't think right," said Father, pointing his finger at Walt from behind his glass of beer.

"How can you think right about a bunch of cardboard squares with numbers on them? Anybody that can think right about that — or thinks he's thinking right about that — is suspect. It's like saying I don't 'live right.'"

"That too." Father was not concerned with logical cleft sticks.

"Deal," said Walt.

"You make the cards work for you," said Father, dealing three cards to them both, two down and one up. "If you think of them as cardboard squares, it becomes a matter of pure luck . . . and luck is always bad."

"I bet ten," said Walt, and pushed a blue chip into the middle of the table.

"Fold," said Father.

"How the hell am I suppose to win when every time I get a hand, you fold—when every time I've got a hand you've got nothing? It's just luck."

"No. You've got two aces . . . maybe a king or a queen besides."

"How do you know that?"

"From the sound of your voice when you bet . . . that, and my cards told me you had something like that."

"Shit," said Walt, shuffling the cards. "Besides, it was only a jack."

"Not much difference."

"So why are you able to 'think right' about cards?"

"Not why—how."

"So . . . how?" Walt was smashing his words out, down onto the table. Nellie left the room and went into the kitchen.

"Because of this," said Father, and pulled out a half-empty pint from his coat pocket.

"Okay. So you're a souse. What's that got to do with it?" Walt dealt them both five cards.

"I can see things better—clearer . . . not just cards, everything."

"I'm drinking. I've been drinking all night. Why don't I have this super vision?"

"I bet three," said Father and moved three white chips toward the center of the table. Walt did the same. "Because you don't live right—you don't think right—and you don't know how to drink."

"Now wait a minute. First you say that drinking makes you think right. Then you say that you have to think right before drinking makes you think right. Shit."

"Give me four cards," said Father. "It's a matter of expectation. If you can't understand that then maybe that's your problem."

Walt gave him four cards and himself two. "There is an A.A. convention in town next month. Maybe you ought to go there.

They'd probably be very interested in hearing what you have to say."

"I'm not an alcoholic."

"Anyone that drinks as much as you do is an alcoholic. It's a matter of natural order."

"I bet four," said Father. "Every day it's a choice. I could quit any time." Walt covered his bet and added a red chip to the pot.

"That's what they all say, 'If I wanted to, I could. It's just that I don't really want to at this moment.'"

Father put a red chip and a blue one into the pot. "It's also a matter of intention. I don't drink to be drunk. It's different." Walt put two blue chips into the pot.

"And just what do you think all the alcohol is doing in there? Rushing around clearing up your eyesight — like sight-savers for the eyeball."

"In a sense it does that, clears my head and gives me a position to look at things from and allows me more freedom. I raise ten."

Walt put in a blue chip, then added a red one. "Sounds like witchcraft to me, only worse."

"If you knew things instead of words, maybe you'd understand . . . I doubt it . . . call."

"Three sixes," said Walt.

"Flush," said Father and laid down five clubs, pulling the chips toward him. Walt was angry, or as angry as he ever was . . . in an abstract way. He kicked at the table leg.

"So you don't get drunk?"

"Right."

"I'll bet you eighty-five dollars that you can't drink a fifth of bourbon without getting drunk."

"That's too much, any man . . ."

"Okay. One fifth of bourbon without taking the bottle from your mouth — the hell with the getting drunk part."

"Let me see the money." Walt took out eighty-five dollars

and laid it on the table. Father picked it up and put it in his vest pocket behind his watch. "In case you lose I may be in less condition to take the money from you, than you from me."

"True," said Walt and brought a fifth of bourbon from the kitchen. Nellie followed him into the living room and after she grasped what was about to happen pleaded that Father forget the stupid game. Father told her to keep quiet and she only asked once, sat down and watched him begin to drink the bourbon. The first half-pint disappeared instantly. The second he gulped like a thirsty man drinking warm milk. The third pint was slower and Father began to gasp through his nose, gulped large mouthfuls and rested the bottle on his lips, buying time. The gasps for air became more frequent and the gulping became not only unpleasant to watch but unpleasant to hear as well. The last ounce of bourbon washed down the bottle like dirty water down a clogged drain.

"You always were a fool," said Father to Walt, "all my children have been fools. Only Reuben." And he looked at me. His face was red. "He's still a fool, but maybe in the kind of way that he won't always be. Maybe." And he winked at me. "But I doubt it." I doubted it too, not remaining a fool, which I knew I was not, but understanding — ever understanding — what Father meant by anything he said. I had this thought while I sat like a Cretan statue looking out of myself at Father, who talked faster and faster; watched as his words ran together into ink blotches. He waved his arms about, tried to light a cigarette, failed, cursed Walt and knocked his beer glass off the table. Of course it took longer than it seems here.

He complained of pains in his stomach. He retched on the table red-yellow vomit and the smell exploded; and with his hands dripping with the liquid he pointed quickly here and there into the corners of the room, mumbling, reached them up to his head and screamed, ". . . The rats, the rats." Then he quit screaming. He quit everything.

Walt went over to Father and lifted his head up from the

table. "He's dead," he said, and tried to sound a laugh that he had somehow earned, failed; tried to say something like, "The argument was of course that it be completed by the living," failed, and tried to pull the eighty-five dollars out of his vest pocket as a final gesture. I shouted then (I wanted to shout then) that the money belonged to Father. Walt's hand shook and the money dropped to the floor. He covered his face and left the room.

And then the Cretan statue looked away from them and at Nellie. Her face was fixed in a hysterical stare whose memory now is like a metaphor of itself, thousands of horrible faces of women with their hands put against their heads to protect them from whatever terrible ghastly things too awful to comprehend without that thin wall of flesh between. But her hands were not raised, and lay in her lap. She sat for a long time and gradually the complexion of her face became more sane. I could see her breathing. Beautiful Nellie. She turned her head towards me.

"Reuben," she said.

"What," I answered roughly.

"Come here, Reuben."

"Why?"

"Touch me." I walked over to her and clumsily took hold of her hand. "What's the matter?"

"Our father is dead," she said.

"So what. It's his own fault. He must have wanted to die. He knew better than to let Walt talk him into something like that. He was the fool."

"Don't talk like that, Reuben."

"I will."

"You should only talk the way you feel."

"I don't feel nothing."

"Then don't talk."

"I don't care . . ."

"I'm going to go blind, Reuben."

"What?"

"I can only see these funny forms, no shapes . . . almost no colors . . . nothing out of the left eye."

"Blind." The idea was like out of a movie — unreal. Nellie was crying.

"Don't be afraid, it's — "

"I'm not afraid. Not at all," she said, tears dropping into her cheap dress. She smiled!!! "I'm going to like being blind." Smiling! If I had been older I would have feared going mad then, but as it was I said,

"It's just shock. It will go away."

"Is he really dead, Reuben? Can you see him?"

"Yes, he's dead . . . how long have you been like this?"

"What?" She was crying again.

"Your eyes."

"A long time. But it's worse now."

"It's just shock. It will go away."

But it didn't.

Chapter IV

...

THE MORNING AFTER FATHER DIED PAUL DROVE HIMSELF TO the Des Moines Depot in the pickup, stopped for a moment at the telegraph office, where John Tickie said nothing but nodded his head, went to Father's desk, and began to manage the depot, though he had probably never been there more than five times in his entire life. We (Nellie, Walt, and I) sort of expected he would do it, not that we expected him to do it, but we expected that he would. Paul was like that. I always had the feeling that I knew why he would do something. Not that I could articulate why he would do it, but because I understood him . . . except the time he laughed at the sheriff.

Walt and Nellie and I took Father's body out of the house and put it in one of the junkers from Paul's collection. We towed it with the truck kept only for hauling the coal that the railroad men kicked off the cars for him, down to First Avenue. Then we unhitched it, pushed it around the corner by hand and let it coast off down into the fog. We listened to the tires against the asphalt, listened till the tire sound stopped, listened while the sound of a giant boulder being dropped several feet into a grass-lined pocket of earth lofted up from below, listened and heard nothing.

"So it goes," said Walt.

Then Nellie turned to him and what she said I couldn't believe — not for her to say. Maybe it was the strain. Perhaps it was the tunnel-like quality that her eyes had taken on that added another dimension to her words. Perhaps it was what she had told me that morning of the blind keeping track of the sun with crickets' legs and frogs' throats that still unsettled me. In any event, though this memory is opaque, she said:

"I hate you. Why can't it be you who is down there?"

"Personal integrity," said Walt, almost sarcastically. Nellie was quiet and we drove home. Three days later he was gone.

The three remaining of us, Paul, Nellie, and myself (Will had been taken to a mental institution after what he was doing was noticed by the authorities, who along with Cedar Stern believed he was mad, but in a very different way from the way he was) were defenseless then — at least more so than before when Father and Walt were at home, especially Walt. And the good people of Des Moines knew this; not immediately, but from stories filtering down from thirteen-year-old boys, of throwing beer bottles against the side of the house — bottles that failed to bring Walt Sledge running and cursing out into the night after them. And they began to think that maybe Walt was not even at home; that maybe he was dead (they knew about Father), or at least had gone away. They grew bolder. A citizens' committee was formed to give the job of Depot Manager to a more qualified person. They argued, decided that having a Sledge operate the depot gave out-of-state travelers a distorted and wrong picture of Des Moines — that the job should not be passed on to Luke Sledge's son, who knew less about the job than other men more familiar with the railroad, and that the insurance companies, being the overwhelming business concern of Des Moines, should have more of a say in the operation of the railroad.

John Tickie sat behind his wire-mesh window and listened to the sound that the wrinkled and indignant faces made as it yammered in through the wire rectangles. He rolled his sleeves up to his elbows, stood up and opened the door. "Get out," he said. "Get off my platform."

"You can be replaced," shouted someone from the committee and someone else pushed him up against the depot wall. "Kill him," screamed a woman's voice.

"Get off my platform," said Tickie.

"Your platform!" yelled an old militant. "Who says it's your platform?"

"Get rid of him."

There were several men, however, who did think of the depot as Tickie's Depot and of the platform as part of that Depot, and as the citizens' committee found time to look around them they noticed through their anger a growing number of these rugged individuals wearing engineer caps, carrying coal shovels, shirts with Rock Island Line written in purple letters across the back, one man with three rings on one hand holding a push broom in vertical position, and a wino with a brick. "Get off my platform," said Tickie, and his words were bigger than before and more difficult to ignore: his request was represented in the grim faces of his troops. The citizens' committee backed off the platform, protecting themselves with terrible threats of physical brutality.

Vengeance.

Needless to say, vengeance's object is never a man, when at all possible. Women, born and nurtured by the devil for his own purposes; built from the rib of a man—from the protective covering of the heart; the snake goddess, looser of poisonous insects; chained to hell with a pomegranate seed; the source of all evil; serpent tamer; lustful and without rationality; intimidating by their very presence (to men through sexual and emotional humiliation . . . to other women through association); harboring mystical powers—witchcraft; capable of dementing the purity of man's thought . . . Guilty. And so it was Nellie whom the good people of Des Moines pushed into stacks of canned goods at grocery stores, yelled obscenities at as she walked down the street, refused to serve in the restaurants, and called on the telephone in the middle of the night to threaten, proposition, and ridicule. An orange cat, Nellie's Cat, was left on the doorstep, its eyelids clipped off.

These small, insufficient gestures finally came together in a tavern on Locust Street where Nellie was pulled inside and lifted up on the bar by eight men. Terrified, she was unable to see clearly enough to even run back and forth up on the bar and stood screaming and kicking out at the laughing hands that ripped at her clothes and jabbed at her crotch. Successful in removing her skirt and slip, they flung beer from their glasses at her face and one man chanced upon an extension cord, which he used to imprint thin red lines on her thighs. Somehow this whipping presented possibilities for punishment and retribution that seemed to the rest of the men more enjoyable and productive than they had even anticipated. They pulled her from her tentative standing position, removed the rest of her extraneous apparel and sportingly took turns with the extension cord. One man used the live end of his cigar to mark her back, but the majority of the people vetoed that practice as too vulgar. Leather belts were added to the whipping brigade; the turns came faster and the two women in the tavern helped too, asking Nellie, "How do you like that?" and telling her that she would "never forget this." But Nellie was screaming; and then she was crying; and then she stopped crying and lay on her stomach whimpering inaudibly under the shouting and laughter. Her silence, I believe, saved her life, and without the screaming the punishment lost its appeal. Several of the men must have had time then, as they waited for their turn, to look at the now bleeding girl in front of them; and at some time, after several rounds of each man hoping his strike would be the last, one of them accepted the extension cord, let it fall to the floor, and the belts were put back on. Perhaps it was guilt then, their fear of the guilt, that drove them to elect a spokesman for the group (an idea undoubtedly inspired by one of the women) to climb up on the bar, turn Nellie over on her back and make love to her — that's what it must have been.

But I hated them. I hated them. I hated them with a black-green and rancid emotion that exploded up inside of me and burned a corner of my heart to a deep purple that never changed color . . . even now, as I write this, I feel it alive, like a cancer, distorting my vision and drawing the tendons in my jaw tight against the bone structure in my face. All bone. And

I had thought that it wouldn't be like this — that this book would make me pure and order those things that are real in an artistic way, and that they would be absolved. I had thought that it would be done. Why has it not gone away? I hate them. But that is not about the story and all that was about that time. I must be narrow-minded . . . singularly concerned with my purpose, and have faith that after it is done (the book), that somehow it will contain it all. Even this.

I went into Walt's old room and found a chrome-plated .25 caliber automatic. My hate had so consumed my ability to reason that had it not been by accident that Walt had left it loaded with the long clip of twelve shots instead of seven I would have left without bothering to change clips. But as it was it made no difference. It was about ten-thirty and I intentionally assumed that every man, woman, and child that was in The Place Tavern when Nellie was beaten and raped, was still there, and that anyone who had come in later, during the time that it took for the cabdriver they had commissioned to drive her home and for me to get the gun and get to the tavern, was at least an accomplice. I parked the pickup across the street. There was no one in front of the bar or on the sidewalk. Picturing myself again as Walt, I stepped across the street, and opening the door with my left hand thrust the gun inside the tavern with me behind it. "Son-of-a-bitches," I yelled, and began to unload the twelve-shot clip into the walls, mirrors, and bottles along the bar of the empty room. "Come out you yellow mother-fuckers . . . Son-of-a-bitches." I might have been crying. I let a couple of bullets wander in through the rest-room doors. But the tavern was empty.

I was confused. I had not done anything, vainglory. The good people of Des Moines were afraid of me . . . they thought I was Walt . . . they were hiding in the next building . . . I was a coward . . . I was a hero . . . shoot the rest of my bullets . . . save them, I may need them . . . go in their homes, kill them, make them pay . . . it's all over, they'll be afraid to ever touch her again . . . I could be killed . . . I don't care . . . I do care. "Come out, you mother-fuckers," I yelled and emptied the rest of the clip. Then I heard some voices outside. Then they got louder.

"This is the police. Come out with your hands above your head." It was ridiculous, I said to myself . . . the police come to arrest me.

I was definitely not going outside with my hands above my head and so I stood where I was and reloaded the clip with bullets from my shirt pocket, in case it wasn't really the police outside.

"Who's in there?" whoever it was shouted.

"Walt Sledge," I shouted back.

"Come out with your hands above your head."

I knew what I had to do . . . what Walt would do. I had to open the door and step outside with the gun ready, and if it wasn't the police, shoot as many of them as I could before they killed me — assuming they had guns, which was probably why they had gone home in the first place. I turned the light off inside the bar so they wouldn't be able to see me so clearly when I stepped out, and shut my eyes for a moment to get used to the dark.

"Don't shoot, I'm coming out," I said, opened the door and stepped outside. In this instant I knew Walt would never have done things this way.

A policeman who had been standing against the building broke my right wrist with a lead-filled club and the chrome-plated automatic fell onto the sidewalk. Another policeman from the other side slammed me face-first against the side of the building. My head struck a brick that some unconscientious mason had left jutting out and blood was coming down over my eyes. I tried to tell them that I was not Walt, but they knew that; and their disappointment in me not being Walt was obvious as they continued treating me discourteously and breaking my ribs even after I had told them about Nellie. I managed to crack one of the men's glasses against his face

and his eye bled. After that I was beaten unconscious and re-
leased from the city jail the following day because the owner
of the tavern could not be located to press charges, and even
the women who had reported my shooting in the barroom refused to file against me. I could not understand that, resented
it, but was nevertheless taken to Mercy Hospital where I was
an inmate for two weeks, and I was almost nineteen when I
got out.

I loved Nellie. She was enchanted in thousands of ways . . . the
way she walked and touched things, holding them as though
they were not objects but forgotten members of herself that
she had misplaced about the house and yard, musing over them
like one does when he stumbles on an old photograph that
sends his mind off remembering times past with a focus acute
and precise, and yet elusive — operating within what Paul and
I called the "season of the witch" until someone wrote a song
called that and said it was something else so we wouldn't use
it anymore. She drifted, wraithlike if you weren't watching her
carefully — just noticing her offhandedly out of the corner of
your eye going from room to room — about the house gathering
up clothes and milkstained cups and other mysterious articles;
and as she worked, looking immensely preoccupied yet in such
a way as to be at the same time concentrating on whatever she
was doing. She would sit on the back porch, sometimes knit-
ting or sewing but always humming to herself, and talking . . .
I think talking . . . me hearing short soft sounds that began
and ended and began again, unrhythmical with long pauses and
consonants, that must have sounded like words to her when
she heard them, knowing their intention beforehand.

The Cretan statue with his "windows to the soul" for eyes
began to see the solemnness that Nellie's good eye had accepted from the one eye's blindness — the bedrock of humor
and playfulness gone. For many hours I tried to find an inkling
of humor in the right eye, the one that could see, convinced

myself that it must be there. "If both her eyes were full of humor and playfulness when they were alive," I thought to myself, "then with only one eye dead, one eye should still have gaiety and humor." But it didn't, and I would look and look out of my windows, trying to see in such a way as to lend humor to her eye. But the more I would try to do this the more aware I was that the humor had fled, migrated in the face of the endless eye winter-deep snowfall. The hazel brown color of her eyes only hinted to me of deep, profound harborings going on behind them. And I thought Nellie must be a philosopher . . . a contemplator of mystical realms . . . a daydreamer of frightening proportions. I once asked her if she wanted to be a philosopher and she laughed. And I wondered how she could laugh when her eyes had no humor . . . and she laughed all the time. The day after she had been raped and beaten I called her on the telephone from the hospital. "Nellie," I said, almost crying from the shame of not having dismembered and drunk the blood of the men who had abused her, and taken their wives and daughters and offered them naked and screaming to the god of intricate sexual humiliations.

And me in the hospital. "Nellie, how do you feel?"

"A little tired, I think." Her voice was already starting to play tricks with her words. "It's been a big day and I'm a little sore from horseback riding this morning. But I think I'll go to the beach this afternoon and get a tan. I'm told I have a good figure, you know." And she was laughing then and I hung up the phone, sure that the joke was at my expense.

It is difficult to imagine why when one eye is blind the blackness is picked up by the other eye, why the process never works in reverse. It is like a disease transferred from twin to twin — the health of one never aids the health of the other. Or perhaps it is a conscious act of the mind standing back and saying: "The dead eye brings me more peace than the live eye — if thy right eye offend thee black it out." And the mind lets the dark liquid of the blind eye flow into that of the seeing. That summer

Nellie's other eye went blind, sealing her forever into a darkness that she had, she said, accepted long before it came.

But I had not accepted it, and wherever I went with Nellie I would tell her what I saw . . . I would be her eyes for her. I continued to do this even after the day she had interrupted one of my extended descriptions and said, "I don't want to know what it looks like, Reuben."

"But it's beautiful," I demanded. "You ought to know what it's like."

"It's not beautiful," she said. "I can remember that much."

After that I was more conscious of making my descriptions beautiful. Looking out from the back porch I would describe the blue sky, gentle rain, the green grass, birds, flowers, artistic pieces of junk, small animals, airplanes reflecting the sun, trees and bushes blowing in the wind, and she would ask, "The City, can you see the City?"

"No," I would answer. "The City is gone — just open fields and sunshine now."

"You're lying," she said, "I can feel it there. I can feel the fog and smell it."

"It's your imagination," I would say. But of course it wasn't. The more I thought about what I was doing — making my narrations pretty, removing the ugly edges and the boring material, keeping everything down to a good-clean-fun level — the more I saw my position change from an informer of the very crucial type, to an entertainer begging for giblets of superficial satisfaction. I talked to Paul about it and he said that anyone giving a description, even when he attempts to give the whole picture, will distort reality . . . that it was inescapable and not, therefore, to worry about it. I continue to worry about it now, but I am sure that there is something else — some compromise between the impossible and the easy that is greater than both. My book is again wandering and I must bring it back to the *Story*.

Nellie learned to read Braille: (Louis Braille, 1829) our house filling with huge volumes of brown paper with pinholes stuck in them. I would watch Nellie sitting on the porch, the sun in her face, looking straight ahead with her hands moving lightly across the brown paper, turning the pages. I watched her face frown disapprovingly at those pinholes, laugh, cry, ponder, become bored, excited, sentimental, nostalgic, sad, angry, horrified, and sleepy. All this with dead eyes. She taught me to read with my fingers. It was a difficult art to master because it disgusted me. I thought it was stupid and for some reason unmanly: the idea was also repugnant to me — feeling words. But Nellie demanded that I learn. She would scold me when she heard me sneaking away from my study table, and I had no excuse. How could I? Whenever I did manage to get out of the house there was always Paul who, with only a look, could send me back in. She sat beside me on the sofa and, holding my hand in such a way that both our first fingers ran over the pinholes — hers before mine — read to me about warlords and whiskey priests and chess players and families with slaves in the South. After we had completed a novel (this usually took between three and four evenings) Nellie would begin to talk as if she were actually there in the book . . . talking about characters and how they were or weren't good people and how nice it would be to live in this or that house. I didn't like those talks, especially when I found myself giving in to them. Nellie was becoming more like that, and many times she would start conversations with me about subjects and places that existed nowhere but behind her harmless eyes . . . and she was becoming more like that and eventually even stopped talking about those places and things. And kept them to herself.

I learned to read Braille, to feel the words with my fingers; the pin dots became more than pin dots and I adjusted to the awkward situation of arriving at a cluster of dots on a brown piece of paper that I did not understand, and looking them up. Unlike most people who learn Braille, I was never able to pretend that the pinholes were secret codes to decipher. They were pinholes.

I developed a degree of dexterity in reading Braille and even began to respond to the way certain combinations of clusters felt. Pinholes could be good or bad depending on their arrangement, and a group of bad pinholes was not necessarily bad surrounded by a different group of pinholes.

I extorted some books from the Des Moines Public Library and learned to write Braille. At first I just punched letters to Nellie and she in turn punched letters back to me, but because her letters so surpassed mine, in beauty and intention, I discontinued our correspondence and began translating novels into Braille — those novels that she could obtain nowhere else. For this she was overjoyed and read them much more quickly than I could translate them. The pleasure she found in these novels I secretly accredited to my meticulous attention to the way the words felt — weeding out and making substitutions for all those clusters of pinholes that were jarring on the fingertips: though I never told Nellie this.

Once, however, as I was sitting at my translating table working on a novel about a fisherman, Nellie came into the room furiously holding out to me a novel that I had translated the week before, a novel almost about an Eastern pilgrimage and full of truisms and platitudes, most of which I had to revise to make readable. Unbeknownst to me, Nellie had read the book a year or two before and had so enjoyed it that she had memorized several of the passages, and was now here to berate me with those passages.

"YOU'VE CHANGED THIS BOOK," she screamed at me. Her hands and face were quivering, intimidating me. Paul heard the beginning and came quietly into the room where he stood beside the doorway and looked at me.

"You've CHANGEDTHISBOOK," she screamed again.

"No I didn't," I said. "I just reworded some of the awkward places."

"YOU'VECHANGEDTHISBOOK," she shouted.

"No . . . only used different words sometimes. All translators do that, some words that will work in one language won't work in another . . . obviously."

"You've changed this book."

"Changing some of the words doesn't change the book. The book is the same . . . its meaning and story are the same."

"YOU'VE CHANGED THIS BOOK. You've changED this boOk."

I stopped talking. It was plain by now that to Nellie I had changed the book. She threw the wretched object at where she thought I was and left the room. With the left side of my face throbbing, I turned to Paul.

"I don't know why you want to translate books anyway," said Paul. "It must be boring."

"So you don't condone 'changing books' either."

"I don't care about 'changing books.' I care about Nellie . . . and you."

"Paul, you're embarrassing to listen to. You don't always have to say just exactly what you feel, with people that already know."

"And I don't care about bravado either. If translating novels word for word is unpleasant to you, and not doing that upsets Nellie . . . then don't do it at all."

"That's too easy."

"I don't care how easy it is . . . nothing's easy. Why not write your own book if the ones you read aren't good enough?"

"It's not that, just a simple matter of touching up here and there."

Paul went back to wherever he was before and I went out onto the porch to make amends to Nellie. By pleading carelessness and stupidity I appeased her indignation and abated her wrath. I asked her if she had ever written anything other than letters and she said that she had. She went into the house and brought out several handwritten manuscripts of one hundred to one hundred and fifty pages. I asked if I could translate them for her and she said that she would enjoy reading them again. I promised to not change any words or make any new paragraphs and the next day began on the one called *Dark Into Myself*. The first page was as follows:

A myriad of colors turn and twist themselves and icecaps of memories dash upon the ground, splintering glass. The prisms haunt me with water. Cool, rushing over me. But the ice is like opium. Mother was dying then I remember with John Charles in the cellar — lying in the water that was ice when it froze. Small birds came and they were yellow and red and blue with high voices and feathers, too . . . but Mother sent them away. Father called to them after they had gone but they could never hear Father. His voice echoed away from their feathers. Crying was in the house. Of my crying there was too, and others. They were forgotten because the walls of the house ate them.

Standing now away . . . faraway . . . it is closer than then. The me then is sad and wanders among the thorns looking for flowers. The same me now seeks out no flowers, hunts no longer among the thorn trees but sees me then and is sad maybe again. Mother is screaming and Father not . . . watching is he . . . and me with brown and gold talons holding in tight to the baby. Sleeping is sacred and I am asleep now, waiting to sleep again. And the little messenger boy with a signpost hands me a letter in velvet. He wants money but I have none to give him. He takes the letter away and will come tomorrow. I will be asleep then though. Touching is important, but I have given that up too, for love.

I finished the page and hurried with it to Nellie. She read it with her fingers and was smiling.

"I remember that," she said.

"Remember what?" I jumped, asked.

"I remember writing it. I remember that feeling I had when I wrote it."

"What's it about? Is it about Mother dying?"

"No. It's about the inside of me. It is the inside of me . . . the inside of me then." I looked at her eyes, trying to understand. I wanted to know the inside of her. I wanted to be inside her as she sat on the sofa and her eyes were dead and she was smiling. I read the piece of brown paper with my fingers and could not understand, could not be there.

"Is the baby me? Was that when you were holding me when Mother died?"

"In a way," she said. "The baby is you but not you at all. The baby then was a feeling when I wrote that . . . a feeling now."

"But I can't feel that feeling. These words don't let me inside you. They don't make sense."

"I didn't write them for you, Reuben. They're for me."

"What good are they to you, you wrote them?"

"Like a diary . . . only better. Diaries are for vain people to list events that happened around them as though they were the grand reason behind why everything happened. So whenever they get to feeling insignificant they can rush to their diaries and read all about all the importance they have."

"But the web you have spun around your world is so intricate and interwoven that no one else can get in."

"And I can't get out," she added, and Nellie's Cat climbed up behind her head.

"Does that please you?"

"It doesn't please me and it doesn't displease me. It's necessary . . . a fact . . . a living fact, you might say."

"No; *you* might say. I wouldn't say that. I would never say that. I'll write you a novel; a giant novel that you can live in — a book that is the inside of me, a great, sprawling, ironclad prodigy of emotion, crammed with myself that you can get into." Strange, that talk.

"What will you write about?"

"About us; Walt, Will, Paul . . . all of us."

"Never write about yourself or people you know."

"Why not? You do."

"I don't write novels."

"Why not write about those things?"

"Novels should be all in the imagination. Don't mess them up with real things."

"Real things don't mess them up . . . they don't have to. You'll see, with only what I know about this family I'll write a novel that will send half the world on a pilgrimage to Des Moines to touch the sacred hair of Nellie's Cat. And the first copy will be for you. All the copies will be for you and it will say 'For Nellie' in the front of it." .

Nellie smiled and looked like she might be asleep if her eyes weren't open. I ran into my translating room and scattered all of those inferior novels across the room. I got my writing tool from a drawer and set a tremendous pile of brown paper in front of me. I began:

Night shadows begged the weeds out of the ground. Around the house were old automobiles, metal caskets made from dead machines. These things facilitated the Sledges' dreary existence.

I stopped writing. Something was wrong. I would just make a minor correction, then I could move on. One of the words was wrong. I changed "dreary" to "desperate." Then the page looked and felt messy — because it is difficult to erase in Braille — so I punched the paragraph with the new word onto another piece of paper. It was worse than before. I struck "desperate" and re-punched the entire paragraph, including the word "dramatic." It was no better and I struck the entire sentence and punched the remaining two sentences on a new piece of paper. The words were not right, and seemed irrelevant.

Only concern yourself with the necessary, I told myself . . .

the essentials. What did "weeds" have to do with what I wanted to say?

From one perspective, "weeds" seemed appropriate, as an image or a symbol—the pinholes that made that word felt somehow right; but from

another angle "weeds" were as inappropriate to what I wanted to say as would be "health food." I knew I must abandon the question of appropriateness and concern myself with expediency.

I struck the remaining two sentences and put a fresh piece of paper in front of me. How should I start? What to begin with? Honesty was the important thing . . . the most important. My novel was to be real, not *just* real . . . ultrareal, more real than anything ever written. I wrote:

This is a real story of real people and real places.

But that seemed dishonest. Who would believe that? I took another sheet of paper and wrote:

This is a real story of real people, my family, and a real place, Des Moines.

And there was something not right about that too. How could I expect anyone to believe that when I didn't believe opening lines like that myself when I read them in magazines? I wanted to write a real novel, not a true story or a true life story. I threw that piece of paper away and wondered again how to start.

I knew that I had a story to tell—a sequence of events to unravel—so I wrote "The story . . ." But the word "The," as a beginning word, was too obscure and impersonal. The word "This," as I soon discovered, was too obvious and interpersonal.

I was becoming depressed to the point of mania. Defeated. All words were hollow. I had spent an entire afternoon failing,

failing, and as I was coming to see, not because of my literary inaccuracy but because of the inherent inadequacy of language itself. And I was right . . . then. I forced myself away from
those thoughts and back again to my intention — my original
goal — to write a novel "For Nellie," a novel that was all of me,
was me, contained me, that she could experience through herself with the sustained awareness that it was in fact not herself, but me. And that thought outlined the blueprints of my
novel — where it must begin and to where it must go. In the
middle of a blank piece of brown paper I punched

(handwritten annotation: i — for uppercase / (I), you need a capital / sign in Braille — I)

and in the middle of the last page of my stack of paper I
punched

⠽ (you).

I was sure that the words were right. Even theoretically (even!)
it seemed that all real novels must be framed in that way, or at
least *do* that same thing; and honest real novels must, therefore, be exactly like that. Somewhere between the I and the
You all the rest would have to go. But I was finished then and
could go no further into it. This was the beginning of a depression that did not leave me (ever completely) until years later.
And I went back to translating Nellie's work.

Chapter V

...

THE RAPE OF NELLIE APPEASED THE GOOD PEOPLE OF DES Moines and we became joyfully ignored. Something like a generation must have turned over, and John Charles escaped all but the greedy remembrances of legislators within the gold-painted capitol building (that cost the taxpayers a king's ransom every year). Walt stopped being talked about as if he had been real and grade-school students boasted to their friends that their fathers knew what had happened to him. Many things were forgotten; more things will be forgotten. I will remember them all, however, because I have not been able to shut them out. If I could, I think I would. Perhaps not.

Des Moines was growing amoebic. Blocks of architectural nightmares bred and interbred, radiating outwards to the east and south and northwest. Large apartment buildings appeared in the west, creating a new breed of snobbery hitherto unheard-of on the West Side. The ranch-style home moved into the country and you could see them like toads squatting down between corn fields. An interstate highway, I-80, was begun and automobiles began zapping back and forth from Des Moines to Newton in less than half an hour. McDonalds Hamburgers found Des Moines. Pool halls were built for families, with ventilating fans and carpets. The far south side became an affluent neighborhood in itself and could boast of an airport and a restaurant that was even in *Gulfs Guide to Good Eating Places in the U.S.* The community playhouse was renovated as was the art building, both of which were, and are, usually discussed in conjunction with the word "controversial," those people not knowing the word, not talking about it. Younkers' animated display windows at Christmas stopped animating and no one drove one hundred miles to see their escalators any longer. The

KRNT Theater, with the largest stage area in the world, deteriorated into old age and no one cared. Riverside Amusement Park lost most of its family appeal and began attracting pairs of patrol cars. Indoor parking ramps made money and movie houses became respectable. Shopping centers and pink physician colonies were invented to service the new Des Moinesians, who in the fall no longer burned their leaves but put them in large plastic bags and left them along the road for the garbage man to pick up because of ordinances against leaf burning that made fire insurance more expensive and so lowered the property value. The "Blue Book" was not necessary to buy alcohol and the bootlegging industry suffered a setback (it did not die, because of high taxes). There were people who called themselves "executives" sometimes even before they were asked, and the car-boys preferred cherry '57 Chevrolets to clean '56 Fords. Pizza parlors were in Des Moines to stay and a series of feeble "coffeehouses" passed in and out of existence every two years . . . or so.

These things happened quickly — so quickly that you could watch them happen. But unlike other things that you could watch happen, they did not go away . . . they were the covering, and obscured the heart of Des Moines, the City, which remained. The embellishment was more elaborate, and Paul, watching the passengers getting off the trains to buy magazines and chewing gum during the layover, never heard them turn to each other and ask, "I wonder what's down there in all that fog?" or "It seems to smell wretched here, like from that hole in the ground. I wonder why anyone wants to live here . . . or why they don't do something about it."

"What would you do about it?" Father had used to ask them.

"I dunno," they'd reply, "Who cares?" and get back on the train. And of course there was nothing anyone could do.

It was possible to be born then in Des Moines and never see the City . . . never meet anyone who even knew it was there — to be entertained from the moment of your conception to the finality of your death. But I was too old by then, and the cavity that held the City was still plainly visible from our house. We had never allowed a billboard to be set in our yard.

These were good times.

Immediately after I completed high school I vacillated between doing nothing and working as a gas station attendant transferring specific amounts of gasoline from a large gasoline tank with a pump on top of it to the smaller gasoline tanks of automobiles. I also removed spots from windshields and checked engines' oil capacities with a long metal measurer called a "dipstick" with gradations marked on it reading FULL and ADD, and ONE QT. For these services I was paid an hourly sum called the "minimum wage."

I was not satisfied with my job and enjoyed talking to the gasoline customers even less than the actual physical work that the job required. So I managed to be placed on "night shift" where I worked from eleven P.M. until seven in the morning. I liked night shift much better because I was only forced to confront two or three gasoline customers in the entire eight hours. As Bill (Jonny) Grievney, my boss, once told me, I was "being paid to be sleepy," and because I slept in the daytime, and so wasn't sleepy at night, I was being paid for nothing, which was what I did all the rest of the time anyway.

Bill (Jonny) Grievney was an older man who claimed to be "young at heart." He helped many of the boys who used to go to my high school work on their cars and chisel away at rusty bolts and cotter pins. He would let them use his tools and put their cars up on the hydraulic lift. He told them stories about when he was young. The boys that he liked the best were always together. They would arrive at the station in a caravan and called themselves the Roadniks.

Sometimes they (Roadniks) would work on their automobiles at night and sometimes they would organize surprise attacks—"rumbles"—on other clubs and swing dogchains around from their fingers while they talked. Sometimes the caravan would go to Newton on I-80 to the stock-car races, and they wore white "blast jackets" with Roadniks written in red on the back, under the picture of a can of Bardol. Many of them had L O V E imbedded across the four fingers of their left hands and the letters H A T E respectively imbedded into the fingers of the right hands. This tattooing effect, as I had actually seen performed, was accomplished by pricking a pin dipped in ball-point pen ink into the fingers along a penciled-in outline of the word. One member told me that his right hand was his "fightin'" hand, and his left hand, because of its avail-ability in his car when his intention was to turn and feel up some cunt, was his "lovin'" hand. Nevertheless, the purpose, I believe, was to indicate that the forces of good and evil, or the potential for those forces, resided simultaneously within the person carrying those words.

I admired the Roadniks and was ashamed for them to see me translating novels into Braille, which was what I did most of the time when I was alone at the gas station on night shift. I told Eddie Thompson—I wasn't sure that he was the leader, but it was a safe assumption—and he told Eric Henderson, the leader, who told the rest of the caravan, that I wanted to join. Then they all came out into the main lobby of the gas sta-tion and stood looking at me in an attitude that might be say-ing "Congratulations" or "Do you have a high school diploma?" Eric Henderson told me that there were "rules" to becoming a Roadnik. The first rule was that I had to have a better car than the pickup and that the car must be at least as "fast" as the slowest car of the caravan, which was Eddie Thompson's, who when I was told this had left the room. The second rule was that I must show "proof of snatching the virginity of three snakes"; this phraseology made the Roadniks snicker loudly and several small caucuses were formed, supposedly to review specific case histories already on file. The caravan then separated outside and back into the garage area underneath a hoisted car.

I drove home that morning and told Paul about needing a better car . . . and a faster one. Paul scepticized on it for a short time and promised that he would drive past the station on his way to the depot and observe the kinds of automobiles the Roadniks owned (I hadn't known). That evening after his work and after my sleep Paul said that he thought it was "possible . . . not too difficult," and something about exhaust overflow and compression performance, which I didn't understand. After dinner he began transplanting dead engine parts out in the front yard. He shuffled his feet along in the dust, surveying his collection, until he saw an automobile that reminded him of some metal part inside of it that he could use, and he'd open the hood or crawl underneath from a side and be disappeared for about twenty minutes. Then I would watch him carrying the part down through the rows of wrecks and set it beside a loose assembly of other parts. Four days later he was finished and asked me to come out and drive it. I came out of the house, and after I learned which automobile was to be mine I must have registered disappointment on my face because Paul quickly added that the Roadniks had only ruled that it must be "fast," which he said it was, and not pretty, which we both knew it wasn't. And it was, fast.

The second rule was more difficult to conform to . . . in fact it took me six months to compile, by devious means, "proof" of introducing three young girls into the sordid underlife of back seats and gas-station-operated motels, decorational emotionality and passionate detachment. The first, Bernice Ornfather, wrote me a poem in iambic pentameter about "youth spent" and "the bleeding sign of age." The second girl gave me no proof of our brief interchange; I felt like that was wasteful. The third, Alice Boone, beforehand signed in durable ink a shirt I had given to her and as that shirt supported us both in the back seat of my fast car it was left behind. The fourth, Diane Vienett, was tape-recorded from under my front seat, admitting in between loud, purely emotional phrases, that the present time, the now, was the first time that she "had done it."

The Roadniks were pleased with the tape recording, they enjoyed it over and over again . . . so much so that I began to doubt that the initiation rules were rules at all—that anyone else had been forced to conform to them—and so forth; however, after conforming to these rules, one day later (after "blowing Eddie Thompson off the road") Eric Henderson ruled another about which there was great laughter from the Roadniks. They asked that I walk down toward the City with a camera and wait for one of the monuments to open, and then take a picture of whatever was inside and bring it back to them; furthermore, it must be done at midnight. I resented this, and resented that my tape was never returned to me, under the pretense of being lost. Nevertheless I hesitantly agreed to my next ordeal.

That night we drove the caravan (I was forced to go last) past my house. Nellie's Cat was sitting in its favorite window, looking out (probably at herself because it was dark outside and light there). We drove on and parked along Third Avenue and got out of our cars. The Roadniks formed a semicircle around me and I sensed a glimmering of ceremony as Eric Henderson presented the camera to me. But the mythical quality was not sustained and dogchains began swinging and clinking from fingers as the Roadniks divided into smaller groups, laughing and feinting punches at each other, as I walked with my camera down into the fog.

The noise from above was soon muffled, then inaudible. Long thick ribbons of fog wrapped around me as I walked. In this silence—except for the walking, the muted, regular sound of my footsteps on the blacktop—I began to feel what I then believed were the lurkings of my inherited anchoritism. The farther down I walked, the more dense the white, cool air, the more pronounced these feelings became. I remembered

Father and the stories of Mother and John Charles and Mary. I could make out then the tremendous wall of the City with fungi clinging like a disease about the cavities . . . massive, gnarled surfaces made of stone and porous concrete . . . and felt familiar toward it — remembered it and remembered playing here when I was very young with Walt and Paul, tossing in pop bottles, taunting the monuments to open. And the monument I remembered too, one of the less foreboding, of a giant four-headed lizard with one head like that of a horse and the other three round, flat, humanish faces, paling in contrast to the pockmarked necks and body. I walked closer and the creature broke silently apart, the base of two of its heads receding into the right wall, and two into the left, one head on each side looking abstractly at its severed self. The fog thicker, much thicker, inside, hardly moved, and there in the opening were the remains — one of the unfortunates who after having found his way into the City had waited patiently for the monument to reopen and let him out again. Perhaps his hope had never deserted him, but his flesh had already begun to loosen; while I, stricken with what I can only explain as guilt, flung the camera inside, turned, and began my climb back up. I heard behind me as I walked the dull explosion of the monument closing — the sound of a huge boulder dropped several feet into a grass-lined pocket of earth. The ground shook once, then stopped. After a while I heard the talking and clinking of the Roadniks.

"Where's the camera?" asked Eric Henderson.

"The zombies have it," I answered. "One of them rushed out of the City and grabbed it."

"A zombie," he insinuated.

"Yes. A dead man that is living, or a living man who is dead . . . anyway, his flesh is cold and he has no respiration."

"Listen, buddy, we don't go along with smart-asses. And we've got ways of dealing with them. Don't we?" he asked and the Roadniks answered.

Somehow I knew that this resentment was not entirely because of the existence of zombies, or the validity of my story, or even losing the camera. It was deeper.

"No, man. We're going to mess you up," Eric was saying.

Within a moment I measured the distance between myself and my fast car; it was large, larger than between myself and the Roadniks, which was shrinking. I felt in my pockets for weapons and there were none. I searched for weapons around me on the ground and there were none. I imagined my situation in relation to my house, which I couldn't see, and the possibility of running home seemed uncanny. "You've had it, mother," I heard a Roadnik say. I wondered what Walt would do and knew as I wondered that he would never have allowed himself to be in my position. I thought bravado might save me — knew it wouldn't. I considered taking a weapon from the first one to reach me. The Roadniks came closer to me and I could no longer make myself think. I was afraid. I sprung at them once, shouting, to make them stop and be confused . . . turned and ran back down into the fog.

Then I could think again, some.

I could hear them behind me. The air became more heavy, making it easier to breathe, harder to see. I was not too afraid to recognize that my senses were operating abnormally — that it would be possible to not see the outline of the City, or the monument opening, and to run inside. But I didn't know how long I had been running before I thought this, or how much farther I had to go; or if I had gone too far already. This thought terrified me more than the Roadniks or anything they could do to me, and I stopped. I could see the wall of the City and it was in front of me. But I wasn't sure. It might have been the other side of the wall. That's stupid. I might have run in and after getting inside the City, turned around. And then my senses were allowed to work and I heard the Roadniks talking and clinking back up the incline; they had given up. But the sound had no direction. I stepped backward several paces . . . then several more, wondering, unable to be sure if I was walking upward. But then I remembered that I hadn't heard the sound of the monument closing, but thought that maybe I hadn't been paying attention. I was walking backward more slowly. I thought about the sound that the monument made when it closed. Then I knew I was not inside. No one could hear the sound of his own imprisonment and not know immediately . . . and no one could not hear it, or could be frightened into going into the City. Fear is too cheap an emotion—fear of external, tangible things (at least those things). I felt like laughing but was afraid of giving my position away to the Roadniks. Then I walked around the wall of the City toward home. After traveling what I thought was the correct amount of time and after opening two more monuments by passing close by in front of them, I walked up the hill and into our backyard. I heard another monument close. Someone else is down there, I thought. I saw Nellie's Cat through the back door sitting in the same window. Nellie was humming to herself when I came in and I told Paul that the fast car he had built for me had probably been destroyed, or shoved into the City. He looked like he was thinking about it, but didn't say anything.

For a long time I did not leave the house, for anything. In the morning I would crawl upwards out of sleep, and, refamiliarizing myself with what it was like to be awake, previewed the possibilities of the coming day from my bed, reminding myself that there were things I wanted to do: listen to St. Louis radio stations, read novels and phenomenological criticism, and build tiny houses and apartment buildings with toothpicks, Magic Wrap, and glue. By the afternoon, early, I would have forgotten that there were things I wanted to do. And I would be stranded on the davenport. Nellie, who could tell if I was awake by listening, told Paul that I had sleeping sickness. I heard her tell him. I had fooled her by breathing in what she thought had been my sleeping way—which it usually was. This type of thing, fooling the members of my small family inside my head secretly, was frequent. I finally noticed, as though around a corner, the dangerousness of this situation. I smoked too much and felt generally unhealthy. But perhaps I had stayed too long by that time.

No, things were good then. Everything was very good up until the hospital; or if it wasn't I have disremembered it. I cannot risk being mistaken. I am sure. There was a clear daylightness about the time, and if the events were confusing, at least they were always separate and distinct.

I looked for a job in the Des Moines *Register*. I did not want to work, but felt that painstakingly reading through the classifieds every afternoon was a moral equivalent. Of course it was not enough to just look — I had to be interested and think about calling up and finding out enough information to convince me I could never handle the job. Usually I waited several days before calling, until the ad disappeared.

FARMHAND WANTED: 262-2032. This ad would not go away. It often changed places in the column, occasionally duping me into believing it was gone. Once, after I was sure it had gone, I even found it by mistake under Miscellaneous. It haunted me and I waited through the night for the paper to be put in the box. The delivery man glared at me suspiciously as I waited in my winter coat and leather aviator's hat for him to hand it out to me, so dark that we could barely see each other except for the reflection of his headlights from the gray snow. I had to call.

The telephone rang three times, but I knew it would not be fair to hang up until the empty space between the fourth and fifth ring.

"Hello."

"Hello. I'm calling about the advertisement you have in the paper."

"Good," he said. "Good. When can you start work?"

"Well, I don't know. What kind of work is it?"

"Farmhand."

"What does that mean?"

"Helping me around the farm."

"I haven't worked for some time and I probably couldn't do it."

"Sure you could. Come out and I'll show you around."

"I won't be able to come until next week, or later, because our other pickup is being fixed."

"That's okay. I'll come and get you in the school bus. I drive a school bus for the school . . . tomorrow morning and you can come back with my wife when she goes shopping. That way you will know how to get here."

"My name is Sledge."

"Okay. I'll look for it on the mailbox. Where do you live?"

"SLEDGE."

"Right. Where do you live?"

"Third house from the corner of Third and Grand." He was invincible.

"Do you know anything about nails?"

"Nails?" I asked.

"I've heard about these new nails with ridges in them. They're suppose to be eight times harder to pull out than regular nails."

"Eight times."

"But if we want to take the crates apart, then I guess it would be eight times harder."

"Crates."

"It might be eight times stronger than it needs to be."

"It depends how strong you want it to be, and if you want to be able to take it apart again. Either you commit yourself or you don't."

"I'll be over around nine-thirty tomorrow."

"What about the nails?"

"I'll get the new ones."

"Tell me where you live and I'll drive over."

"I thought your car didn't work.'
"I'll fix it."

Ansol Brenner's name had been written across his mailbox with a Magic Marker. A N S OL and B R E were large, carefully performed, with embellished capital letters, NNER was squashed into the remaining two-and-a-half inches and tapered to the bottom of the box in a violent arch. Someone had shot a hole through the red flag with a .22. A white picket fence surrounded the house; the gate had fallen off and was cast out of the way, beside a thousand-gallon Econogas tank. From only talking to him on the telephone I knew that the fence had been his wife's idea, that she had wanted to be able to say, the farm ends here, and all this belongs to the house, and they are not the same. Ansol had not torn the gate off. It had hung there for a long time, but when it fell off he didn't put it back. Pieces of wood and things of metal, a water pump, a metal wheel, a garage/machine shed with a sagging front roof, large coils of baling wire, an elevator, and a porch swing, lay sedately half covered with snow ridges and peaks in the yard and around the red buildings. He had let the Red Man Tobacco Company paint his barn for him. It had been funny paint that turned orange. They, had also painted RED MAN TOBACCO across the side of the building above a picture of a pouch of tobacco; this paint was still clear, but had cracked.

I knocked on the door and a very small woman flew across the room, opened the door and asked if I wanted some coffee, or cookies, or coffee cake. I told her I was Reuben Sledge and that I was looking for Mr. Brenner. She knew all about that and shoved a handful of cookies from the counter out at me, asking me to come in. I did and was immediately surrounded by her and food. She said Ansol was down the road at another set of buildings. I went to find him, carrying a thermos of coffee, a pocketful of cookies, and three sandwiches.

Along the side of the road before the farm lot crouched an

empty house, and like an old man's the weight of its body had become after a while too difficult to keep up straight and its skeleton sank and bowed into and out of itself. These houses make us sad. They have not thrown their families out. They have not broken down, or their walls let cold air whistle inside. Their water pipes have not begun to leak, or their furnaces stopped heating. They have been deserted by people whose lives had begun to fall apart, and had run desperately off into the city like frightened crows, thinking that they would be better there. And of course no one would live in one of these houses after that — unsure if there wasn't something wrong with the houses — some sort of thing in the walls that inno-cent people can pick up, little by little, like strychnine, until they go bananas. So the houses rot from neglect. The water pipes rust. Mice eat through the electrical wires, and once one window is smashed it sets off a chain reaction that breaks the others, even the attic windows that take four or five throws before hitting.

Several dozen cattle — a mixture of whiteface and Angus — stood in no particular arrangement beside the barn. I listened to the banging of metal hog feeders from another building. A giant free-form ice sculpture reached halfway from the ground to the overflow pipe on the storage tank. The windmill was turned off and the locked vane kept the wheel turned perpen-dicular to the wind.

"Mr. Sledge."

I turned to face the sound, then realized it was my name. Ansol was standing in the opened tractorway to the barn and waved to me to join him . . . conveying in the same motion that any time between then and next Wednesday would be soon enough.

"Hello," I said.

"Take a look at these nails," he said, and put one in my hand.

"Like a fishhook," I said.

"Just like a fishhook," he said and took a hammer from his

overalls. He drove one of the notorious nails into an upright beam in the barn, up to a quarter-inch from its head.

"Try to pull that out," he said, handing me the hammer. I pulled it out. It seemed eight times harder than a normal nail.

"That's harder than a normal nail," I said.

"Eight times harder," he said. Then we went deeper into the barn, and after showing me a buggy wheel that reminded him of a memory he thought he had forgotten, and a piece of metal hung on the wall that he said was to remind him when he looked at it of the biggest, hardest rock that he had ever found in a field and had taken him four days to get out of the ground and haul away and put in the creek, he showed me a pile of lumber, mostly oak, that he had rescued from the weather after it had once been a small work shed. He began picking through the boards, separating those clean and those with nails still in them. I saw a rat run out of the pile.

"There goes a rat," I said.

He did not stop sorting, but said, "Multiply by 1000 for every rat you see to get the total population of rats."

"Over how long?" I asked. He stopped sorting and stood up and lit a cigarette and gave me one. I asked him if he wanted a sandwich, but he didn't. I asked him if it wasn't a suspicious thing to smoke in a barn. He said that it was one of those rules like smoking in bed or always painting corners first — rules made to protect idiots. He confessed that his wife could not allow him to smoke in the house because of her fear of emphysema, which she was sure, in bizarre instances, could be contracted in a sniff. Then we talked about rats, and tried to figure out if you could only count two rats if you saw them standing together . . . if you saw them one at a time they might be the same rat. We couldn't decide if it made any difference. We sat down on a bale of straw and drank coffee and ate sandwiches, still smoking the cigarettes, unable to know if we exhaled smoke or cold breath.

Ansol Brenner was fifty-seven, looked a well-kept sixty-two, and drove a school bus in the morning and afternoon for the neighborhood school. (A rural neighborhood is much larger, in area, than an urban or suburban neighborhood: the number of people is probably no different.) He was inefficient in the old sense of the word; not incapable, but unwilling to be seduced by work — unwilling to be singleminded. Those things that needed to be done were constantly put off for those things that needed to be thought about. And unfinished projects did not pester him to be completed, but represented, in themselves, thoughts he had not finished thinking, like how to get a true estimation of the number of rats in a building. Mrs. Brenner wanted him to hire someone to do the work, but Ansol, his children gone and his neighbors efficient in the new sense of the word, wanted someone to be inefficient with, even if he had to pay them. He felt he could afford it.

We ate the sandwiches. He told me how the barn had been built . . . by early afternoon we had progressed some thirty feet to the corn bin filled with cracked corn, of which I was to transport between fifteen and twenty shovelsful twice a day, mixed with a half-bag of supplement, to the bunks for the cattle, along with two bales of hay from the loft, to be put in a separate bunk. A pickup came down the road and pulled in. A large man in a canvas hat came into the barn and directly asked Ansol if he had a hundred bales of hay that he could buy. The number was difficult for Ansol to know about. He looked up to the loft, as though the boards in the ceiling would help him visualize what a pile of one hundred bales would look like; perhaps he wondered what his hayloft would look like if one hundred bales were gone.

Our visitor knew more about this number and Ansol's hay supply than either of us did, and walked across the barn, explaining in the matter-of-fact manner farmers have when they are being social his own need of the hay and Ansol's lack of a need. He stopped talking when he could see me well and pulled the front of his hat down closer to his eyes, creating a kind of arbitrary frown. He came closer until he could see me very well, and stopped. I pulled down my aviator hat.

"Aren't you one of the Sledge boys?" he asked, as though he were holding a weapon.

"He's *one* of them," said Ansol, no longer looking at the ceiling.

"What's he doing here?"

"He's going to work for me," he said. "And he'll help you get those bales tomorrow. If you want them —"

"What . . ."

"— at forty cents a bale."

"I'll come get them Saturday. My boys and I will get them." He took out his checkbook.

"Pay me later," said Ansol. The man went away.

"That's Bob Bush."

"I wish he could have met my brother," I said, watching the pickup pull onto the road.

"Walt?"

"How did you know?"

"You're Reuben, aren't you."

"How did you know?"

"Only one you could be. You're too young to be anyone else."

"So what," I said, as though I had an empty weapon in my hand.

"What happened to your father?"

"You mean you don't know?" I asked, ironically.

"I know he's dead. I heard about you pushing him down into the City."

"Who told you?"

"Somebody who knew somebody that saw you do it."

"He just died, that's all."

"Nobody *just* dies," he said.

"Don't they," I said, arranging the words like a question, but not helping with my voice. "None of my family would be in there if it wasn't for farmers like you refusing to give my father land."

"There's a difference between John Charles and the rest of you."

"Very generous of you."

"Look. We'll see a lot of each other, on one hand. But if you say I got to tell you what a great guy your brother was — I won't do it."

"There's a lot I could tell you about that . . . things that you don't know. You only know —"

"I don't care. I don't want to know," he said, and walked away from me to begin arranging the boards into two piles. I stood still, carefully crunching the rest of the cookies inside my coat pocket. Then I went to help him.

"I saw another rat," I said.

We built farrowing stalls with the boards. This took us three weeks — twenty stalls. I did the regular chores by myself. One or two days a week Ansol would take a day trip with his wife, Ann, and granddaughter, who had been bequeathed to them after his daughter divorced her relationship with her husband and did not want the burden of the child, restraining her movements, hindering her chances of remarrying, and reminding her of how they had adopted the girl in order to save the marriage. And after they had got the child (at a young age because they wanted a fresh start) its skin had started to turn dark, never black, but some color they could tell would never go white again . . . darker than it ought to be. This was likely not the last, but one of the last thinly balanced dominoes that finally toppled the precarious tower of their lives together. During the one-week divorce proceedings Annabelle was with diverse and deliberate attention introduced into Ansol's house, in such a way as to appear at the end of the week that she belonged there.

Mrs. Brenner had told me this one afternoon in the secrecy of her kitchen. This unfolding had been carefully planned, as though she had gone over the sparse material in her mind for the last nine years, both making sense of it to herself and finding the most delicate, dramatic way to tell it — which after several years become one and the same thing. Ansol and Annabelle were together in the school bus then, and Mrs. Brenner, between my last gulp of milk and a piece of cake, warned me to keep the story away from Ansol, who though he would not ever fully understand it, might at least see far enough into it to recognize a hint of the ghastly business of child manipulation, which would send him into a period of rage comparable to the time he had seen his son from across a field setting fire to a wingless owl lying in a puddle of gasoline, and had run screaming across the corn stubble to beat the child with his fists and kick him unconscious, and had for weeks after that time refused to come out of the house, sitting and rocking back and forth in his rocking chair, staring at a portrait of his father without actually seeing it — more like looking at it because the chair was pointed toward the wall and the picture was on the wall and he was watching the wall.

Many days I was left to work alone. Mr. and Mrs. Brenner and Annabelle were of the age when traveling is important, and they took day trips. Things were good then. Everything was good before the hospital. The farrowing crates were completed. The sows had another two or three weeks before they needed to be watched. I learned how to work. Those *duties* I had could be completed in one hour; my manner of doing them, however, took seven hours, without an unoccupied minute.

On these days I would leave home at seven-fifteen A.M., beginning to drive when it was still dark. Out of the city and onto the gravel, the ice and snow became first gray, and then a ghostlike pale. I drove with my window down and could smell the cold light coming as though out of the ground because it was not in the sky — not until after I had parked the truck and gone into the Brenners' house where I plugged in the coffeepot that Ann had filled for me the night before and checked the refrigerator — where, waiting for the coffee to perk, I watched the color sneak into the sky out of the kitchen window. Then I drank the coffee and washed the cup and pot.

Outside, I started the tractor and let it warm up, though tractors run fine, cold. Then I drove down to the other buildings and hooked up a lowsided wagon to it. Behind the barn I parked the wagon beside a hinged wooden window opening into the corn bin. I walked around to the front of the barn and took the ax from the inside wall and carried it to the water tank to break the ice that had formed during the night, flipped the broken pieces out onto the ground, and carried the ax back.

After eighteen shovels of cracked corn I closed the door and checked the huge mousetraps made for rats. I drove out into the lot and spread the corn by standing in the wagon and throwing the corn out with the shovel so that it sprayed out across the entire bottom of the bunks. Then back for the supplement, which had to be shoveled down onto the noses of the cattle and let fall down between their heads onto the corn.

With this infinitesimal restraint I looked for watery eyes, indicating vitamin deficiency, fixed broken bunks, fed the sows, cleaned the barns, being sure not to drive the spreader into snow deeper than eighteen inches for fear of getting stuck, ate lunch, sharpened the plow and disc, checked the water in the storage tank, refed the cattle, and checked to be sure the bedding was dry.

Some days the Brenners would be gone during the week and I would make sure Annabelle had not forgotten to wake up and leave for school. Mrs. Brenner had told me that Annabelle, because of her insecurity, would often hide food — take pieces of hamburger from the table, wrap them up in her napkin and hide them in her bedroom. In case she ever ran out. The basement was also a favorite place of hers to hide food; the thousands of jars of canned fruit and jams provided perfect cover.

I never forgot this and even while I was driving her to school I would watch her quick eyes, wondering if she was looking for food. Sometimes I would offer her cookies and sandwiches that had been left in her refrigerator (Mrs. Brenner said that Annabelle would never go out into the kitchen to get food herself, and would only hide food that had been given to her, either by being put on her plate at dinner time or given to her as a snack in the evenings). She never refused, and put the cookies or sandwiches deep into a gigantic pocket in her coat. I never heard her speak, except tiny, instant words when asked a direct question by Ann or Ansol. She never answered me.

I was almost embarrassed to feel myself becoming excited to see spring come. Ansol told me everyday for three weeks that it was too early to begin plowing, that the ground was still frozen. And everyday I would walk around the fields and jump up and down on the dirt, feeling sure that the ground had thawed during the night. I was glad for the rain because it would help dissolve the ice. Things were good then, so good that I did not notice a terribleness within the Brenners' house. Ansol had slipped quietly into the house to get us some food—quietly in order that his wife would not hear him and try to give him some leftover coffee cake that neither of us had liked and she was trying to unload. Even Annabelle wouldn't eat it. She would hide it, but she wouldn't eat it. Mrs. Brenner was talking to her daughter on the phone: Vickie, who had recently remarried, wanted her child back. Mrs. Brenner explained to her that it was not healthy for Annabelle to be traded around—that Annabelle was at an age where her friends were important to her, and being taken away from them now—when for the first time she did have a few friends, shy, rabbit-like girls that she visited occasionally and who came to the farm and played very quiet games in her bedroom—would be wrong. Vickie demanded she have her daughter back, and Mrs. Brenner asked why it would be different this time—that the girl's color was still not white and . . .

and Ansol heard her. He walked out of the house with two

sandwiches, walked into the nearest field and stood holding them as though he had forgotten he had them, as though they were extensions of his hands. I went out to him and asked again if the ground was ready, jumping up and down on it to show how it gave.

"Who cares?" said Ansol. He did not offer me a sandwich or look at me.

"I care," I said.

"Go clean the barn," he said, and I did not see him for two weeks. Mrs. Brenner said he had gone away, into Des Moines. But then he came back and told me that it was time to plow.

"You take it out first," I said.

"No," he said. "You go ahead. You help me through this spring."

"Don't talk like that."

I hitched the plow and drove out into the first field, one of my favorite ones, with steep hills and a creek running through it. I let the plow down.

I don't remember anything else about this time.

I woke up in the hospital; Nellie and Paul were sitting in the room. I could not see very clearly and it took a long time to know where I was.

"Where am I?"

"In the hospital."

"What am I doing here?"

"You had an accident," said Paul.

"What!"

"The tractor fell over on you, on a soft shoulder of a hill."

"How long have I been here?"

"Five days."

"Five days! What happened to me?"

"You've had a concussion, and a skull fracture."

"What."

"We were afraid you would die. The doctors didn't know," said Nellie.

I told them to go home and passed out. Two days later I saw my doctor. I had been sleeping and he was looking at my chart and seemed to have been awake for the last thirty-six hours.

"Hello," I said.

"Hello," he said, and put the chart back onto the hook at the end of my bed.

"I'm so tired all the time," I said. "And I tried to get up today and was too weak and too dizzy."

"Don't try to move around yet," he said.

"What's the matter with me?"

"Your head's not well."

"Come on, doctors don't talk like that."

"Your brain is still bleeding. Try this," he said, and put his hands out in front of him and swiveled them from his wrists in half circles, in unison. I tried and could not make my left hand follow what my right hand was doing.

"I've never done that before," I said, sure that it was a trick to keep me in the hospital . . . something that doctors practiced in Med. School. He muttered and wrote down something in my chart.

"That doesn't mean anything," I said.

"Probably not," he said, condescending and flat.

For the next two months I practiced twisting my hands back and forth. And every time he would come in, I couldn't do it. Sometimes he would talk to me and would seem as though he had forgotten. Sometimes he would even walk out of the room — then come back and say, "Can you do this?" and move his hands.

"Why can't I remember those five days?"

"That just happens," he said. "It's natural in this type of accident."

"Will I ever get it back?"

"Probably not. You're lucky to be alive. I even expect your memory isn't too clear about the first couple weeks after that."

I was ashamed to admit that I had no idea of how long I had

been in the hospital, how many spinal taps, or how many days I had slept completely through.

"What does that mean?" I asked.

"Nothing," he said, but I was sure from his face that he was lying, sort of. But that might have been my own apprehension. It wasn't. He said he scratched the bottom of my foot with a key, but I couldn't feel it.

Ansol came to see me at least twice a week and talked all afternoon. He was uncomfortable in the hospital and stood up every time a nurse came in. Once, before he had come, an orderly told me that he, Ansol, was paying for my hospital bills and calling up every day to see how I was doing. The orderly told me that Ansol might be doing this in order to make me think that he was a good fellow—so that it wouldn't occur to me to sue him, which he said could bring me in some fifty thousand dollars. I told him that I did not want to sue, and the orderly said that he would tell Ansol that I had decided not to—just so he would know he wasn't pulling anything over on me. I told him not to say anything and that if he did I would break his head.

Nellie came everyday and would sit with me even when I was asleep. Sometimes after I woke up I seemed to know Nellie had come and gone, not wanting to wake me. This frightened me because I was afraid that she had come, that I had talked to her, and then had forgotten, retaining only a sense of the memory. I would ask her the next day or call her on the phone and she would tell me that I had not been awake.

When I left the hospital it was winter again. It was also dark, and I had left by way of the fire escape to avoid the notice of those people who knew I still could not move my hands correctly. I wanted to surprise Nellie and Paul and decided to hitchhike home. Twice I became unstable and leaned against a building while my equilibrium rearranged itself. At Sixth Ave. I stood with one foot on the pavement and one foot on the curb to avoid the possibility of being arrested for illegally hitchhiking, a law that allows the Des Moines police to make money and harass people in the name of safety. I placed one hand on my hip and extended the other above my head with the thumb perpendicular to the ground. This was the classic stance, the form of which was worthy of the phrase "hitching a ride." I disliked many of the contemporary antihitchhikers, who not only refused the humility of this attitude, but also felt no obligation to entertain the driver after they were picked up; they offered nothing in return for the ride, the effort, or the gasoline money; they demanded to be recognized as serious, merely by their position along the road; their faces did not even betray a desire for a ride, as though they had come by some misunderstood quirk of fate to be standing, half dazed, along a roadway. The pages of these people's activities are always very short and often they will not answer when asked where they are going, but indicate by grunts and groans when they are getting off, with no explanation or story behind their passage. When I drove I never gave them rides.

I resolved not to be like that, an antihitchhiker.

I stood in that spot from nine until midnight. Then I walked down the street, where it would be easier for the cars to stop. From every group of cars that approached me, I would pick one out and tell myself, "That one will pick me up." When this plan failed I applied it in reverse, saying, "That car will never pick me up," and then "Those cars will never pick me up." I tried staring straight into the eyes of the drivers, forcing them to encounter me, and they stared back and drove by. I was becoming tired and dramatically exaggerated this circumstance. They registered compassion for me and drove by. My head began to hurt. I was angry and disgusted and tired and hungry. I sat down on the street and haphazardly tried to light some paper lying in the ditch by flipping live matches into it. I began to curse and say obscene things to myself. An old Mercury stopped after an unmistakably long time. I climbed into the back seat and told the aging bricklayer I wanted to go home. I put my head against one of the back windows, feeling as though my head might explode. "Things are changing," he said, "for the better. There are better ways of doing things nowadays. More sensible. I can remember when hitchhikers used to stand with their thumbs stuck up in the air about their heads. And what's the use? Everyone knows . . . ."

I went to bed immediately on returning home, without waking Paul and Nellie with the joyous news of my arrival. I slept soundly and was not discovered in the house until the next evening, when I woke up and emerged into the living room. They were happy to see me. Paul was suspicious and called the hospital. It informed him of my escape. We argued and I stayed at home.

I continued to be dizzy and could not remain active for even short periods of time without headaches — splitting headaches, that began as a small needle of pain inside the back middle of my head and spread in a muffled explosion around the upper skull, as though looking for a way out. Seeing was difficult during these attacks and talking was impossible because of the intense irritation caused by vibrating the pain with the words.

Yet I was still not aware of the depth of the destruction — of the penetrating overcast wrought by the accident . . . only hints that the concussion was more than a headache, was more than a metal pin placed in my skull to hold it together, more than the dizziness and jumbled coordination. Dr. Sheldon came to see me once and scratched the bottom of my foot with a key. This time I felt it. He said I was getting better.

"What about those five days?" I asked. "I still don't remember them."

"You probably never will. Forget it."

"That's a bad joke."

"Stay in bed and don't walk around for more than ten minutes at a time." He looked again as though he could tell me something else, but maybe it was because he looked tired.

"Why don't you get some sleep?" I asked. He said something to Nellie and Paul in the living room and then left.

Because reading books was too painful, and no bedridden person enjoys listening to the radio because it constantly reminds him that he has nothing to do, I built toothpick houses, buildings, and apartments.

At first I constructed simple structures. Then I had Paul bring me some balsa wood and I added stairs and elevator shafts and balconies and real wooden walls with windows. I built awful rooms and rooms that might be nice to be in.

Successful in varying degrees with these projects, I began a super structure, a windmill with a shaft and a small wooden hand crank to turn the wheel around. I recognized that I had many structural and aesthetic problems to solve and . . .

woke up and saw the completed windmill sitting on the floor beside my bed, more shoddy than I had imagined it would look, with even a couple of glue smears. . . . I called Nellie, but she could not help me. I called Paul and he said that I had built the windmill during the last three days and had carried it into the living room once to work on it in the better light, and had sent him out for thin thread-wire to use in the base. My memory had disintegrated another part of its stuff.

Nellie called Dr. Sheldon and he came; he sat down at the kitchen table and Nellie gave him some coffee. "He doesn't remember the last three days," she was whispering to him when I entered the room.

"What's wrong with me?" I asked him, beginning to take offense in his practice of not sleeping before coming to see me.

"Don't worry. It's usual in this kind of accident to have a blackout . . . before you are fully recovered."

"What *could* be wrong with me?"

He waited, and then with a visible effort started his tired voice again. "In accidents like yours it is sometimes possible for the victim —"

"Don't use that word."

"Shut up — to gradually become cut off from the outside world."

"What!"

"There is a possibility that you will become an emotional vegetable."

"Do something."

"We have. The pin inserted in your head will keep the bone from chafing against the brain tissue; but there is no assurance that the damage has not already been done."

"What damage?" My head was beginning to hurt.

"A protein imbalance within the electrochemical structure of the mnemonic area of the brain. That's all we can say about it now. We don't know any more about it."

"What does that mean?"

"It means you may have already started to become a vegetable."

"Just because I can't remember — how does that mean I will be a vegetable?"

"You don't like the word. What it means is that you will not be able to learn; not be able to talk because you will forget what the person you are talking to has just said; not be able to enjoy simple pleasures like eating because you will not be able to remember what particular kinds of food taste like; not be able to do anything at all related to progressions or change. Immediate sensations will be your only pleasure — like a hot bath. You will forget the members of your own family. Nothing will matter. And most of all you will never know that there is anything wrong with you, because you will be unable to remember what the world was like when your proteins were ordered. Maybe vegetable is the wrong word."

I was trying to be brave. "How will I know if this is happening to me?" I asked. "How will I be able to tell if the process has begun?"

144 • DAVID RHODES

"The first indication that your outside world is changing is when you begin to lose hold of those things you already have."

"Come on, doctors don't talk like that."

"You will begin to forget the things that have happened to you or to your family . . . not only the dates and names, but whole segments of time. But the small things will come first."

"Send me the bill for this visit."

"Mr. Brenner's. . . ."

"Send this one to me," I said. He left and took a long time shutting the door, letting cold air in the house.

I translated this to mean that if I could remember everything that had happened to me, I could keep myself from becoming autistically frozen; in other words, I could consciously divert the protein disease by keeping my memories intact. If a chemical balance could affect my mnemonic clarity, then clarity could also affect chemical balance. I could do something to cure myself. The constant pressure of my clear memories would force the deranged proteins back in order and keep the healthy proteins from becoming contaminated.

This work was very difficult. The concentration required to just get me back to a distant memory, even with the help of gimmicks, birthdays, seasons of year, physical situations, and logical thinking about what must have been, was enough to insert the needle through the back of my head. It was impossible, with the needle in my head, to move around inside a memory, to remember what it *felt* like to be alive then . . . and I would give up, telling myself that beginnings are always hard.

But the headaches, I reasoned, could be part of the disease — obstacles set up by the deranged proteins to protect themselves, allowing them to influence more proteins. So despite the headaches I went into my memories and turned them over and over like a steel rasp inside my head. I would not be defeated. I scheduled myself: eight hours a day. I became a memory master. I flushed out people and dialogue so deeply hidden and obscure that even Nellie could not remember. (This was dangerous, because there was no objective correlative, and the possibility of a personal delusion loomed around it. Autism. It was safer to choose a well-known event and remember the *generalities* of the situation in detail.)

By the middle of the summer the headaches had let up and only bothered me occasionally. But by then I had another worry. For instance: I would spend eight hours remembering what had happened on February 14, 1966, two years and seventeen days ago; one week later, when I was remembering another day, I had no assurance that the memory of February 14, 1966, wasn't fading. Furthermore, to remember the last six months I would have to remember what I was remembering during each particular day; and remembering a memory of a memory — no matter what the memory — always felt the same — more so when I remembered remembering the memory of a memory.

I was consciously putting myself into an emotional deadlock in order to avoid becoming a vegetable, which amounted to the same thing. Perhaps all plants were at one time people who tried to keep their proteins ordered, and because they could not act in the world, were not concerned with their own immediate situations, and did not have brothers or sisters to take care of them, they began dying of starvation and exposure. This race would have been destroyed except for the mutants and Darwin's Law. Their feet grew into the ground and the earth and air and sun sustained them, without them noticing. Today we eat plants and by osmosis are able to remember.

I needed to do something — something in the world that mysteriously had to do with memories, but at the same time would not turn back on itself. Something that would take a memory and finish it, file it and keep it intact. And this would have something — I did not know what — to do with words, which were the only things I knew that could capture memories without *completely* destroying the feelings, the substance of the past. I had to intermingle with people.

I went back to the book I was writing for Nellie, still wanting to write it for her, but now wanting also to write it for me, in order to go on. But where could I begin? It had to be short enough to not take up the rest of my life, and so reduce me to a kind of typing vegetable. But it had to be long enough to contain the memories and order the deranged proteins.

For a trial I punched out an account of when Paul had fallen in love with a girl who was young and rode a Japanese motorcycle and had green eyes. I took it to Nellie and she read it.

"That's not the way I remember it," she said.

"That's what happened," I demanded.

"Yes. The events. But it's still not the way I remember it."

"That's not important."

"Don't write things that aren't important."

"It doesn't matter."

"It does."

"It doesn't."

I knew it did. But I could not recognize importance. All memories were important and in that could not be screened, except arbitrarily. Somehow I had to choose those emotions and memories that in themselves contained and carried with them all the less important ones. I could not even conceive of how this might be solved. And beyond this I needed a language that would contain the events of the memories in such a way as to not interfere with Nellie's remembrance of them, at the same time containing my own. I needed an attitude toward the past, and an approach to the words I would use to represent it that would do this. In some way words would order my proteins, words would give me to Nellie, words would become in themselves more than the memories, which alone endlessly convoluted.

I thought about the first word of my book, I. Was it the right word? Was answering that question the same as evaluating myself? I needed a solid footing. I needed an approach, an attitude and a voice.

Because of my inadequacy I turned to the work of other men. I tried to make these novels compensate for and represent the world. Through them I pictured myself interacting with real people. This attitude launched me into the greatest depression I have ever known, and to feed this condition I had many books. My room was full of them . . . books that had been hatefully sold to me after hundreds of ignored overdue notices signed in person by the head librarian; in fact, every book I opened began: *I was sickened unto death,* and continued to present the unquestionable, irrevocable truth of that statement. And rather than feel relief in that I was not alone, an uncertain comradeship, I was further depressed because of the abundancy of this feeling in the world. There seemed no escape from this. Then there was no hope of escape. I could not talk to Nellie, or Paul. I could not bear the daylight or the outdoors. The dead of summer had arrived and I slept continuously through the day in the damp basement, keeping away from the heat. No, it was not sleeping that I did then. It was mind-writhing, thought exercises that exercised on themselves on themselves over and over and over . . . endlessly repetitious sense and nonsense. I implored my depression to question itself — to ask how it had come, why it had come: I reasoned that the accident had done this to me, that it was because I did not know how to do anything; then I reasoned that this was not the reason, it was that the accident had made it impossible for me to want to do anything. I knew that that was too easy, that it had nothing to do with that. My depression laughed at my calamity. And that depression was all the more formidable because of its promise of the coming of a conception, an attitude a thousand times more horrible.

I thought of depression like that. Though a part of me, and

though through its eyes I viewed my miserable basement world, still I was able to see that it was not me . . . rather a "thing" that was not of my own doing, that defined me, not I it. From this position I could hear it speak to me, saying, "The City has sent out its head executioner. Dread her coming; she does not return."

My body, pledged against me, turned a month-old rat-gray from the neglect of sunshine and the constant embattlement of the slimy air. My teeth rotted and my fingernails broke up into little milk-white chips. Persistent headaches eroded the thinking fibers of my brain, collapsing the synapses, polluting and diseasing my liver; the pain was a companion to me, collecting my perverted thoughts tightly around my mind's eye, letting not one of them escape, letting not one of them dissolve . . . playing them back to me again and again and again against the backdrop of that clammy delirium. Even the prayers, the prayers, those feeble pleadings for otherness, were returned alive and were tortured beyond the luxury of despair. "Dread her coming. She does not return." Nellie and Paul were not with me then. I endeavored to write in order to keep my thoughts progressing and moving away from themselves, but the effort of fighting against the depression was more painful than the depression itself: "Whether I will be able to win the control of my life is what must now and forever concern me. Today I can see that my life is going out and on from me toward and into dark and evil biddings and writing this does not help." I wrote that.

I am amazed that creation myths have never been correctly written, that despair is far too immediate to have been taken so lightly. And if the true creation myth were written it would be similar to the following:

In the beginning was the Word. This Word was a very
special Word and the only Word of its kind because
there were no other Words but it. This Word could read

itself. It could also speak itself and listen to itself speaking itself. It could look at itself and watch itself without reading and sometimes it would look at itself and think about itself. Infrequently it would think about itself in as many different ways as possible, but because it could not count, it was impossible for the Word to know if it had thought of itself in as many ways as possible. It was also difficult for the Word to know if it was thinking about itself in a new way or if it was remembering a previous way of thinking about itself . . . or remembering a memory of a way of thinking about itself.

Once, after a very long time . . . so long that it is unimaginable, the Word became afraid of thoughts it was having about itself. The Word was so afraid of these thoughts that it could not keep itself from thinking about the fearful thoughts again and again, over and over. It thought about the fearful thoughts so hard that a piece of one of the letters of the Word was chipped off by the shaking of its intense thinking. In the entire history of the universe, that is of the Word, because that was all the universe was, this had never happened before. The Word did not know that it had chipped and as it looked away from itself — a direction that up until that time did not exist — the Word saw the piece of itself. Because that Word had not noticed losing a piece of itself it imagined that it was looking at a piece of something, or rather simply a something that was not of the Word. This thought was pleasing to the Word — far more pleasing than any thinking it had ever done. A world of experience was opened to the Word. It watched the piece and wondered what it would do next. It wondered if more pieces would appear. It wondered where the piece had come from and if it was going somewhere.

This piece of the Word, being a piece of the Word

and so similar to the Word in all respects, could think about itself and remember itself and watch itself and watch itself watching itself. It could also watch the Word and think about the Word. After several unimaginable periods of time the Word and the piece of the Word chanced to think about each other in exactly the same way . . . at exactly the same time (what time there was). It was then that the Word noticed that a piece was missing from itself and knew that it had been thinking about the piece in the wrong way for two unimaginable periods of time. The anger of the Word began on the First Day and continued until the Seventh Day. So great was the Word's anger that its shaking broke the Word into seven billion pieces. One of those pieces became the earth as we know it today . . . the rest became red dwarfs and other bodies of the universe. There was no longer the Word, and the Spirit of the Word was all that remained of its original shape.

As time would have it, man came into existence by a chance meeting of molecules. Being of the earth, which was of course of the Word, man was similar to the Word in all respects. He could imagine himself and think about himself and imagine himself thinking about himself. He could think about things that were not of him too, he thought. The Spirit of the Word soon became aware of the existence of mankind and watched them closely, especially one man named Omar whom the rest of mankind revered as "highly intelligent." When Omar was seven hundred years old the Spirit of the Word told him that he must be the exemplar of his people and rule with an iron hand. For nine years Omar ruled the earth with an iron hand and was wonderful in the presence of the Spirit of the Word. But one day when Omar was walking along the beach, content with his thoughts, a green whale shouted to him from the sea. "Go away," said Omar, "I am content with my thoughts."

"Of course you are," said the green whale. "Any fool can see that, and be that. But I know things you have never dreamed of."

"As I am the iron-handed ruler of my people," said Omar, "perhaps you had better tell me of these things."

"They are better shown than told," said the green whale.

"Then show me," said Omar.

"Take up one of the sticks that I have caused to be washed ashore."

Omar picked up one of the pieces of driftwood and used its pointed end to make marks in the sand, following the careful instructions of the green whale. Then the green whale went away.

That evening when the Spirit of the Word came searching for the iron-handed leader of mankind it found him sitting on the beach staring down at the word OMΛR written in the sand. "Omar," screamed the Spirit of the Word, "that you have attempted to be me I can never forgive you. I cast you from my sight, but not of your own." And the Spirit of the Word grasped Omar about the face and turned his eyes inward. Omar turned from the Spirit of the Word and stumbled off into the forest, vengefully searching for the green whale, bumping into trees.

I had moved one of the spare beds—the one that had belonged to my mother—into the basement. My only light was provided by a one-hundred-watt G.E. bulb hanging from a mouse-chewed wire above my bed. The glare from this light was purblinding and I wrapped toilet paper around it to act as a shade. This eliminated the glare but rendered the walls so gloomy that my condition could not bear it and I unwrapped the light. Other than this and a sewage pipe that leaked around its upper joint there was myself and nine hundred and eighty square feet of concrete. And I looked at the concrete; my thoughts looked at the concrete. The irregularity of this surface, I came to believe, was my only salvation. No, that is the wrong word—a poor word, salvation: "only salvation" is especially wrong. Ask any manic-depressive, or any other person, for that matter, who has been imprisoned alone in a room for an abnormal time; and he will not use the word "salvation." He will say that he counted rivets, nails, and lines, that he found the faces of dragons and men in the shadows, that he knew in detail every blemish, crack, and disfiguration, that he could predict the changing patterns of light throughout the day, even perhaps that he could hear the walls speaking to him: but he will not say that the walls were his "salvation," that they saved him. He will not give such a noble title to those walls that he bled for every particle of notice he could stretch out of them . . . the memory of hatred will always be too immediate for that.

I began, I am sure, by watching spaces—by letting my eyes settle into a natural focus of the wall, sections of about four feet square, ignoring the fuzzy frame around the area. Of course this was not actually watching but mostly eye resting. Afraid of the involuted thought ricocheting that happened behind my closed eyes I left them open, thus keeping a constant rapport with myself—a sense of place that remained the same from hour to hour and therefore allowed me a sniveling degree of security that varied only in relation to the morbidity of my thoughts. These concrete areas soon became too familiar and I could no longer identify myself with their gray texture. My entire basement room became too familiar and ceased to be able to define me . . . walking into my room became like shutting my eyes. But I had one release; and I drew out those infrequent times when my body would ask to be taken upstairs to the bathroom where it drained out into the toilet its extinguished body fluids to be washed down the leaking pipe through my basement and out into the underground. I could even force myself to gulp cupfuls of water into my stomach, knowing that it would rinse yellowing through the cinder-like cells of my unfed self and afford me another tramping up the stairs and a gazing out from the bathroom window at the backyard and the fogcloud of the City.

My recovery, as I call it now, was not recognizable at the time. It began as I took note of the malformities of the walls: where clusters of rocks jutted out from the otherwise smoother surface (the concrete forms had not fitted properly together when the walls were poured and looked like three panels, no one parallel to the other two): where an occasional hammer blow had powdered a round, white hole: where the sighing of the upstairs had torn long cracks into the foundation. These were important, even necessary . . . but more important than any of these oddities was their intermingling, the relationship they made to one another . . . and deep down in my warbling brain the significance of these relationships was of ungodly proportions. They were everything. It was the immediate concern of all my waking hours that none of these relationships should escape me. I must know them all. They must be recorded . . . recorded fact. I undertook the task with an almost religious fervor. I used string to map the interconnectedies of my basement quarters. With a small square of clear tape I would fasten one end of a piece of string to a particular abnormality in the wall surface, such as a hammer hole, and then connect the other end of the string to another abnormality in the wall, thus establishing a simple one-to-one relationship by means of the string. To each piece of string I would fasten a small piece of colored paper, and all of these papers were numbered. A number corresponding to the number on the piece of colored paper could be located in a special notebook and the relationship defined by that string would be described: "a soft and a hard," "two hards," "lines and points," "lines and oval," "one healthy and one sick," "two sick," etc. I had difficulty in sticking more than eight string ends to a constituting member of a relationship and found myself ignoring relationships I knew to exist. I noticed that not only two abnormalities could combine to form a single relationship, but also three, four, five, six, and so on. So I tied strings to strings and attempted to describe these elaborate relationships in single words: "bleakness . . ." "sterility . . ." "movement . . ." My basement filled with strings. And it became important that my bed be part of the plan and I tied strings to the bedposts, and the windows and the door had to be figured in too. I had to ignore everything in the extremities of the room because I could no longer get to them to fasten strings. The strings began obstructing my vision and began forming relationships among themselves and I connected them together and labeled them, "string 49 and string 13 . . . flight," "string 53 and 38 . . . geometry." The strings became so dense that the dark spaces defined by where there were no strings became paramount. Only these were of course impossible to map. I had left myself a small tunnel through the strings from the door to my bed and one afternoon (I could tell it was afternoon because of the way the light crept along my strings) I noticed Paul standing in the door-opening end of my tunnel. My depression should never have allowed that . . . it had made what I thought then, a fatal mistake . . . an error of allowing me too much freedom.

"Come out of there, you jerk," said Paul. And I did. He bullied me into eating proper foods and coming with him to the depot in the morning. I sat on the middle platform bench all day long, alone, noticing the world indifferently as it receded from and rushed at me. Paul came out at noon and ate a sandwich with me. In the afternoon he came out again and we went home.

Depression: disease of commonplace, where those small, insignificant, good things of life turn around on you — little old ladies and milk-fed babies become tormentors: sleeplessness is a curse, and not an uncomfortable evening spent swallowing aspirin; doomed thoughts are the cause, and are the condition, and prevent the cure. The only hope that was possible for me came in the form of a defeated anticipation: how much worse can it be? Surely this is the bottom, the lowest rung. But even that was a dead consideration.

From this position on the bench I watched a young woman of questionable beauty walk onto the wooden platform from a Rock Island Line coach. A flopping leather handbag shouldered on her left side counterbalanced a small valise of the sort one imagines having mirrors and combs stuck onto its inside top. To protect her yellow dress from the dingy steam wafting up from under the train . . . collecting her arrival confusion about her in an air of supreme indifference, she headed for the depot, her shabby shoes inclining inward, awkward, though somehow with perfect posture. This I saw, and immediately forgot as soon as her movements carried on beyond my plane of vision. The station cat appeared among the baggage racks, cautioning the jerky motions of the baggage man as he tossed the suitcases off the iron-wheeled carrier. So I watched her. After what I took to be several hours — dusk had come and colored the Des Moines gloom with lazy pinks and shadows that stretched out in long roundish shapes, as though painted in by some mad cartoonist whose humor had begun to escape even himself . . . Paul came out of the depot and sat beside me.

"If you can loose yourself for awhile from your apathy, there's a girl inside who seems to be in trouble."

"What kind of trouble? There's trouble everywhere. I have mine, you have yours. The world turns on . . ."

"I think she can't get ahold of whoever she knows in town and doesn't have any money for a cab."

"So what."

"So take her where she wants to go."

"Is she bothering you?"

"Yes."

"Take her yourself."

Paul went back inside the depot, defeated. I returned to

waiting for his quitting time, when we would go home . . . and my vision was filled again by the woman with shabby shoes. She fidgeted her weight from one side to the other, stumbled several paces in one direction then back again, her hands grabbing repeatedly at her face. She had left her valise in the depot and came to stand fixed not five feet directly in front of me. There she began to cry, clutching still at her face with those hands.

My God, I thought to myself, and was struck with the absurdity of the situation — the obvious choreography that was implied. However, I was dismantled. I was frantic to be free of it. I wanted to get up and run away, but the fear that Paul had arranged the entire episode turned me from the impulse. She continued to cry unselfconsciously, with no indication of leaving. I could not bear it any longer, not the crying, as such, but the demands it was making on me.

"Why are you crying?" I asked, with negative concern. She batted her hair back away from her eyes and looked at me.

"Never mind. It makes no difference even to me. It's so clumsy to cry. I hate it."

"Why are you crying?"

"I don't know. I think I'm crying because I have no money. I don't know anybody here. And I'm even afraid of you."

"That's completely ridiculous," I said.

"Most feelings are ridiculous."

"I'll help you."

"Help me what? How do you know what I need help doing?"

"I don't. Tell me what you want and I'll try to help. Either that or go away."

"Do you mean just tell you what I want?"

"I have ten dollars. Do you want it?"

"Ten dollars."

"Ten dollars." She sat down beside me and started crying again and also telling me of how she had been sent money for a train ticket by an old boyfriend she had had in college who said he would meet the train and how he hadn't come and how she had called his number and the telephone was disconnected and how she had no money and had been living with her mother who was now in a county home because of hardening of the arteries which caused her (her mother) to think that unreal things were real — that memories were real — and how she had been fired from a job as a secretary because she couldn't keep her mind on her work and because she didn't get along with the other employees because "they were awful, and little people," and what could she do with ten dollars anyway. By then Paul had locked the door to the depot and was standing watching me with his hands in his pockets.

"We'll take you," I told her. The three of us climbed into the pickup — her in between and Paul shifting gears carefully, making sure not to touch those shining legs.

At 913 Forest Avenue we left the pickup and rang a doorbell that could be seen from across the street because of a small green light behind the semitransparent plastic button. The door opened and a withered lady pushed her head out to greet us. "Who is it?" she asked.

"I'm here to see Frank Warlock," said our companion.

"He doesn't live here," the head snapped back.

"But he must," she whined, "he must. I've written to him at this address. He answered my letters . . . and he sent me money to. . . ."

"He used to live here. He doesn't live here now. And I'm glad he's gone, too."

"Please, can you tell me where he's gone?"

"Nope."

"He must have left an address. For his mail."

"Nope. No address. Just one morning he comes downstairs with a suitcase and says he wants one-half the rent back. I told him no doing . . . that if he wants to leave that's fine with me, but no money. 'Fair's fair,' I said. I wouldn't all of a sudden charge him an extra month's rent, would I? I can tell you that nobody in this house misses him either . . . leaving his socks around and everything. Who are these there with you?" She waved a finger outside at Paul and me.

"They brought me here from the train depot. This one works there," and she indicated Paul.

"Sledges," she said. "Sledges. Who you're looking for doesn't live here. Sorry," said the face and was pulled back inside, and then the door was shut.

The clutching at the face was beginning again. I grappled with several evaporating emotions and was appalled that Paul was not taking control of the situation. I had to act fast before the crying and I told her that she could come home with us and that Nellie, our sister, would watch out for her and that tomorrow I would help her arrange to do whatever she wanted to do but that worrying about it tonight was of no consequence and to just relax and get a good night's sleep and at any rate there were no trains leaving that late at night and hotel living, especially in Des Moines, as everyone knew, was not to be desired. (This, as I now reason, is more because of the rural attitude to transient living than because of the actual, physical condition of the hotels themselves — which may or may not be all that horrible.)

Nellie was suspicious and flew from place to place around the living room saying things like, "No money? . . . Warlock . . . I've never heard of a Frank Warlock . . . Have you, Reuben? Warlock! Have you ever heard of a Frank Warlock?" We stood and watched her, waiting from the kitchen. And it finally dawned on her that Tabor (I had learned her name) was actually in her care. Then, though she continued moving here and there, familiarizing herself with her hands, looking as though she were trying to see, because there is nothing else to think looking at her face, she began shouting orders at Paul and me to get the sheets for the spare bed (Walt's) and take the bed into her own room because of the scary noises that rickety old house made at night . . . and to see what was to eat in the kitchen, and if there was nothing to go to the store and bring in some clean towels from outside on the clothesline and stay out of the bathroom because Tabor surely would want to take a bath. All of these things we did. And when we had completed them Nellie was sitting on the sofa with Tabor and Nellie's Cat (which was hating Tabor in the way a cat hates someone) talking about Chicago, which was where Tabor was from and though Nellie had never been there because of her reading she knew things like that the lakes caught on fire every so often and that the political situation of the city should somehow remain above serious reproach for reasons that I did not understand. Of these things they talked with an earnestness that only women can have, about anything. And I wondered how Nellie could be like that.

Paul made some soup, which we ate in the kitchen. I was quiet all evening and remained up long after Tabor and Nellie and Paul had gone to bed, watching. Then I went down into my cellar and fell into a broken sleep.

She fascinated me. For days, weeks, I could think of nothing else. I followed her about the house, watching her do the things that she did. I drove her around Des Moines while she looked for a job. We talked together at night and sometimes sat on the back porch in the afternoons, looking down into the fog. And though I explained the City to her many times — as did Paul and Nellie — the idea never settled in her and like slow, heavy bubbles would rise up to the surface and explode, again and again; and she would return hours later and ask, "Do you mean to say that there's a city down there?" And we would have to explain it again. Sometimes she would sit on the back porch by herself, leaning forward and staring down into the fog, almost as though she were excited, but quiet, and remain there all afternoon while I sat inside the screen door, keeping an eye on her.

Soon then Tabor became aware of my incessant fascination; and did, I am sure, play upon it in thousands of ways, her character down to the simplest gestures, changing often seventeen times in a day, her talking voice altering sometimes in midsentence; but done with such ironic subtlety that I could never be sure if those alterations were ever anything more than phenomena of my own imagination, a change of perspective influenced by the passing of an imperceptible bat's wing of memory across the path of my experience. All of this is confusing, I know. But how else could it have been? How else could she have remained to me so completely foreign, so completely incomprehensible, even unimaginable, while resembling me with fingers and eyes and speaking words that I believed had meanings? Some sort of pride — a woman's pride so different from that of a man that it appears like humility — must have led her to taunt me in this way. But how can I admit that now? How can I admit to myself that she knew of everything she did — that she conceived of every movement, every intonation, before it happened? Preempting my responses so finally and at such a distance as to be able to force me to question even those few, most basic things of her that I had hoped could be taken for granted: beautiful, slender, and loving. The idea is frightening though not as much as the possibility that she had no center at all — that she was actually all of the things and ways she appeared to be. No, I could have never believed that.

I am wandering. I must be concerned only with the events — just in relating how things happened; nothing more. It must be finished.

I would look at Tabor, looking in such a way as to perhaps seem like staring to her. She would talk to me, her eyes flashing and quick. She would do things around the house, the same things that Nellie would do, but recklessly in comparison; like taking an opened book from the floor and replacing it in the bookcase. The act was the same, but in the way that it was carried out, the two, Nellie and Tabor, differed so greatly that these supposedly identical actions appeared to have no relation to one another. But that was probably because of her legs. They were long and slender yet not so much and were always alighting in different, unlikely positions — as if posing — that filled me with stomach feelings of soft and warm and round and water moving and I could not take my eyes off them for long and then they, the eyes, would be called back again. The breasts too, did that. Many things of her, did that.*

All of this should have told me something. Perhaps if it had, what happened later would not have happened, at all. But it didn't, and we wonder now how all those ancient people could go on believing that the world was flat, what with all the clues,

---

*It may be assumed that all phenomena of printed language have in them-selves a direction, and that that direction is often predictable. Directionless, unpredictable writing is not a real possibility — even in a foreign language. As soon as one symbol, or word, is clearly set down, a condition of limited choices governs those words which can be allowed to follow. One of the di-rectional possibilities is always that of a hoax. By this time you are familiar with that. This particular section, as you have already assumed, must in one way or another address love. Either that or be a hoax, in that the direction set up is never realized. (See *The Borrowed Prose*, by E. Donaldson). And you may well ask, what does anyone from Iowa know about love?

I am profoundly qualified to discuss love, and have taken my degree from the abandoned farmhouses of my soul where I have gone looking for an emo-tion empty of irony, an experience able to contain that perpetual distancing called consciousness. Hate, envy, pride, greed, sorrow, despair, joy, melan-choly, fear . . . they are all there, chemically occupying space in my brain, and to discover them it is only necessary to shut my eyes and listen. But love is synergetic and completely unpredictable by looking separately at any of its components; it is a bizarre interaction between two completely separate, autonomous, self-contained, and madly lonely people . . . for no reason and to no end. . . . I know that. That is to say I have had a suspicion — a suspicion grounded in the eyes of old couples on summer porches in wicker rocking chairs, a calm that was denied to me — a terrible conspiracy, a murmured talking in another room. I wanted myself to be sitting on porches and sleep-ing in brass beds . . . under old comforters. I searched for love in the corners of pride and despair — the two most Grand Canyon-like emotions I know. I asked Nellie and she said that it couldn't be communicated . . . a conspiracy, perhaps a brain tumor, malignant cancer, a personality inadequacy, or a dis-eased liver preventing me from that realm of living. And so like a small boy and an abandoned farmhouse I learned my subject. And so like a small boy I was happily frightened. And so like an old fool I was not horrified.

and I did fall in love with her—love that had nothing to do with knowing. That, in itself, was not destructive. It was wanting to be loved in return that became like a cancer, and that more than anything caused what happened later. This is so difficult.

And there were indications of affection and love from her. Some. She stood very close to me once and without warning reached out and stroked her relaxed hand across my chest, lightly, as though touching the fabric of the shirt, even tracing around the seam of the pocket—looking quickly from the path of her hand and to my eyes. It was affection. These times were infrequent, so infrequent that I would worry that they had never happened—that they had not happened in the way that they did. But then she would do something—something small, always small—and reaffirm her affection for me. I did not trust her eyes because they were inchoate. I did not trust her words because they were universal. I would only believe her when she touched me. And then not for long.

Nellie and Paul had gone to bed and Tabor stayed in the living room talking to me. We sat together on the davenport. I was not watching her but was attempting, with shut eyes, to understand what she had just said, in order to talk. She sat close to me, her legs curled up underneath her, leaning forward on her side. My thoughts were hurled against images of her legs; images that were not words.

"I like things that seem like you could jump in," she had said.

Jump in, jump in, I thought . . . jump in.

"Like a truckload of pillows?" I said.

"No. Real things. I only like clouds that look like you could jump in them. And fields," she said.

Jump in. Jump in. Fields jump in. Jump in fields.

"Do you like cornfields?" I asked.

"Only from a long ways away. Not up close."

Not up close.

"Then you don't like anything up close," I said.

"Some things I like up close. Most things I like from far away though."

Faraway . . . jump in . . . don't like . . . don't like.

"How about cities?" I asked.

"Only very large ones — ones that from a long ways away all you can see are buildings. No spaces . . . where you might fall and hit the ground." She said, and I finally understood . . . the glass was removed from my eyes.

"I'd rather float over things than jump into them," I said, proudly.

"Float over them!" She shouted, angry.

Quickly I added, "Yes. Or float around them."

She frowned and stuffed her legs further up under her. I knew I had made a mistake, some leap of association that she had not followed. Finally she said that "floating wasn't real." I agreed, and admitted that jumping was, and assured her desperately that I was not teasing her or making fun of what she was talking about. Then I asked if she wanted me to shag on out to the kitchen and get some ice cream and she thought that was a funny word.

But words were trapping me again. I could never hope to understand Tabor with words. I could never be sure of her affection for me with words; and that was all I cared about. An idea occurred to me, slowly, like all great ideas; I was struck with the simplicity of it: I could take Tabor into the basement with me, into the tunnel of strings and into the bed. I could make love to her once and never worry about her love for me; or at least have a good, solid reason not to worry. Then I could be sure. Yes.

We went downstairs and into my room. I thought then that it was strange she did not ask about the strings — that she looked at them more with enmity than curiosity. I began explaining the strings anyway, but she interrupted me by shoving her hand up inside my shirt and I gave it up.

At first my own passion and activity kept me from noticing that my plan was not working, that it would not work. Only after I was satisfied—after a dulling quake of sexual apathy had calmed me, and I loosed myself from her and fell over on my side—did I see that expressionless, ghastly face. No, not expressionless, but capable of holding any emotion, all emotions, and most of all aloof. Probably I should have shut my eyes then and remained silent, giving in to the love I felt for her. But I didn't; and I asked her what she was thinking, and she said she was thinking of a "huge field of clover." She said she was thinking of lying in a huge field of clover. God help me, I resented that. I tried to shut it out, didn't, and went to sleep.

Tabor did not want to return home. She said that she was twenty-six and too old to return to anything, especially her mother who by just being around aged you three days for every minute spent living. During the next few days Tabor found a job working as a waitress in a cheap travelers' inn that sold salt-water taffy pumped full of air. Despite all of our, Nellie's, Paul's, and my, complaining and pleading, she would not live with us and moved into an apartment in downtown Des Moines. She told me that she could not "handle" being with me because it so heavily taxed her emotions, which at this time were, as she said, "very unstable." She said that she wanted a month or so to become familiar with her new environment and that after this we would get together again and be happy. I believed her when she said this. I still believe that she was not lying—that it was very real to her. I do believe this. I believe it.

"But we will write letters," she had said.

I waited for these letters. It seemed that I waited a long time. Then I received one. I lifted it like food from the mailbox. I carried it with me to the basement, noticing the way she had written my name: Mr. Reuben Sledge, knowing this was not important in itself, and after I was settled in bed with a cigarette I opened it. The paper cracked as though electric. I read it carefully. Then I put it down beside me on the bed and thought about it. It was a good letter, written with a genuine sense of me. It was a loving, affectionate letter. I thought about it more, remembering especially several lines. I thought of these lines and thought why she must have written them: her purpose. Then I could not be sure if I was remembering them correctly, the exact wording. I picked up the letter again and put it down. This time I did not wait so long and picked it up again. I read those lines. Then I read the whole letter again and put it down. I picked it up to refamiliarize myself with it. I circled words and drew arrows, making connections between the mapped thought patterns. I assigned differing connotations to reoccurring words in order to see if their meanings changed within different sections. Repetition itself unnerved me and I wondered why she had chosen to so limit our communication, as though keeping huge parts of herself from me . . . especially in so short a letter. Where she used "a" instead of "the" I became disturbed because of her obvious conscious/ unconscious choice to be impersonal.

I did this for three hours. Then I left the basement and went outside and sat in one of Paul's wrecks, busying myself by taking off all of the knobs on the dashboard and putting them in the glove compartment, which was partially torn away because of someone carelessly ripping out the radio. I could remember every word of the letter, and could even picture the way the words looked on the page—even the punctuation (which I had begun to think was more important than I had suspected, because of wanting to or not wanting to run thoughts together). I wrestled with these things.

But still I went back to the letter, to make sure. It was exactly as I remembered it. That frightened me a little. Yes, I knew what the words were; but I did not know what they meant. I did not know why she had written them, not altogether; some sections were in themselves very clear, but every assumption I would make about her in one section would be contradicted in the next and I could never understand how she could fit all of these together and still love me. But the words themselves were exactly as I remembered them, and that frightened me.

I read it again. Then I poured lighter fluid on it and burned it in my ashtray. But it did not go away, although it has now. I watched it burn and stirred the ashes into small black flakes.

I took a pen and several sheets of lined yellow paper, legal paper. I wrote to her, a long careful letter. How exacting I was! With what precision my hand formed the letters! With what cunning I performed paragraphs and complex sentences! Could a madman do this? Could any but the most solid of men, under the pressure that I was, write such a letter? With what concentration I read over the letter and sealed it, mailed it, and stayed to watch the mailman take it from the box. He saw me glaring over the flagged container like a vulture and he was very careful with it. The next day I wrote another but did not mail this one, keeping it for myself.

After eight days I received another letter from Tabor. I noticed that my name was written in the same way, only this time with a zip code at the bottom. That, in itself, did not mean anything: she might have learned it during the last week and wanted to use it even though it was unnecessary. I took it to the basement and with a cigarette and a jam jar half filled with Ten High I opened it. Ravishing down through the green words I devoured whole sections at a time, slowing down and taking hold of the words only at the end where she had written "Love," and signed her initials. I tried to remember. I was sure she had written "with love," before. Yes, I was sure of it; even though I had burned the letter. Did she remember that? Is it possible that she had forgotten it? No. No one forgets anything so important. There was a reason for the change. I could not understand. My head felt like someone was pushing on it.

I went back and reread the entire letter, carefully. I carried it to the back porch and read it there. I tried to remember Tabor in bed with me. I read the letter again.

Somehow, buried among all of those things I did not know, I managed to learn that Tabor was not happy living in Des Moines, that she felt uneasy about the shape of the buildings and the coldness of the people. She confessed to feeling "lost and confused . . . frightened even of my own apartment's walls." Once, though I no longer remember in which letter, she said, "I must have help. I will not turn to you until I can stand alone. I must have help." This did not bother me; I praised anything that would hold her to me, unhappiness too.

(How hard this is to write. How ridiculous, digging around in my backyard for security while a revolution was breeding inside my house.)

I received another letter. This one was better than the other two; that is, she sounded more miserable. I put the letter down, feeling more at ease than I had in months. Thinking back over the letter, I continued to feel at ease until I noticed that my thought was being called back to a particular paragraph. And this paragraph, the more I remembered it and thought about it, filled me with dread . . . though I did not know the reason for this dread at that time. I reread the fearful thing. It said:

These green walls of my apartment are awful. Everything is awful. I will never be happy. I was never meant
to be happy. Why am I telling you all this? Am I trying
to hurt you? My life seems like it is running out of me
and I am going down.

What was it about this paragraph? Then I knew. "I am going down." Tabor had gone into the City—she had been telling me all along. I thought back over all the letters. Their meaning became clear, of course. She had gone down into the City, and I ran upstairs, outside the house, across the yard and onto the blacktop, running along the rim.

At First Avenue I turned down into the fog. Running was faster here, of course, and the heavy air filled my lungs well. I did not tire. Though anxious, I felt full of life and lean as a wolf. I ran on down, not noticing the wall or the opening monument.

Chapter VI

...

GRANTED, MY PERFECT STUPIDITY IS BY NOW UNQUESTION-
ably clear in your mind; and from here on in you would be
foolish to let anything pass before you without a cautioned
disrespect for anyone so blatantly ignorant in the ways of the
world. Listen. Listen, because if I can just get through this part
I can be finished, because these things are important, and the
only problem of relating them is an ancient familiar one — my
inability to see myself because of my eyes being directed always outside. So to continue I must stand away from myself
for awhile and pretend that things do not matter so much,
when in actuality they do. I do not mean to cheat you or make
you feel as if I walk around all day picturing myself as breaking
through (or into) literary norms. It is because inside the City it
is dark and beyond its walls I do not know myself, and must let
the goings on inside speak for themselves . . . let them be me if
you will. And so I must begin:

He ran down and for a time was not afraid because he did not
notice that he had passed through the monument and into the
City, running on deeper into it. The darkness forced him to
run more slowly; then finally to walk, looking around him at
the thick black fog. The sound of the monument closing made
him stop altogether. The echo of the sound let him know ir-
revocably where he was; and the quality of the ghastly noise
attested to the kind of place that it was. As this noise continued around him, he thought in horror of his ignorance — his
belief that someone could be saved from this, by him. And because of the fog the sound went on and on, coming back to
him from the farthest, smallest corners, from walls, alleys and
empty streets, all hidden in the darkness. From each place the

sound had gone, it came back again and again. And in mockery he knew Tabor was not here—that she had never been
here—that she could not be here. No amount of discomfort
could bring her to a place where she would hear that sound.
He knew that. She might stand on the rim and listen while
the sound came up into the clean air, and even be fascinated
and hear it with the cunning of a hunted animal, but she could
never hear it from inside. He knew her that well.

"I have been tricked," said Reuben, after the echo had
subsided to such a constant drone that he thought it might
never end, or that he might never end hearing it. "I have been
tricked . . . I have been tricked . . . I have been tricked." The
City whispered back to him from the heavy, dark, cold fog. The
mockery of it, he thought, and wondered if any living thing
had heard him.

Like a frightened blind woman he groped his way to the
right, where he pressed up against a solid wall—brick, he ascertained by his fingers, from the edges and grooves. He reasoned to be able to feel his way along this wall and lead himself
back the street he had come in on, and so arrive at the base of
the monument, where there might be a gray light. From there
he thought to manage an escape. After some dozen steps of
this plan he reached a corner—an intersection, he thought,
with four buildings at right angles to one another. Fear was
beginning to clutter his thinking. Yet he was aware of this.
He ventured away out from the building, walking at what he
hoped to be a straight-across path ending at another corner
where he hoped to continue on. His frantic hands could find
no building. He became more afraid, and ran forward several
steps . . . nothing. Then several more, nothing.

He turned and ran back, but could no longer find the corner he had abandoned. He stood still and attempted in the
darkness and stench, the smell of dying and rats' fur, to collect himself. Then he heard a new noise, a fast heavy walking
noise, iron wheels on brick, abandoned everything and ran,

listening, like a bat, to the sound of his own footsteps on the brick street, running downhill. He ran into one building front and glass splintered. The echoes returned. He picked himself up and continued running deeper on into the City, wondering if from his accident there was blood.

And as he ran he heard new sounds — new sounds coming from further down in; softly at first, but building in pitch and power until everywhere the black fog was exploding with it. Screaming . . . directionless, impersonal, terrordriven scream- ing . . . a sound that he would later discover to increase when he ran — later when all the more ungodly things were familiar and he could notice, as though standing on a hill looking at a sunset, variations. I am afraid, he thought to himself. I will be afraid; but I will not be mad.

He began walking and tried again to collect himself. He had no idea of the place where he was; neither did he have a hope of finding out. I have been tricked, he thought, tricked inside and tricked into losing my place after that. This must be the end.

At first he felt that his eyes were adapting to the darkness — that he was almost able to see. He stopped. Only the sound of the screaming was audible and already he could imagine how someone, after many years, could be used to that. Can it be that I am beginning to see in the dark? he wondered. It was an uncomfortable thought, so foreign to any world that he could conceive, that if it were true it would mean that everything was up for grabs: human reason, compassion, form, substance . . . the whole rotten mess (if even that could be said about a place that wrong).

But it was not true. Reuben Sledge went on, and after a time clearly there was a real light somewhere in front of him, down from him. The blackness was giving way to a uniformly sterile gray, and he could see window spaces in the buildings, darker than the building sides. There was no curb for the streets. And ahead of him, perhaps a hundred yards, was a streetlight. This may be worse, he thought; this may be a sign; but ran down between the gray buildings toward it. He found that there were more lights, normal distances apart and on both sides of the street. He stood back, looking. Down from each light fell a conical area of well-lit fog, down to the brick street. Away from him he could see four and almost five of these light cones, before the fog engulfed the rest of them in its gray mouth. A gray cleanliness covered everything. There was no breeze or wind, and no paper and dust-ball ruins — mementos from the living — cluttered the streets. The screaming was louder there.

Reuben walked down and into the first light cone, passing quickly through it and into a darker area, wanting to keep out of the strong, milky light, to see but not to be seen seeing. He walked quietly along, stopping frequently . . . farther into the City.

Across the street from him, near an opening into an alley-way, Reuben noticed, or believed he noticed, something move. He stopped walking, but the shadow stopped too. He moved again, and the figure moved. My shadow, he thought, believing the phenomenon to be solipsistic, merely distorted by the intense fog and the effect that the continual screaming was having on his mind. He stopped again, and the dark figure stopped, but, he felt, not at the appropriate time; its movements seeming slightly jerky. He led the shadow several steps farther, first slowly, then quickly, then stopping, up to a light cone on its own side of the street. Reuben stepped forward again, and into the light stepped a humanish figure, an old man with yellowing skin that stood everywhere no more than one sixteenth of an inch away from his bones, completely naked, his eyes wide, staring and jerking his head back and forth, his scrotum falling down between his thin heavily veined legs like stretched clay. The figure opened his mouth but Reuben heard nothing more than what was already there. The old man stood back against the building side and slowly raised one of his bare feet up as though he might climb straight up the side of the building like a human fly, scraping his toes along the brick. Then he jerked forward several cautious steps, scurried on out of the light, on down the street and into the heavy grayness, without making a sound.

Reuben thought to himself: things are not so bad here. He leaned back against one of the building sides, out of the light. I will be afraid, he thought. But I will not be tricked again. He continued in this way of thinking: *Things are not so bad here; I have met the first inhabitant of the City; things are not so bad as I thought.* He concentrated on this and looked out down the street, seeing how carefully planned and set were the buildings, the streets, the black reflecting surfaces of the windows . . . and there were street signs! They said Grand Ave., Locust, Fourth Ave. There were names for where he was. *Someone* had purposely named this place! The thought comforted him and he hung onto it. Someone had built this place. . . . Someone had built it and someone had named it, called its parts by familiar names. It was charted. But like a man who has decided that he may view the world beautifully, those very things that originally gave him inspiration turn around and show their ugly backsides: Someone had built it! He shuddered, his first and last real stand against the encroachment of the fog through his clothes and into his skin.

He reasoned that to continue moving was purposeless, and would only more bewilder him: better to remain where he was and collect himself. He took a cigarette from his jacket pocket and afterwards threw it away because his matches would not light. Ten minutes later he picked it, nearly soaked through, off the brick and gently laid it back in the package, in case he might be able to trade it later for a rope or a woman or a pair of shoes or something. He waited and watched.

"Are you a devil?" asked a voice from inside a broken window in the concrete wall. The voice was soft and spoke carefully, in the way of a child.

"No," he answered, and turned toward the window several yards from him down the street, just at the edge of a light cone.

"Then never mind," said the voice, and Reuben listened

through the screaming to hardly audible running footsteps inside. He went to the window. Nothing.

Food. The concern dropped on him as if out of the sky. And because of it he began to feel hungry. He fought against it, telling himself that it was not true hunger, only a kind of test, a way of foreshadowing what it would later feel like. Food. How could he eat? Nothing could grow down here, he was sure of that, sort of; and if something could grow, what would it be like — what kinds of things could live here? Don't think about it, he told himself; I must think of other things. (But what else is there to think of? There are concerns of the body and concerns of the mind, and all concerns of the mind are concerns of place, and Reuben knew nothing of the workings of his place.)

"Hello."

He heard that. The sound echoed. Away from him in the offing of his sight he saw a white form coming towards him. "Come here," it shouted, and might have been feminine. And although he did not know about where he was, or where he might end up if he left there, he ran again deeper into the City.

"Wait," the thing called and he ran on and the running seemed to be downhill but he did not care. He ran down between the light in zigzagged patterns to keep in the darker areas.

Reuben assumed that it would know the streets much better than himself, that he must go into a building where he might lie in wait behind the door with a chair or a knife. He ran past gas stations with pumps like giant fire hydrants and movie theaters with empty marquees, looking as though they might work if only someone would work them. He ran around a corner and finally down a narrow alley, not opening again into the street; brick beneath him and on both sides, finally in front of him, too. The light did not penetrate into this alley and water dripped down from the roofs. Puddles lay in the low places. There must be, he thought, and found a wooden door, not built large enough for a man. He put his hand to the metal latch and it opened. Crouching, he went inside, slamming it behind him and looking madly about for a weapon. All of this was done very quickly. The sound of the door shutting echoed down the alley and into the street where the gas stations and theaters tossed it around in the screaming. Stupid, he thought, to be so obvious.

Quick, muted shuffling noises came from behind him. A wooden box was knocked over. Whispering. Running feet. Whispering. Reuben found a piece of two-by-four several feet long and wielding it like a mace advanced forward. "Who's there?" he asked. "Come out."

Whispering.

In the corner behind a partially standing large workbench, huddled together like frightened cattle, were three men, small men with dark eyes, but men just the same.

"Leave us be," they pleaded. "Leave us be."

"Hide me," Reuben implored them, relieved to be among his own. "There's something after me. You must hide me."

The men came cautiously out of the corner, moving as one irregular organism, with diastole and contraction.

They whispered together and came closer to him. "You've got to hide me," said Reuben, looking finally down at the club in his hand and throwing it away.

"Hide you from what?" carefully asked one of the men, extending a hand six inches away from his body, as though pointing.

"Something's chasing me."

They huddled closer together. "Did you bring it here?"

"I don't know, it could have heard the door slam. Where can I hide?"

"What did it look like?"

"It was white and. . . ."

"Are you sure it was white?" The men were breaking apart now and talking more loudly.

"Well, some light color, and —"

"It wasn't black?" asked the biggest of the three, no more than five and one half feet tall.

"No. Do you think I couldn't tell black if I saw it?" Reuben was less afraid now, because of the changing tone of the men: they were obviously not worried about the figure he had seen, and also seemed knowledgeable about what to be worried about and what not to be . . . at least more than himself. They surrounded him, wearing light blue coveralls, the kind worn by mechanics and farmers, with heavy laced boots. These boots, he noticed, were not always matched pairs.

"A new one," one of them muttered to the other two.

"How long you been here?" asked another.

"Not very long."

"You don't know much about this place then."

"No."

One of them picked up the piece of wood and held it.

"Why did you come here?"

"I was tricked. It's a long story and. . . ."

"No, why did you come into this room? Of course you were tricked. We all were, one way or another."

"Not in the way I was."

"Why did you come here?" The man with Reuben's piece of discarded wood began to look menacing.

"I was being chased, and put down that piece of wood and stop walking around me like that." The two-by-four was thrown down on top of the workbench. The sound echoed around the room. Reuben listened to it.

"It's better in here," he said. "The screaming's not so bad. If we close up this window more, with padding, I mean, we could keep most of it out."

They looked at each other. One of them said, "We don't even hear it anymore . . . you won't either, after you've been here awhile."

"I'll never be here that long. I'm getting out. I don't really belong here."

One of them smiled, but it did not frighten him.

"My name's Oskar," said the taller man, and extended his open hand. Reuben grasped it. Oskar returned a weak squeeze and quickly withdrew his hand. "These is Georgie and Irv. Excuse us for acting the way we do; but we ain't seen anyone come through that door for so long . . . and we got our fears."

"What I want to know is — "

"There's lots you want to know," Georgie said. "And we can make it all clear to you, 'cause we been here a long time . . . Irv longest, but — "

"How long?"

"First things first, we decided. There's not much pleasant to think of here, so we spent time planning how we'd handle telling someone, a newcomer, about this place . . . and you can't go so fast; I mean because we know, we can protect you — from knowing too fast, that is, and so getting yourself into a mess of trouble."

"What more trouble can . . . How much worse can it get?"

"There's trouble and there's trouble," said Irv. "That's part of what you got to come to know."

"Stop being so mysterious."

"The first thing to know is that there's nothin' to be afraid of."

"So why were you hiding under that table when I came in?"

"I'm still talking," said Irv, and the three men sat down on steel-rung chairs, kitchen chairs. The room itself was similar to a large storage closet, with one window, nailed closed, looking onto the street, through which light from a nearby streetlamp stretched into the room, sending long shadows across the cement floor and the few pieces of collected furniture. The light did not penetrate into the farther corners of the room. Reuben climbed up onto the workbench, trying to distinguish those other objects in the room of solid substance that were not recognizable because of the partial darkness. And though these pieces in themselves were inconsequential, and he had only to walk over and examine them to discern their true nature, still he could not help, while looking at them, attempting to know them. One, he reasoned, was a wooden box. Irv talked, letting out carefully ordered pieces of information. The facts, thought Reuben. Once the facts are known — the problem seen for what it is — solutions will occur. Problems are situations that have too few facts. Hopeless situations are merely wanting in facts. This is a good place to collect myself, he thought.

"The first thing you must know is that you can never escape. Call it belief if you want."

"That can't be true," said Reuben, getting more comfortable on the bench.

"After you know that, the rest is merely a matter of course."

"I'll decide that for myself," he mumbled, waiting to get on to the facts.

"Naturally."

"What did you mean when you said that there is nothing to be afraid of?"

"He didn't really mean that," said Oskar. "He meant—"

"Excuse me," interrupted Reuben, putting his hand into his coat pocket. "Do any of you have a dry match?"

"No."

"Well, a stove or something. I want to light a cigarette."

"There's no heat."

"What do you do in the wintertime?"

"It's colder then, but we manage, because the fog keeps whatever heat there is, down here . . . for the most part."

"Streetlamps. Where there's electricity, there's heat."

"Light bulbs don't get hot enough to light cigarettes."

"No. Break the bulbs, cross the wires, I mean."

"And chance blowing out all the current?" asked Irv, indignantly, as though the suggestion were something of the order of rape, or goatfucking.

"Put in a new fuse."

"In where?"

"In the fuse box."

"What fuse box?"

"Follow the wires."

"They run underground, under buildings."

"Dig them up."

"With what? There are no tools like that here." They seemed as though they were being patient. This made him nervous.

Irv continued: "He meant to say that you might as well be afraid of nothing, because it doesn't matter. The iceman moves in the City as quietly and quickly as you can imagine him doing it, in dark clothes. If he chooses you, nothing will help."

"You will have your fears," said Oskar. "No one wants to die. But they will not help you. Only stay off the streets; you are safer to be unnoticed in here."

"Come on, stop it! Who is the iceman?"

"Not so fast. You should be thankful. Most people never come this far into the City. Most never venture farther in than the monuments, where they quickly starve to death waiting for them to reopen. Most never have the facts explained to them. You're lucky."

"Maybe. Who told you the facts?"

"We have had to learn them by surviving," said Oskar. "But mostly Irv learned first. He's been here since 1965."

"November," said Irv.

"That's a long time," said Reuben. "Why didn't you leave — that's almost five . . . How did. . . ."

"Think over what we have told you. Later we will tell you more."

Oskar, Georgie and Irv set a large box in front of them and began playing euchre on its top, with cards made by tearing paper along a straight edge and marking each square with a ball-point pen. They shuffled the pieces of paper like children, by spreading them out on the surface of the box and moving them around with the open palms of their hands . . . with their eyes closed because several of the key cards could be recognized by sight. They kept score. They've been here a long time, thought Reuben, watching them, unable to distinguish in the poor light the individual cards from the mass of them all. They can see better than I.

He sat for a while on the bench, then carried a straight-legged chair over to the window and looked out into the street. He listened, and after a long time he could hear the men talking, as though the screaming had subsided.

"I'm thirsty," Reuben said.

"Here," said Irv and tossed a metal thermos half filled with water across the room. It hit the floor and slid across and struck the wall next to Reuben's chair. The sound echoed like ten thousand flying bats in a small mirrored room. The water was cold. He thought he heard a new sound from out in the City. He would hear it and then he wouldn't, each time a little clearer and a little louder. When it seemed to be very loud Irv, Oskar, and Georgie heard it, finished the hand, and went outside. They told him not to follow.

Then, from the window he saw a shape that filled him with horror; it walked into a nearby light cone and was clearly a metal-wheeled ice wagon being pulled by a horse with blinders — an albino, he thought, by its pink eyes. The mostly white horse was half covered with a dark velveteen-like growth, like spongemoss or old sofas, which almost completely covered the bottom of his body and neck. He had been meticulously trained (or was walking under the divine guidance — the fear of God); his purpose was sure and no driver directed him — there was not even a place on the wooden wagon for a driver to sit, merely a plain wooden box with metal wheels that clanked from brick to brick. It passed close to the window, and far down the street Reuben saw it stop next to Irv and the other two men, saw them open up the back and take out something, shut the door and disappear. The albino walked out of sight and he was alone for what seemed to him like at least fifteen minutes. Then they returned and resumed playing cards.

Reuben thought of when these men would tell him the workings of the City. It was an unpleasant position to be in, he thought — waiting for someone to decide when you were ready to learn facts.

"I'm hungry," said Reuben. "What do you eat . . . to have stayed alive for this long?"

"Think about it," said Oskar, and the three went to sleep in one of the corners. Reuben fell asleep in his chair.

He slept a long troubled sleep, though he did not know the duration. The sound of the ice wagon woke him, only this time Oskar, Irv, and Georgie did not hear it and continued sleeping. Reuben slipped from his chair and silently opened the door, stepped into the alleyway and ran lightly down onto the street. The screaming was louder outside. He walked around the corner and away from the storage room; it seemed like he was walking downhill. He stood where he had seen the men before, when the ice wagon had stopped, and waited for the horse.

It came closer to him and he looked at its eyes, then looked away, feeling, however, that it was just himself — his personal, particular revulsion that made it like that — that other people would be able to think these eyes were not horrible, because of their color. The albino walked on by him without indicating in any way that he had noticed, but stopped so that the back end of the wagon stood directly in front of him. Water dripped from the corners and splattered onto the brick. An iron bolt held the two doors closed. Reuben opened them and swung the doors aside. The metal screamed. He staggered backwards, not wanting to, the stench overwhelming him. Inside was a single layer of block ice, covering the bottom of the box, some eight inches deep. On top of this lay bright red, and gray, molding meat, partially wrapped here and there in newspaper. Blood enmeshed into the ice and trickled onto the street when it melted. He did not dwell on this, but stepped back away from the wagon and vomited onto the bricks. A high, thin whistle came from deeper in the City and the albino was down the street in a full, dead run, the back doors swinging and banging against the sides of the wagon. Reuben knew what this was. He did not need to be told, yet he demanded that someone, one of the men, tell him. He wanted to hear it out loud. He ran back and opened the door in such a way that the three woke up and sat back against the wall.

"That ice wagon," said Reuben. "What's in there?"

"What do you think is in there?" asked Oskar.

"I know what I think. I want to hear you say it."

"What do you think—"

"Say it! Say it, you son-of-a-bitches!"

"It's human flesh."

"And you eat it!" screamed Reuben.

"We eat it," said Irv, with no affect. "And you'll eat it, if you want to live."

"If you can call that living, *living*, then . . . you'd have to say it wasn't."

"Call it surviving."

"It's cannibalism!" said Reuben. "Don't try to fool me with words. Cannibalism!"

"We told you to stay inside and wait. . . ."

"Until I was hungry. Not just hungry, real hungry, thinking that I'd eat it then."

"You will."

"Never."

"You must understand that you can never escape. You will be here forever; there is no way out. It doesn't matter what you do, in here."

Reuben might have argued. He might have talked to them, and told them that he did not believe that . . . but they would have said that it made no difference what he believed, that the situation would be no different, that it was not necessary to believe anything, only to survive. They would have said that facts were facts and that whatever attitude you took toward facts did not change them, like the earth being flat and everything else.

But he did not. He sat in his chair and looked out into the

street. He asked them questions . . . slowly, with long periods of silence in between, while they played cards.

"You can eat that?"
  "Yes, it will keep you alive."

"Why couldn't we wait in front of a monument, and wait for someone to come along and open it?"
  "It's a matter of probability. A monument opens, on the average, once every three weeks, and even then it is unlikely that with seven to choose from you will be at the right one."

"But you MIGHT be at the right one."
  "That's a romantic attitude. You can't afford to be a romantic down here. We live from the thinking of romantics, their flesh."

"What if there were no romantics?"
  "Then, well . . . we have our fears."
  "Do you mean that —"
  "The iceman. He collects the meat. It is his wagon. If he runs out, then . . . well, better one dead, than all."

"The whistle, a thin high —"
  "The iceman."

"Who is the iceman?"
  "No one has seen him, except glimpses."

"If. Just say, just suppose, you could eat that. Why couldn't you take it with you — to the monument — enough food to wait . . . no matter how long?"
  "The meat would spoil and poison you."

"Why does he do it?"
  "Who?"

"The iceman."

"Would you do it?"

"No."

"That's why."

"If, suppose, you were to walk to one of the monuments. How would you get there?"

"Only the iceman knows his way around in the dark. There are no lights except in the center area of the City. Many of the streets are dead ends, or lead in circles, and you cannot see. There are no street signs there. The ice wagon only delivers food in the lighted areas. You would starve; or worse, there are madmen here."

"Why are things like this?"

"They just are. Do you want to play cards?"

"No. Not yet." Reuben did not look back from the window, took a drink from the thermos and threw it back. It rattled across the floor.

Again he heard the wagon, and again his companions left the room, waited for it to stop, and were gone for what seemed to Reuben like fifteen minutes.

I have come here to collect myself, he thought. I have come here to learn the facts, the workings of the City. These men (and he watched them through the window at the wagon) would keep me here. They would imprison me. They would have me think like them — that there is no escape. For some purpose they want me, and they are idiots. They do not know the workings of the City. They would understand a river by standing on the bridge. I hate them. I hate them. They can teach me, but I will never be like them.

Later. The door opened and closed. Irv, Georgie, and Oskar walked into the better lit front of the room and resumed their gaming at the table. Reuben could see bloodstains on their fingers and knew that before, when he had first come into the closet-like room from outside, he could never have seen differences so easily. His eyes were in some way adapting.

"In exchange," said Reuben, "for what you have shown me, I can tell you stories of outside."

The three looked at each other, and then back at him. "Stories of outside are very important to us here," said Georgie. "Of course all stories are about outside. There is no sense talking about events here."

"Maybe," said Reuben. "But I can tell you what it's like outside, in case you've forgotten."

"There isn't much to think about here," said Irv, "and it's immoral to tell bad stories, because they will be repeated over and over in your memory, and they will make everything just that much worse."

"This story won't bum you out."

"Don't talk like that," said Georgie. "Don't ever talk like that."

"Anyway, do you want to hear it?"

"Are you sure it's a good one?" asked Oskar.

"It's good," said Reuben, "it's just the way it is outside . . . of course it's good. And it's about love."

"Go ahead," said Irv, "but make it a short one — long ones are hard to remember, the details."

"Nellie once had a boyfriend. . . ."

"Nellie?"

"That's my sister. Anyway, it's surprising that she had one, because after her blindness became noticeably worse, and—"

"Wait a minute," said Oskar, "are you sure this is a good one?"

"It's a good one," said Reuben, "and you can't be that sensitive — there has to be some of that stuff — in order to make it authentic."

"Well, maybe," said Oskar.

"If you're going to be that critical," said Reuben, "then I

simply won't tell it: but then you'll miss knowing for sure what it was like outside."

"Go ahead."

Far away in the City Reuben heard the beginnings of a sound that would much later be the clattering of the ice wagon. The other three did not hear; their auditory capabilities, especially Irv's who had been there the longest, were not good, possibly because of damage caused to their eardrums by the screaming. The men looked at the floor and walls while he talked, paying close attention to detail, their hands touching their faces.

"It was remarkable because Nellie did not get around enough to meet hardly anyone, and the only people that even recognized her were shopowners and cashiers, where she went about her daily business. Her eighth-grade class had forgotten her long ago. Anyhow, it was remarkable when this fellow went bananas—"

"Stop that," said Irv.

"—fell in love with her. To condense this a bit; he was the only son of John Tickie, a man who had given my father a job and had later hired Paul to work in his place—who even defended him against the good people of Des Moines—"

"Don't be ironic," said Georgie; "it's cheap."

"In any case he was her age, about twenty-six then, and played an electric piano in the background of country Western groups in taverns. Somehow she had met him, probably about town on the streets because Nellie never went into taverns. The first time that either Paul or I saw him was one breezy afternoon in autumn, no clouds in the sky if I recall, when he arrived at the house in a panel truck. It was his own truck, but it still said Anderson's Donut Wagon on the side. We were in the yard at the time, and he got out of the truck." The sound of the ice wagon was growing louder, yet still the three men did not hear it.

"To condense this a bit: he was short, and a little stocky—actually he looked a lot like his father, at least in shape. His hair was already thinning, and we shook hands. He explained, in the matter-of-fact way of speaking of his father, that he had fallen in love with Nellie and wanted some help carrying the electric piano from his Donut Truck to the house." The three men looked at the floor and walls, concentrating; because listening to someone talking is like that, like cardplaying, in detention centers, cheap hotel rooms, joints, and homes for dying, where time makes no difference one way or another unless you notice it. Sleeping will work for that too.

"These trips between the house and the van carrying the piano (we had seen him carry it himself, when he thought we were too busy, but the memory of that always prompted us to help) were the only times we ever heard him talk. We learned he played in bands for a living, because he would rather play that than work, though playing that kind of music, he said, smiling, was kind of like working. Even that first day we didn't ever hear him talk to Nellie. We just left them together in the living room and ten minutes later we could hear him playing." Within the space of the next three minutes, Irv, Georgie, and Oskar heard the sound of the approaching ice wagon. As each heard it he lifted his head toward Reuben and watched him, wondering if he had heard, then fell back to watching the floor. Reuben thought, it was not much time since he was last here. There must be something around this area which keeps him. Perhaps he has his wagon loaded in this part. He stopped thinking of it.

"The music he played was pleasant, but in a much different way from that I had heard before. If most music could be said to be a kind of singing, then his music could just as easily be said to be a kind of thinking. No one would call the sounds that fit between when he started playing and when he stopped, a song. It wasn't. It, like thinking, had no unity, no tune, no theme, no recognizable rhythm pattern, no variations in pitch, nothing like that; just sounds thinking among themselves."

The noise outside grew louder.

"If I try I can imagine them now, sitting in the living room, she in our overstuffed red chair, Nellie's Cat up behind her head keeping an eye on things, and he behind the brown electric piano, leaning over it. I could come in and sit down; neither of them would move. I could tell from watching Nellie very closely that she was smiling, and from this knowledge I studied Willie's face and finally saw the same thin faint smile on his own lips. Their bodies rocked forward and back, almost imperceptibly, in unison, though the swing of his rock was longer than hers. Almost like they were humming together."

The sound outside was very loud now and the three stood up and went over to the door in the darker part of the room, watching Reuben, who crossed over to them and stepped out onto the wet bricks.

"And this went on three or four times a week for almost a year. I can remember being happy at home, when Nellie and Willie were together in the living room. Father had died. Walt was gone, and there was only Paul and me sitting about the house, feeding off of what was happening between Nellie and Willie. That was before she was raped and beaten, of course."

"Wait a minute," said Oskar, walking.

"It's O.K." The clatter of the ice wagon was filling the streets. "And so then after she was raped we didn't see him for several weeks, and we all missed—I was in the hospital at the time for doing in the people who had hurt her, almost killing many of them."

"Wait a minute," said Irv, stopping to walk and turning directly toward him. "Are you sure this is a good story?"

"Ultimately good," he said, and they continued walking, Georgie, Irv, and Oskar huddling closely to him, looking down at their feet, listening closely while he talked. The ice wagon turned onto the straight long street that continued on down to them, the sound being more clear and direct then.

"To condense this a bit: when he finally did come we asked

him, while carrying the electric piano, where he had been, and explained to him that we had missed his playing. He said that he had quit his job and had not been eating well. Because? Well, because, he explained, of what had happened to Nellie, and how, play as he might, he could not understand how anyone, much less a group of individuals, could do such a thing. Detaining him at the door, we asked why that would not bring him to see Nellie, to comfort her, rather than drive him away. He answered straight out—"

The wagon was in sight. They stood still and waited for it to stop beside them. Reuben looked away from the horse's eyes. He did not know how long it had been since he had eaten. Oskar opened up the back doors; the metal hinges screamed. Again the smell nearly caused Reuben to faint. I am weak, he thought. I have grown weak, too weak for what lies ahead of me. Two handfuls were taken out. Irv tore a piece off with his teeth and then blood dripped from the corners of his mouth. Oskar cut a slice with his jackknife and wedged it into his mouth. "Here," said Georgie handing him some, "eat it fast." The flesh was cold in his hand. "Check for mold," mumbled Irv. Reuben thought: there are many ugly places, desperate living conditions. But those situations cannot be used to justify themselves, because there is no end to that. Yet escape . . . to escape . . . for strength to escape. This kind of thinking had been done before, but other men . . . had even been given a name, of sorts; the matter was that he knew he would need something in order to go on, and this had made an irrevocable change in him, and things he would never have done before jumped into his area of possibilities. The wagon door was shut and after two light cones the horse was engulfed in grayness, his echoing still going on. Reuben put one of the limp, cold, dripping pieces in his mouth, and the taste—if anyone could call it that—ran through his entire self like some kind of a shock. He could not vomit, because there was nothing inside him, only the thin walls of his stomach; that, and he feared if he started that it would never stop. He began to gag. "Quick," said Georgie, "keep talking; it's the only way to keep it in."

I hate you, Reuben thought. Desperately he began: "He was afraid of a personal confrontation — one in which Nellie would, or might, attempt to embrace him. We plugged the piano in, went out and started the generator. The music from inside was terrible, discord and chaos." Reuben swallowed.

"Again," said Irv, wolfing the last of his. "Another piece. The first is too much like an experiment." Reuben took another.

"Inside (we watched from the kitchen) tears were coming down Willie's cheeks, onto his shabby shirt, and awful sounds were coming out of the piano. Nellie, still bruised, got out of her chair and went over to him. Despite her almost perfect blindness she quickly found him and gently put her hands on his shoulders. 'Don't touch me,' he said." Reuben swallowed a second time and let the rest fall onto the street.

"'What's that?' she asked, running her hands more quickly up and down his arms.

"'Tumors!' he said, jumping up from his bench. 'Those are tumors. Don't touch me!'

"'How can you, when you know me so well, say that?' she asked and touched him again. He turned around and pushed her backwards. She fell against a chair and onto the floor. He looked at her and ran from the house—"

"Wait!" said Oskar. "There's no way this can be a good story — not with what you are getting into now. Stop!"

"No, you have to listen," Reuben said. "This is the way that it was. . . . Finally, back at his room he locked himself in and sat for days staring at his right hand, the one with which he had shoved Nellie. He stared at it and he hated it. He did not have his piano to play, and he went down into the basement of the rooming house and tied his right arm to the inside of the oil furnace, through the bottom door that had been used for taking out ashes before it was converted from coal. He tied himself

with wire, and with his foot reached around the furnace and
kicked on the ignition button. That arm was completely burned
off, the smell filling the basement. On his other hand (trying
to undo what he had done) the fingers were melted and when
the horrified people came down into the cellar they wrapped
his hand in a towel without separating the fingers so that later
his one remaining hand was webbed."

"Change the ending," said Irv. "Change the ending." His
voice was like a dying judge.

"That's the way it was. That's what happened. Isn't it strange?"

"Change the ending."

"Sorry. It's not my world."

"Then leave us."

"Don't you have any more facts to tell me about this place?"

"There are no facts — only the awful situation, and you
make it worse. Go away, or change the ending of that story. You
didn't have to show that side of it. No one made you." Georgie
was sitting down on the concrete, looking at his hands.

"Maybe not," said Reuben. "But I've been with you too long.
I have to get out of here. I don't belong here."

"There is no escape. That's a fact."

"I'll never believe that. Leave me be," he said and walked on
off down the street, passing buildings he had never seen before
and would not remember. I can find water in the low pockets
of the streets and roofs, where the condensed fog collects, he
thought; a hard rain will also make it down.

He was not so afraid now. Although he had become considerably weakened and wondered even if he could manage
to run successfully should he be prompted, still his body was
one of those light-framed endurance modules that at one hundred twenty-five pounds could go on almost indefinitely. He
walked down deeper into the City, noticing as in the back of
his mind that the noise did not bother him, that he could even
live with that.

He entered into an environment that was different in

character from those he had previously encountered. Large grain bins of galvanized steel, barbershops with barber poles, Bible-supplies stores, produce markets, one-aisle drug stores, weigh stations, antique shops filled with buggy wheels and milk cans, a machine shop, a Ford sales lot . . . Reuben saw an old tractor behind a dry goods store and heard an uncommon noise, which in several blocks he was able to trace to coming from a two-table billiard room, open to the street behind a large glass window that let a remarkable amount of light inside from the streetlamp directly in front. Someone was playing pool and Reuben went inside, listening then to the squeaking sound of chalking a cue.

"W-w-w-w-w-w-w," began a high-pitched whining inhuman sound. Whatever it was had stepped back against the wall, out of sight. Reuben backed towards the door, finding within him a potential he had supposed himself to have lost . . . the ability to run.

"W-s-s-w-wswhat you w-w-want?" the voice said, but not so clearly. Reuben wondered if he had not managed to hear intelligence in a senseless squabble. The noise stopped. Asthmatic breathing began.

Reuben regained the door opening, and bracing his arms against the frame in such a way as to help launch him into his running, aware that he was clearly visible to his protagonist, said as clearly as possible, "I will not hurt you. I want facts."

"Facts?" asked the voice, with definite intention. Reuben tightened his grip on the door frame.

"Facts about this place," said Reuben.

"It's a poolroom," said the voice, some of the sounds passing upward into the inaudible range. What can make that kind of sound? wondered Reuben; surely nothing that was real in the usual sense . . . having once lived outside the City wall.

"I know that. Stand into the light," said Reuben. It began walking.

The farther green-felted table acted as a light catcher, collecting most of the penetrable fog about its top, and the thing was not recognizable until it had reached the second table and by then the outline of its head so completely took over Reuben's senses that he was for what seemed a long time unable to notice even the overall size, which for all practical purposes was near normal. Waterhead, thought Reuben. The figure moved closer and laid a cue onto the table, releasing it from a tiny hand. Its two eyes were small black dots one and one half inches apart and directly in the middle of the huge, elongated head. These eyes looked out away from each other. Its mouth hung open and the hollow of the bottom lip made it appear like a round, red hole. More disgusting than all this, however, was the nose, which without bone or cartilage was two blaring sockets through which passed a wheezing sound equaled only in its ghastliness by the color of the skin, which was indeed that of a freshly rotted apple. Saliva dripped from the mouth onto the floor. My God, thought Reuben, why did I ever come here?

"Do you w-w-w-want to see a trick shot?" asked the thing, picking up a billiard ball in each hand, completely filling each palm.

"O.K.," said Reuben, because he had not collected himself enough to say any more. The waterhead carefully placed one of two balls against a cushion and put the other one up against it so that the two formed the beginning of a line perpendicular to the rail. Then he placed the cue ball at a forty-five-degree angle from this and banked the first ball into the opposite corner pocket without disturbing the second ball.

"Amazing," said Reuben.

"I've got a better one than that," said the waterhead.

"I haven't got time," said Reuben. "Sorry. All I need to know is facts, then I'll leave you alone. See I spent such a long time with these three men, and they hardly knew . . ."

"You mean Oskar, Georgie, and Irv?" the head asked, and put down the cue stick.

"Yes," he said.

"They're idiots."

"I know. They told me that no one could ever get out of here."

"They w-w-were right about that. There's a lot they don't know, though — possibilities that they aren't aware of because they never come out of that storeroom."

"What do you mean, they were right about not being able to get out? It's stupid, a City that no one can get out of, full of fog, where people eat each other. It can't be."

"It is," he shrieked.

"Maybe you think so, but there's a way out. If someone learns the facts."

"W-w-what facts?"

"The facts about the workings of the City."

"W-s-sw-what about them?"

"To begin with . . . do you mind if we go outside? I feel kind of conspicuous standing here in this light."

"So you can't see me?"

"If you don't mind."

"O.K. If you'll watch some more trick shots after a w-w-while."

And they went outside, the waterhead walking behind Reuben, his misshaped feet slapping against the bricks, into a dark area where Reuben could no longer see him, only hear his high, broken voice.

"See, I don't belong here," said Reuben. "I didn't intend to come."

"Perhaps that makes a difference."

"It does. I'm sure of it."

"Then I guess it does. I guess if you are sure of it, then it's a fact."

"What can you tell me about this place?"

"What can you tell me about outside?"

"What do you want to know?" asked Reuben. "It's not important."

"What do you want to know about here?"

"Why didn't you stutter that time?"

"I forgot about it. W-w-why?"

"Never mind. I want to know how to get out."

"You can't."

"That's crazy. If you asked me how to get in here from outside, I wouldn't say, 'You can't.' If there's a way in, there's a way out."

"What if I asked you how to get out, outside?"

"That would be a stupid question," said Reuben.

"Then you might say, 'You can't.'"

"What's the matter with you?"

"I have water inside my head. It won't go away."

Reuben knew that he would have to be careful. He felt that the waterhead might know something about the workings of the City, but he was sure that that information would have to be carefully taken out of his head, before it was twisted around.

"How did you come here?" asked Reuben.

"I walked."

"Why did you come here?"

"I should have come before."

"Why?"

"I was tricked. See, from everyone that knew me, and everything I knew, I was not supposed to live very long . . . not longer than ten years at the most. That's what they told me, and what I read."

"So?"

"So I worked in a circus and waited to die but I never did, and each day I never did, so finally I decided that if that w-w-was the w-w-way that it was then I w-would come down here."

"Why?"

"W-w-w-wouldn't you?"

"No, I was tricked into coming."

"I mean, if you looked like me."

"Oh. I see what you mean."

"I mean there's more freedom down here for me, without the circus and people running me out of stores because they think that maybe I'm pestilential."

"But if you wanted to get out."

"I would never have come."

Reuben thought again. He had not been careful enough, and any information there was inside the head was not coming out.

"What is your name?" asked Reuben.

"The squid."

"The squid!"

"Yes. My parents, when they saw —"

"Never mind."

"I thought you wanted the facts."

"Tell me what this place is."

"What do you mean?"

"I mean is it a City of the Dead?"

"No."

"What is it?"

"Tell me about outside first. Then I'll tell you."

"What about outside?"

"Anything."

"O.K. There was once this minister, that is he used to be a minister, but then he became a fanatic. . . ."

"Is this true?"

"Yes. And every night — you could set your watch by him — he would come out of one of those buildings on Market Street and walk up to Grand. Where he would stand in front of the Fanny Farmer Candy Store and preach of the damnation of the world. The nighthawks — bull bats — would be out by then and be swooping down into the streets, between the buildings and across the roofs, and he'd curse them and call out to them like

they were people, to go back to their homes, out of the darkness, and sleep until morning. Then the teenagers would climb
out of their cars and jeer at him and flip cigarettes from their
fingers at his coat; and he would curse them, and they would
push him against the building and around in circles, being
careful to keep behind him because though slow, he was nevertheless heavy and would flail out at them. And they would get
bored and go back into their cars and he would rave on until the
night help—the scum of the earth—came out of the restaurants and movie theaters in cheap dresses and hats and hurry
down the street from him. Then he would go home. And after a
while no one saw him again."

"Is that true?"

"Yes."

"Good. It's just the way I remember."

"Now tell me about this place."

"In the days before altimeters," the squid began, "on w-w-
winter days when the snow covered the ground and clouds were
so thick in the air that everywhere you looked was w-w-white,
everywhere, it was possible for pilots, after a difficult bank, to
become confused about which way was up—because of there
being w-w-white everywhere they looked. So pulling back on
the stick they would crash into the ice and snow, thinking it was
the clouds; or sail with the landing gear lowered up through a
layer of clouds. This place, the City, is neither the clouds or the
ice, it is in between."

"Be clearer," said Reuben.

"This is a place where some people are living and some
things happen."

Reuben felt, for the first time in the City, that he might cry,
or scream, or make some outburst. "Why," he asked, "why do
you torment me when I am already so beaten down by being
here that all I can think of is leaving?"

"Why would you think I would be compassionate?" asked
the squid.

"I didn't," said Reuben, his voice shaking. "I didn't. And I don't."

"There is one man here who can help you," said the waterhead. "His name is Johnson Johnson. He helps many others. Find him."

Reuben walked away. The squid followed him for several blocks, begging him to come back to the poolroom and watch trick shots. Reuben knew he did not have to; that it made no difference. But more important than this was something he had learned from the waterhead, in the order of a fact: one had to be careful about the nature of facts. For instance, if anyone knew of a way out of the City, they would not tell him, because they would not be in the City at all, and if they were — if they knew how to get out but were not escaping — then they would be either mad or have mad reasons for not leaving, in which case they would not tell him anyway; and what he would hear would be that "no one can escape," whether that were the case or not. Other facts, he thought, might also be like that. What he must do was let the free and easy talk of those others in the City, speaking of what they believed to be the case, fill his mind, so that later he might reformulate the material, and split. It was such a good plan, he thought, that he could hardly control his face, which smiled.

Enough of this aimless walking; Reuben reasoned that his purpose might better be served by standing in one place and watching and so learning the workings of the City by examining it through one locale, in detail — the way it is possible to learn more about a man by observing him in one situation at length than by catching running glimpses of him in different places. There was something protective about the plan too. He could see and hear anything that approached him. He sat down and leaned against a wall. The wet, clammy grayness leaped into the material of his clothes and by osmosis filled the pores of his body. And he fell asleep and woke up and fell asleep again, hardly dreaming at all.

He woke up and the sound of the ice wagon was twice as loud as it would have been if he had been awake to hear the beginning of it. He wound his watch. Later, he saw the metal-runged carrier coming down towards him. It had not turned off in another direction; he felt comfort in that; he was in a chartered part of town. The street sign above him read High Street; people would be by here. So well laid out, he thought, and so seemingly unnecessary; but perhaps that was like thinking that the inside of a watch isn't important, only necessary for the case, face, and hands.

The albino, without seeming to notice his person sitting in a dark area, stopped with the wagon doors close within his reach. How can he see like that? Reuben wondered. He stood up and felt stiff, opened the double doors and withdrew a small piece. Then he shut the doors and the horse continued on down the street.

There's something good about that animal, thought Reuben, and had many more thoughts about the beast and even incorporated it into a dream before he again heard the metal wheels, three or four hours in the distance. The horse frequented this area of High Street three times before Reuben decided that he might follow it, and so discover other inhabitants of the City, on the delivery route. Sitting still was not working. It was not teaching him anything. He might perhaps be led to the iceman who, he reasoned, might be persuaded to abandon his project and help him, them, escape, by taking the entire horse and wagon to one of the monuments, and so having the food, the preservation of mind for the long vigil . . . him or Johnson Johnson, if that name actually corresponded to a real person, and was not an illusive watery substance in the squid's head. He thought more and was sure he would rather meet Johnson Johnson, and hoped to be out of the City long before he even happened to come upon the iceman; then noticed that the wagon and horse would be long out of his sight if he was not quickly up and after them. He pushed himself away from the building and ran down the street, just as the albino and following rectangular box turned a corner and went out of his view.

Reuben recovered his distance from the animal and was soon walking calmly alongside it, thinking that he, the horse, had intentionally slowed its pace to make it easier for him . . . though without turning his head. This was the first moment since he had passed through the monument when Reuben felt that kindness had been shown to him, though he could not be sure, of course, that it was not his own desperate imagination.

Oblivious to these thinkings, the animal plodded on, dragging behind it the dripping box. How could a dumb animal be so meticulously trained? wondered Reuben. How could an animal be made to do this? Why would it go on living? How could it go on living, day to day, carrying such a burden? What does it eat? Surely nothing can grow here.

They went on. Reuben felt as though he were growing stronger, taking strength from the horse's huge body, like lying flat out on the earth and letting the energy leap upward into you. Something is good about this beast, he thought. Something is good about it beyond its ability to endure. If it knew the workings of the City it would tell me. Overcome with compassion, Reuben gently reached out his hand to pull a piece of the moss from its neck. It came easily. The albino screamed and turned his head, the eyes red with fear and pain. A tiny scarlet trickle of blood ran down its neck from underneath the flap of dead skin that he had pulled loose.

"Oh no!" said Reuben. "I'm sorry," and stopped momentarily. "Oh, my God, what happened to you?" But the albino had resumed his walk and former attitude and showed no indication of wanting to explain how scar tissue had come to cover half its body.

Reuben caught up to his companion and walked along beside. Once, but just once, the albino looked wildly over at him and shied away, for fear that he would again reach out, but then resumed staring fixedly ahead. It expects nothing better, thought Reuben; it anticipates that the pain and abuse will continue forever, and still it drags that immoral wagon. The prince of hell could not want such a thing even in punishment — even in fun. What kind of place is that where things happen that should never happen even in the dark of the sun? It doesn't have to be like this.

"I'm sorry," he said to the albino, and mingled in the clanking of the metal wheels were the echoes . . . I'm sorry . . . I'm sorry.

"I had no idea — how could I? It was compassion that had me do it, and an accident that it backfired. I wish it had been me. Can you believe that?" . . . Can you believe that . . . Can you believe that? The animal walked on, his eyes hidden from Reuben by the blinders. Reuben looked at the tiny stream of drying blood flickering out of the flap of "moss." The mark would remain forever, a stain of proof against him.

The horse and Reuben went on, without stopping, for so long that Reuben began to wonder if the horse in fact knew the streets, because it never turned, and continued walking straight ahead, or almost, and Reuben remembered being told about huge circular streets. He broke a window and marked the jagged edge with a piece of cloth from his shirt. Much later he saw the window again, was sure it was the same one, but the cloth was gone. Reuben wondered again about the horse. But before it came seriously and conspicuously into doubt Reuben had a haunting thought, and unable to suffer it he decided to test it and fell back to walking behind the wagon. The albino soon walked down a side street and stopped. It was true. The horse had been following him: the mockery of it!

No one came out of the nearby buildings, and the horse moved away. And then another giant perception crawled into his mind: the people might hide if they saw the ice wagon followed by someone; and he fell farther behind and kept in the darker areas of the streets, walking on the sides of his shoes. The albino stopped again, this time in an area of City suburb, in front of a fat, squat house fully illuminated inside, effecting an eerie, unnatural contrast to the rest of the area. The yellow light inside stretched out into the fog and looked like a huge lantern at sea. Noise came from the house. "Wait," said someone inside, and even from two streetlamps away Reuben knew he had heard the voice before, once. The door opened and out of the house came a woman, her yellow hair falling in rolls down over her shoulders, moving with the timidity and nobility of a deer, dressed in a very cheap white dress, sewn together with red thread, her eyes brilliantly dark; like a wild moon, thought Reuben . . . so brilliant that they must color anything that they look at. She held out an armload of green to the animal.

Plants, thought Reuben, she has plants.

"Hello," he called, waiting before he approached the house to see if, like himself, she would take flight at the sound. She did not, and returned: "Hello, come out. Who are you?"

The horse finished chewing and moved ahead. She stepped from the front step on to the street and called, "Mildew," and the animal stopped and backed the wagon toward her. "Stop," she commanded, and opened the back doors and took out a neat handful of meat which she carefully wrapped in brown paper carried from inside. Then bidding good-bye to the horse, she turned to face Reuben, who had by this time progressed to a distance of less than three yards from her, where he stopped.

"You are still here," she said. "I knew you would be."

"Of course," he said. "I'm told that there is no way out. So here I am and who are you?"

"Mary." Somehow he had expected her to say more, but she stood quiet, smiling easily into his eyes. Reuben waited this time before begging for information and pretended that he too was as relaxed and serene as the woman. (This is what he told himself . . . what he listened to, however, was that he might be becoming hardened, that he did not need to talk about escaping so frequently only because he did not think about it, so much.) His plan, he conceded, might be long-range, and the time between his escape and now might be able to be lived in less unpleasant ways.

Mary set the package down on the front step, then sat down beside it. "Why did you run?" she asked.

"Oh, I don't know. Just a game I play with people."

"You should not play games that others don't understand."

Reuben agreed that she might be pointing out a particular character fault of his and asked how long she had been there.

"Johnson brought me here, not so long ago."

"Johnson Johnson?"

"Yes."

"He brought you in here, in the City?"

"No, no. He brought me to this house; before that I lived in closer to the theaters."

"It seems so long since I was in a real house," he said, mostly to himself. "Why don't we go inside?"

"No, you can't come in with me. Johnson would kill you; that's why he brought me here, for himself, I mean. He is very jealous."

"And you don't mind?"

"Mind?"

"You don't try to escape?"

"No. Why should I? He is beautiful, and I have no need for other men. But friends, we can be friends. And he doesn't keep me by force. I can leave whenever I want."

Reuben was not listening. He was thinking of how different it would be . . . if he could be in a house, a house with chairs and tables and pictures and rugs and lights (he could see the lights, lighting the entire block). If only he could be in a house, where people lived, with someone, where it might not be so damp, so cold, so insufferably gray . . . that he could think in a house where the walls, yellow walls, could keep his thinking close about him. How could anyone think in this fog? — stealing your ideas and diffracting and dissolving them until they become so less like thoughts and more like fog that they begin to help echo the screaming, though he hardly heard this now. This fog, he thought; there is nothing like small cats' feet about it. That would be like comparing a parakeet to a Chinese dragon . . . if that will work, then everything is up for grabs.

"You do not listen to me," said Mary, who had been talking. "But at least that's better than most of them . . . complaining and pleading to be helped out . . . an awful way to act, don't you think?"

"Perhaps they are afraid," he said.

"If they *are* afraid, and I can't see any reason to be, because I am not, and neither is Johnson, and if they are afraid then they do not have to be so obvious about it, all the crying, I mean. It just makes others unhappy."

"Perhaps they are so afraid that they don't think about that. Perhaps they are so afraid that they can't think about that. Their fears preclude that."

"Do you like people who talk like books?" she asked.

"What!"

"Who talk as though they always say important things . . . things that others should pay a lot of attention to."

"Well. . . ."

"Johnson does that. And maybe I have been thinking that I don't like it; importance can only go so far. Sometimes we like to sleep, and twitch . . . and laugh."

"What theaters?" asked Reuben.

"Movies. They show old-time movies in the theaters."

"How many are there?"

"Three and sometimes four."

"Oh," Reuben said, thinking again more than he was listening; watching Mary, noticing that she was one of those people with an indeterminate age — knowing that age is usually right about twenty-nine or thirty. He had a profound respect for indeterminate age, for any place that he had not reached, and he deferred to her; her cheeks looked as though they might be very warm and had color that concerned him, because he had worried that he might never see it again.

Mary talked to him and though his attention was not careful, the soporific sounds from her tuned throat fought like an opiate in his mind for control, won, and he lay out on the street with his head in her lap, and she talked and laughed, about the movies she had seen and of the stories Johnson had told her of the City and outside . . . good stories.

"Take me inside," said Reuben. "I'll be all right if I can just get inside." And she threw open the door and let him in, shutting it behind them.

If he had been tired before he went inside . . . he woke up. Plants grew out of the cracks in the floor; plants uprooted the floorboards, grew up the walls and across the ceiling, and fitted and wrapped around long, tubular white lights. "Plant lights," Mary said, that Johnson had given her when she came into the house, and after she had turned them on the plants came from everywhere as though the City were a stretched membrane and the plants, like pressurized water, behind, finding a tiny hole, spurted out. She told him to take his shoes off, and not to mind stepping on them because they did not mind. Oh God, thought Reuben, why did I ever come here? But he could not leave . . . the house had done to him what he had hoped, and now he was caught. Pleasure and warmth are like that; ideals become desires and wants become needs and it overcomes you to watch them change, or tell when one is clearly not the other two.

"How long have you been here, in the City?" he asked.

"I have always been here," she said.

"That can't be."

"Then I do not remember being outside," she said.

"It must be horrible, not to remember," but as he said this he knew that it wasn't.

"If Johnson finds you here, there will be trouble."

Reuben was wandering through the rooms, looking at the plants, letting them comfort him.

"There won't be any unless he wants me to leave, and then only if he wants to make sure that it will come out that way."

"Do you ever think about words?" asked Mary, whose thoughts seemed to snip off at the base after she had used them, making it easier to get into another one. Reuben stopped and sat, fell into a chair, half crushing a banana-shaped leaf attached to a rubber plant. I should not have come here, he thought. I will never get out.

"Sometimes," he said. "Why?"

"I mean funny words."

"I don't know any funny words," he said. "There are no funny words."

"Yes there are," she said, the sound of her tuned throat filling the room with her wild, belligerent joyous rebuttal. "Feet," she said (Fe-e-e-e-e-et) and began to laugh and sat down on the floor with the plants.

"Feet?" said Reuben.

"Feet," she said, between laughing.

"Feet," he said and was beginning to see it.

"Feet," she said, laughing louder because saying it was a good part of the fun.

"Feet," he said, thinking how foolish it was.

"Feet," she said.

"Feet," he said, laughing now, feeling, how good this is, what we are doing.

"Feet," she said.

"And you know what else is funny?" he said.

"What?" she asked, gasping for air.

"Foot," he howled.

"Foot?" she asked, hardly managing to bend the sound of the word up into a question.

"Foot," he said.

"Foot."

They laughed, and Reuben told her stories but they are not important. They are stories that people have to tell about themselves, letting them carefully come out, revealing secret parts of them . . . revealing, but not like a window into the soul. They have been told too often for that and they are embarrassing to those people, like us, who know more about him than those stories could approximate, because they are partially fictional, merely shadowy extensions of the concrete reality of Reuben.

Fully clothed, they fell asleep lying in the plants, wrapped in each other's arms. I must get out of here, thought Reuben, before he drifted off to sleep and dreamed sweet good dreams about outside, about Iowa, the windmills and cheap whistles, and how his father had, every night while eating dinner, taken his pocket watch out and wound it and set it to the sound of the train whistle, put it against his ear before replacing it, like a diamond, into his vest or overalls.

"Let's go to a movie," said Mary.

"No."

"Let's go to a movie."

"O.K."

"Why didn't you want to?"

"I thought we might get lost and not be able to come back, but then I knew that you could get us back."

"Do you want to eat some food before we go?"

"Sure . . . say, can we eat this?" and he gestured around him.

"That is animals' food!" she said. The issue was closed and they began to eat from out of the brown paper, Reuben not wanting her to watch him and turning away. Then they put on winter coats — she had an extra one for him — and went outside where it was noticeably colder. "Are you sure we can get back?" asked Reuben.

"Yes," she said. "I can get us both back—if you do not do something that would make me leave you behind." They walked around a corner.

"Don't worry."

They heard the dull explosion of a monument closing. Reuben stopped.

"That's a monument closing," he said.

"Yes," she said. "Do you want to go see if we can talk to who came in, instead of the movies?"

"We could never find him."

"Maybe we could, if he comes farther in."

"He'd be afraid of us."

"Yes. But they are funny to watch, like the Three Stooges in a haunted house."

"It's not right to talk about people like that."

"I met one who was not afraid. I asked him if he wanted to talk and he said, 'Go away.' That was a long time ago."

"What did he look like?" Reuben asked and then thought no, it couldn't be; but it reminded him.

"He was nice looking."

They arrived at the theater, The Orpheum, which had neither lights nor billboards and looked to all outside appearances disused. But the doors opened to the touch and they went inside. They stood in the doorway opening into the theater proper. Several small bunches of people were already there but good viewing positions seemed to have had nothing to do with the places they had chosen to sit . . . the darker areas were popular, along the wall. Reuben thought of leaving Mary in order to go up to the projection booth; who would do this? he wondered; who would take time to show movies? He did not leave Mary, and did not want to answer those questions. They walked down the aisle and sat down as near to the center as they could, without being too close to anyone else. Some of them were screaming.

"When do they start?" asked Reuben.

"You just have to wait until they begin; sometimes that's a long time, sometimes not. We don't use watches here."

"If you were always in the City, and if you don't use watches here, how do you know about watches at all?"

"The information filters in."

"And books," said Reuben.

"And books."

"I guess it's like a boomerang . . . I don't use them, and have never been where they do; still I know what they are, and what they do."

"What's a boomerang?"

"It's not important," he said, wishing the movie would begin so that the people would quiet down. He could not help noticing them, some doubling over in the foldable chairs, rocking back and forth, crying.

"Those awful people," said Mary, "coming here into public places to scream and yell and make it so the sound for the movie must be turned up to an almost painful level to hear. Their carrying on, whimpering and crying, they make me sick. I wish they would go off and let a roof fall on them."

"How can you say that about people who are suffering?"

"Suffering — what's suffering — what's to suffer?"

"This place. This place is bad enough."

"This place! This theater is the best one. The others are dirty and full of teenagers chasing up and down the aisle and cutting seats and writing scary things on the walls."

"I mean the City."

"Oh. Well, Johnson and I aren't suffering, and it's not that we are different. They just come here to show off." Reuben thought he might be starting to dislike J.J. or at least have unsympathetic feelings about him.

"Show off!"

"Why else? Why else would they come here except to show off?"

"Public places make you feel safer."

"Then why do they carry on like this if they feel safe . . . they're just showing off."

"Maybe you're right," he said, finally aware that it made no difference to anyone what he felt . . . that the suffering would not go away, or the showing off, whichever it was, and they had come to watch a movie, not debate abstracts. But more important than this . . . he was beginning to understand how he might be immune to it all; he felt as though he might flat out not care.

The movie began. Reuben turned back but could see nothing through the small rectangular hole in the gray porous wall but the light, which despite the brilliant intensity could not cut cleanly through the fog and lost more than half of its picture to the air before reaching the screen. Laurel and Hardy: *Bacon Grabbers.*

By the introduction of the steamroller into the movie Reuben felt that his laughter had surely damaged a vital part of his stomach, but was unable to do anything but exacerbate the rupture. Two old ladies walked up the aisle, one helping steady the other, both crying quietly and stumbling into the folding chairs bolted to the floor. The steamroller smashed Laurel and Hardy's car and Reuben could laugh no harder; his voice box had been evacuated. He leaned forward and buried his head into Mary's hair. "Don't, Mary," he tried to say, but she had managed already to free his constricted erection into the cool air, grasping it with both of her warm hands, watching it like some kind of live animal in front of her mouth.

"Don't do that," he said.

"It's all right," she whispered to the animal, "Johnson knows you are here. He knows everything here. He must not mind or he would have already come for you."

"Just not here, Mary," he said. "Just not here."

"It's dark. It is dark enough."

"Come on, Mary, let's go, back to the house."

"It is good here."

"It's better there."

"Watch out," she whispered, cooing.

"Stop that. Mary, stop that." She stopped, and helped . . . at least stayed out of the way while Reuben recovered his emblem of desire.

"Hurry," said Mary, "we must get home, before it leaves."

"What?"

"The feeling," she said . . . then added, "My feeling." They left the theater and walked out into the street, laughing and hugging each other.

"Don't you think we should lock the door?"

"Why?"

"Johnson . . . in case he decides to drop in for a visit," Reuben explained.

"It wouldn't make any difference. He goes anywhere he wants. If he wants in here, he would come in. There is nowhere he cannot go."

"Just in case, why don't we lock it anyway? Perhaps his supernatural powers will be working at a low ebb today."

Reuben locked the front door. "Why," he asked, "does it always seem like wherever you go — that it is downhill — effortless."

"Hurry up," she said. "I'm losing it." She led him to the sofa and began unloosing him again. "I can feel it," she whispered, the sounds coming up from her tuned throat. "It's coming back to me."

"Let me — ," he began.

"No," she said, "relax. Johnson never lets me, like this. Let me. Relax."

"But there's nothing for me — "

"Talk to me," she said and pushed his pants down to his knees.

"What about?"

"Anything."

"Like what?"

She had stopped talking. Reuben was stroking the back of her head and playing with the collar of her dress, turning it over and twisting it in an arbitrary rhythm.

SLEDGE. Written in black durable ink behind the collar where the manufacturer's name would have been if the dress had been manufactured, SLEDGE. We, Reuben thought, have marked all our sheets and pillowcases in this way, and the only sheet he knew that had come into the City had been in an automobile.

"Mary, where did you get this dress?"

She was not talking.

"Mary," he shouted, "where did you get this dress?"

"What difference does it make?" she asked, very irritated at being forced to talk.

"Because it's one of the bizarre coincidences that no one would ever believe; but makes me wonder if you aren't my sister."

"What!" she said, beginning to whisper.

"I had a sister named Mary that disappeared and my mother thought she wandered into the City."

"What did she look like?"

"I never saw her."

"Was she beautiful?" Her voice was nearly a hum now.

"I tell you I don't know. We have to stop this."

"You don't know for sure; and besides it will be better this way."

"No."

"If it bothers you, later, you can forget it."

"There's something very stupid about the way I was made. I forget nothing . . . nothing . . . stop, Mary." She sat halfway up.

"If you make me stop, then you'll have to leave," she said, coldly.

Reuben thought of going back outside and shuddered at the thought . . . and there was no way of being sure one way or another if Mary was related to him . . . and after all, what difference did it make? Once you have gone so far down, what difference another few feet?

"Go ahead," he said.

"Tell me about my family, while I do it," she whispered.

My God, thought Reuben, she had decided on it: I should never have come here. "The teeth, Mary, be careful with the teeth."

"Talk to me, Reuben . . . but not like a book."

"Grandfather, Luther Sledge, was a trapper; not a good trapper, but that was more a matter of concentration than technique. It was as if there were an invisible area around him within which he lived, and trapping was not large enough to fill it. His face, with flying beard and moustache, was so diffuse as to suggest that it could not possibly contain a whole person. Most of his time was spent, as he called it, 'woods wandering,' and those few furs he did collect were traded to a Sac Indian named Eyeron, who ran a trading post on the Rock River of Wisconsin.

"One afternoon Grandfather rode to the trading post on his giant Percheron, in a sour mood because of the rain and the mud. His inclinations were met with those of the Indian who, because of the weather and business and life being what it usually was at the trading post, was in a comparable if not gloomier mood. Grandfather had brought six beaver, two muskrat, and one rather ragged mink. The whiskey that the Sac offered Grandfather for these was one bottle short of the amount that he believed fair; this lesser amount falling under the term 'blamed robbery.' Eyeron proposed that a shell game be played and that the difference — one bottle — be decided in this way.

"Grandfather agreed to the game, but having a certain degree of dexterity in manipulating the shells himself, demanded that Eyeron search for the pea. Two rounds of the best out of three were decided upon and Grandfather lost four straight times. This made his already ugly mood worse and he demanded another game at stakes that would make it worth his while to concentrate. Amos, the Percheron, was placed on one side of the balance and our grandmother on the other. The game produced the obvious outcome and the lesser amount of whiskey was traded to Eyeron for a rope which, with one end tied to Grandmother and the other to Amos, Grandfather took off into the woods. (I believe this was unnecessary—that Grandmother was more than happy to leave the trading post, life being what it was there, and that she was a moral Indian and would never have attempted to escape. But Grandfather must not have known this, or if he did, was more content not knowing it.)

"Grandfather communicated little with his wife and so was considerably taken aback when after completing a house he discovered that his wife refused to go into it. He spent many hours attempting to trick her into coming inside. He would playfully wrestle with her, throw her upon his shoulders and make a run for the door, but she was too fast. He would pretend to be in agony, as if a pan of hot fat had somehow fallen on his head, hoping to win her over through sympathy. She did not come. He bought beads, hung them about in plain sight through the open door and would stroll easily out into the woods, where he would lie in wait, hoping to be able to dash up and lock her inside after she had wandered in to secure the beads. After his final attempt to starve her while eating huge chunks of meat inside the opened door, he gave up. Then she came in, refusing only to sleep inside. Grandfather conceded this, completed a leather tent which she also wouldn't go in, and finally built a lean-to off the side of the cabin where they slept during the storms. There were three children before Father and all of them learned to sleep inside the house.

"Grandmother, unaware of Luther's woods wandering, saw from her position that her husband, instead of being gone two days (which was the time it usually took to collect the furs and reset the traps), would frequently be gone for six or seven. I say frequently, but possibly not more than a half dozen times a year.

"This was frequent enough for Grandmother, however, who finally convinced Tom and Peter, the oldest of the boys, to follow him. They reported that Grandfather traveled down Raccoon Creek recovering furs and resetting traps for a mile and a half. His movements were steady and precise. It had rained the day before and it was easy for the boys to move rapidly and silently behind their father. A pale wind came up from the north, cool, and like a machine Grandfather's movements slowed down. Everything else remained constant, his actions were unchanged, only the pace slowed. Amos, the horse, made more stops along the creek to push the water around with his nose the way horses will do when they don't really feel like drinking but want to taste the water and blow bubbles in it. Tom and Peter found more time to sit in one place and think about whatever they wanted to think about other than what Grandfather was doing. It was fall, the leaves had turned a myriad of colors and had mostly fallen from the trees. Canadian geese were flying south for the winter and honked out their passageway to the clusters of white clouds that tailed along behind them. Grandfather's rhythm began to break. His hands lifted the inch-and-a-half steel traps, struggled halfheartedly to disentangle the dangling animals from them, moving like one's hands do very early in the morning. He nearly lost a thumb attempting clumsily to reset a steel spring and finally gave up altogether. A ground squirrel caught his eye as it ran back into the brush. Grandfather followed it in and Amos plodded along behind him, picking at the dry leaves on the bushes as he went. Several days later, the boys, after covering an area of approximately ten square miles, some of which was traveled four times, observing nothing more than a fox-and-geese game, played with no snow, no tracks, and no geese, went home.

"Father was nineteen when the first logging company moved into the area. Grandfather burned their house and moved back farther into the woods. Then the farmers came and Grandfather moved up against the Mississippi River. The steamboats became more frequent and Grandfather moved across the river and into Iowa. After three years of attempting to establish a workable trapping line without encroaching on someone else's line he sold his traps and moved back to the Wisconsin side, where he sat and watched from his porch the steamships bellowing their way down the river, smashing through rafts and ice and rowboats. Soon afterwards he died. Grandmother refused to leave the cabin from that moment on, and Tom and Peter built a trading post that soon became a customary stop for the boats running between northern Minnesota and Missouri."

"You don't have to stop just because *this* is over," said Mary. "Go on —"

"No," said Reuben, refastening his pants, and standing up. "It is too hard to talk about, anyway."

"It's a good story."

"I know; but it gets bad, and it ends here, and how much worse can it be?"

"You're starting to complain and whine. Why?"

"Maybe . . . even if I was happy . . . maybe happiness isn't all there is; I mean there might be a revolution going on inside you, while you were being happy."

"That's the way Johnson talks . . . like a book, only worse."

"Yes, you make me happy, Mary. What else can you show me, what else can you do for me? What next?"

"Don't be pathetic," she said, and Reuben looked at her eyes, which were brilliant, like a dark moon.

"Look; come with me and we'll find a way out of here."

"Leave this house!"

"Yes . . . this house is nothing; you ought to see the houses outside . . . you ought to see the light outside."

"There's light here."

"Not real light! Not clear, clean, warm sunlight . . . and colors."

"There are colors here."

"Not real colors — everything's gray, gray . . . gray."

"It is not."

"It might as well be; compared to outside. And no screaming."

"No screaming. You mean no one shows off outside?"

"That's right. People only scream from hunger, illness, fear, pain, loss, and injustice outside, no in —"

"If all those things are outside, why do you want to go there?"

"To be free. We don't eat each other outside."

"What do you eat?" she asked, but answered for him. "You eat animals, and plants, and you don't wait until they die, you kill them, millions of them. I know all about that."

"But they wouldn't live, except for that purpose," he said.

"That's not right."

"Enough of this. Come with me. See for yourself. It's impossible to describe what it's like outside, words won't work. Come and see. You can always come back."

"Johnson would never let me go."

"To hell with Johnson."

"How would we get out?"

"I don't know. I thought you would have some ideas."

"I'm sorry."

"You don't?"

"No."

"Do you know how to get to the monuments?"

"No, but Johnson does. He knows everything about the City."

"The squid told me that he helps people."

"The squid?"

"A waterhead."

"Oh."

"Does he help people?"

"I don't know what he does; he never talks about it."

"Take me to him."

"If he finds out we were together."

"I thought you said he already knew."

"Maybe. But maybe he didn't."

"Take me to him. When I find a way out, I'll come back for you."

"I probably won't come," she said.

"You can decide later."

"I want you to stay here."

"No. I've already been here too long . . . you never did tell me where you found that sheet."

"You never asked me to tell. I found it in the back seat of a car."

"What else?" he asked.

"What else?"

"What else was in the car?"

"Nothing."

"Nothing!"

Mary looked at him. "The iceman," she said. "He might have. . . ."

"That long ago! How long has he been here?"

"A long time."

"Surely you've been here longer."

"No. He was here before me . . . how else could we live?"

"Take me to Johnson."

"Will you come back?"

"Yes."

"I cannot take you to him. But I can take you to where you can find him, or he can find you."

"That's good enough," Reuben said, wondering if it was.

They left the yellow house and walked onto the brick street, past wooden buildings and cathedrals surrounded by iron fences with stakes sharp on the top held together in elaborate curlings of metal, street signs, gutters, stagnant water, tire irons, machinery and broken typewriters, through the screaming and the smell of dying and death . . . and the fog, like memory, pulling all these shapes into itself, taking them in, dissolving the very skeleton of their substance into its

gray haze. All things belong to the fog, and all things mat-
tered little but that they were part of the fog and the fog was
everywhere.

They ran. The running was effortless but the screaming increased. They preferred walking. Mary slipped through the fog
and down the alleys like a mink, knowing as if by sense those
turns and obstacles where the fuzzy light from the streetlamps
did not reach. Reuben was reminded of his ancient fear of madness, creeping to him from the echoes of their footsteps, soft-
ened and delayed by the fog; terrifying regularity — sounds
made by effortless walking, taken into the fog and brought
back to them foreign and bent out of shape, as though they,
the sounds, had never come from them.

Mary left him across the street from a warehouse, and told
him that Johnson had always told her — when she wanted
to see him — to wait there, and not to look for him, and that
after awhile he always found her. Mary walked back toward
her home. Strange how well she knows her way around, he
thought, wondering how she would ever find her way back. As
he watched her slip around a corner and out of his sight, he
was afraid that he had lost, given up, something that he could
never recover. He felt sad and angry; sad at losing Mary and
angry at losing so much time without learning any new facts,
not even a new attitude. "You, we, cannot get out," she had
said before she left. "That can't be," he had said; "it's ridiculous,
a City no one can get out of. It doesn't make sense." He was
right where he started.

Facts, he thought, thinking like a book in things that were
important to catch — must be feminine. He could not exactly
explain this nonsensical revelation, and figured it arose from
his particular relationship with and attitude toward the two
things.

Mary had brought him to a likely part of the City to find
someone; people walked past him occasionally. He even saw
the squid walk through a light cone and into the warehouse,

coming back onto the street shortly after. Reuben did not stop any of these people. I must be single-minded, he thought. I would never find the way out if I just wasted my time with people who don't know the facts . . . I must find Johnson and am tired of standing here.

The warehouse was metal. All warehouses are metal, real ones. It had a sliding door and he rolled it open just enough to allow him to enter; the rusted pulleys resisted his effort and screamed. Inside were stacks of small brown packages. In the aisles between the packages, a little over head-high, were light bulbs hanging from long wires of broken and cracked insulation. He felt one of the packages with his hand and it was soft. "Johnson," he called out, but received no answer. In the middle of the warehouse, where all the aisles eventually led — some of them winding around from distances over fifty yards away — was a metal and glass room. A wooden sign reading office hung over the door suspended from a double chain fastened to the ceiling. He went there. The door was open and the room was empty but for a desk with a rolling top and many tiny drawers, a chair, a piece of paper on the wall, some machines, and a man sitting in the chair. His upper body crippled down over his crossed legs, his right arm clutched toward his chest, his hand limp. The nodding of his head was slow and easily rhythmical. Reuben looked at the piece of paper and at first thought it was a calendar.

The man didn't notice Reuben and he kicked the door haphazardly to announce his intrusion. The man's nodding continued, his eyes open, staring fixedly at some place on the floor in front of him. Reuben stood quietly, watching his body rock quietly back and forth, making audible creakings come from the chair at the extremities of his nodding. This movement and position suggested at first a figure racked with intestinal agony so great that he had abandoned himself, and unable to fight the pain, had given up his body to carry out the internal throbbings of the disease, back and forward, clutching with his arms to keep the pain intact. Like a maimed dog. And Reuben, like the friends of Job, watching. But his expression denied this—denied even a hint of suffering—his pupils frozen wide open and unfocused, covered with a thin film of glass . . . keeping the distance. Whirring noises came from the machine. Reuben looked at it closely and it seemed to be some kind of a clock.

"Johnson," he said. Johnson turned his head towards him, uninterrupting the rocking which continued while his eyes fought to focus, his mouth opening and closing, gasping for understanding. "In the drawer," he said and let his head fall back toward the floor. Reuben went to the secretary and pulled open two of the small drawers with white marble knobs, then three. Inside the fourth drawer were a candle, spoon, and syringe, the spike colored from dried blood. "In the drawer," he repeated and Reuben pulled open the large center drawer and took out the brown package torn open from the top, filled with white powder—no, filled with heroin; no other word is suitable; no other word can mean heroin—smack, H., joy powder, horse, scag . . . these words act like a whitewash, a cover-up, a pacification for the sublime violence that can only be said by Heroin.

"I want to get out of here," Reuben said.

"In the drawer," he repeated and Reuben sat down on the floor and waited for the glass to clear from this man's eyes. I must be single-minded, he told himself. Escape is all that must concern me. I must not stay here any longer than necessary to obtain the information . . . to learn the workings of the City. In the well-lit fog Reuben watched him rock on and on and on, each nod becoming unnoticeably slower, until the movement stopped altogether and Johnson slept with his head resting against his knee, breathing easily. Outside, the sliding door opened and footsteps came through the warehouse and brought a man into the office room, a farmer by his dress, with overalls and soft muddy work boots. He pushed a punch card into the time machine, took it out and looked at it. Then taking a pencil from one of the small drawers wrote something down on the sheet of paper on the wall. Then he left.

Reuben went over to the paper and read the inscription, a name and a date, transferred from the time machine: Lewis 7/15/70. He shuddered at the possibility that he had been over six months in the City. While he waited for his sleeping companion to gain consciousness three others came into the warehouse and into the office and wrote their names and the date onto the sheet of paper, each without speaking, ignoring him. Six months! At first the thought made him more aware of his desire to escape. He shook the sleeping figure in the chair but he fell onto the floor, continuing to sleep. *Six months!* He listened to the metallic zing and whirring of the punch clock.

Reuben took a card from the stack outside the office and placed it in the clock: 7/15/70 . . . 7/15/70 . . . 7/15/70: each time he put it in, it wrote 7/15/70. One day. One day. He could leave, he told himself. But he had no place to go. This must be the end, he told himself. Johnson did not move. Reuben took the untied necktie from his neck and tied it tight around his upper arm. He mixed an unknown amount of heroin in the spoon with water from a canister in a lower drawer. He lit the candle, and holding the spoon above the flame, stirred the mixture with the end of the pencil, watching the white grains dissolve, milking the clear of the water. Putting the spoon down on the floor, he drew the serum up into the syringe, filling it three-quarters of the way up; then holding it upright, he spurted a small amount of the liquid out and down onto his hand, making sure that no air remained in the tube. He felt for his vein and pinched the area around the swelling vessel. Sure then of its location, he eased in the spike until it nestled one half inch into his arm. He drew back on the plunger and saw the black blood fill the bottom quarter of the calibrated tube. He undid the necktie and eased the solution into his body. He withdrew the spike and put it on the floor, sat and waited, rubbing his arm. But the wait was not long. He rushed, and in the last tiny moment of his waiting he saw Johnson open his eyes, the glass gone, and sit up. Then the warmness. Then the quiet explosion ran through his body like a horde of baby ducks, and the fog and the glare and the churning of the punch clock swarmed into a calm sensation that reminded him of no time at all . . . of no City. And he leaned back against the metal wall smiling at Johnson, who had climbed again into the chair, holding his head.

For him, the screaming subsided, and if he thought anything he thought to wish that he would never come down again. Sunlight flooded into the warehouse with natural golds and greens and yellows and reds, filling the gloomy corners with spirals of colors, lines of solid light, and clean transparent air. He breathed and was joyful. He could feel his lungs work. His liver was clean.

He could move his hand where he wanted, and it would go. What control I have, he thought. I can do everything, anything . . . move my hand, look at Johnson, run, jump, scream, laugh, sit with my legs curled up or straight in front of me, lean back, stand up, lie down, but they were all equal possibilities. On the other hand he felt that he might not be able to move at all. What he did do was sit on the floor and give in to the marginal rhythm of nodding, aware that at any moment his stomach might revolt.

He knew he was sick; but he didn't care. It was all right. Then the sickness itself went away and that was all right too. The lights, the air, all right.

He was not in the City. He was not in Iowa. He was not anywhere . . . no place, and that should have frightened him. That should have told him that everything was not all right . . . that it was necessary to be fastened to a place, to the ground and the people, as necessary as for a color . . . more than necessary, essential.

Men and women, sometimes children — rank, ancient, tough children — came into the office. He watched them and they were always shy, walking closely to the walls, keeping the opened door in sight; hollow-eyed people. He tried to talk to them but they pushed the cards into the punch clock, wrote down their names on the paper, and hurried on out of the office, on out of the warehouse, hugging closely to the warmth of their bodies a small brown package, their ragged clothes trailing behind them, like clowns in winter, running off into the City.

Like an amateur he did not sleep, and fought the dull beckoning and learned of its need as he saw the sunlight wash from the warehouse, the fog creep up from under the secretary and fill the room, heard the faint crying grow louder, smelled the stench, and retched onto the floor . . . crashing. He held his head, his throat dry, swallowing nothing, cursing and extinguished.

"You want something to eat, Reuben?" asked Johnson.

"No. Just leave me alone, please," he answered.

Johnson went out of the warehouse and Reuben could hear the clanking of the ice wagon on the bricks of Sixth Avenue. He got up and sat in the chair, tired but afraid now of sleeping. On the sheet of paper he read, *Reuben Sledge: 7/15/70*. Someone had written that. He took another card and placed it in the time clock; 7/15/70. One day! One day! And it wasn't over yet. There is a limit, he thought then, of how much one can endure. Johnson returned, eating the red meat.

"Take it easy," he said. "You'll get used to coming down. You'll learn to sleep through it. Everyone does." He looked down where Reuben had been sitting. "And why don't you clean that mess up?"

"No one can get used to this."

"Perhaps. But something happens. It won't always be this bad. At least you'll learn to sleep."

This was little consolation. "I want to get out," Reuben mumbled. "Help me out."

"There's no way out. I'm sure you've heard that before, too, but can't believe it. Well, it's not a matter of belief. It's a tangible. There is no way out. It matters little if you believe it or not . . . only to you. What you think will never alter the circumstances. But you can rise above it . . . in your mind."

"Above the clouds," Reuben said, sarcastically. "Upside down. Seems like a bad joke."

"I see you met the squid."

"How did you know my name?"

"How did you know mine?" The two looked at each other.

"Do you know how to get to the monuments?" asked Reuben.

"I've been there several times . . . to the First Street and Sixth Street monuments."

"Can you show me?"

"I can take you with me sometime," he said, and leaned against the secretary.

"What's the idea of the names and dates? Who wrote down my name?"

"I wrote it down. Every two months or so I check the chart and see who has picked up a package . . . and when. If more than three months have gone by, then I write the name on the board outside for the iceman."

"Wait! That's not necessarily true . . . I mean that they're dead. It could be. . . ."

"No one gets off," he said. "No one gets off. Sooner or later they will overdose or starve . . . but no one gets off."

"It's that attitude that keeps people here. Things don't have to be like that. Like this. Just because some junkie writes down my name on a sheet of paper—"

"Not necessarily," he said. "But you *will* take more, and most likely you will starve to death. Not necessarily, of course, but you will."

"Anorexia nervosa," Reuben said.

"Nothing as complicated as that. You won't eat because you won't think of it. The weaker you grow, the less ambition you will have to get better. Malnutrition, vitamin deficiencies, and heart problems. The time when you're not nodding will be spent sleeping."

"And you?"

"Probably the same way. But I'll last longer than you . . . longer than all of you."

"Odd."

"It's just that I operate this warehouse, this City. I have something to do other than survive. And that allows me to survive longer."

"If you want to call this survival."

"Consider the alternatives," Johnson said.

"There are no alternatives to survival. That's why the quality of survival . . . the kind of survival, is important. A junkie of metaphysical proportions doesn't impress me much."

"Success doesn't concern me. Not even my own."

"Look, my head's killing me. I can't go on like this much longer. Do you have a place I can sleep . . . away from here?"

He did, and gave Reuben directions to his apartment. He rose to leave and Johnson called him back from the door.

"How long has it been since you've eaten?"

Reuben was ashamed to say and stepped away, without admitting his dull hunger. He would get some food on the next delivery.

"What do you care?" he asked.

"Company. If I could keep you here, I would."

Reuben stood still for a moment, regaining a more sure sense of equilibrium. "I'll be back," he said, and left the warehouse. Walking two blocks to his right and one to his left, he found the building number, and with the brass key he had been given opened the door, turned on an overhead light, and fell asleep without turning back the purple bedspread. The apartment was hot and the sweating air troubled him while he slept. This room was orange.

When he awoke Johnson Johnson was there sitting across

the room from him, looking at the objects around him on the glass coffee table and linoleum floor, watching them, although they did not move or change in any way. He's been here a long time, thought Reuben; he has sat for long hours alone in here with no entertainment but what he could dredge up out of the past. And objects are never just objects; they are symbols for circumstances of mind . . . they suggest memories. They become memories. They become inseparable from those specific emotions that we cannot forget. They remind us, perhaps from the shape. It is impossible to look at familiar objects without memories coming yammying out of them.

"You do know how to get to the monuments," said Reuben, and J.J. looked up.

"I've been there."

"Take me."

"Sometime," he said, and took a syringe out of his jacket pocket, then a bag. Soon after, he was filling his veins.

"Can you tell me how to get there?" asked Reuben.

"No. There are no street signs and — "

"Say. You've got matches!"

"So what."

"Where'd you get them? I was told that there was no heat here."

"It's not true. Have some," and he tossed Reuben a pack. Reuben took out his cigarettes and lit one.

"Want one?" he asked.

"No."

Johnson rushed. "Anyway," continued Johnson, "you get to them on intuition."

"Then I could get there myself, as easily as you."

"Someone showed me the first time; after that it was easier. It would be impossible to try to make it on your own . . . the first time."

"When can we go?"

"Soon," Johnson said. "Right now I've got work. I'll be back."

Then he left the apartment, trotting off down the gray street in his tennis shoes, and was gone.

Reuben was excited. He would get to the monuments. He was hopeful, and ate some flesh that J.J. had left. Then he waited and tried to remember the name Johnson Johnson, where he had heard it, before the City; and then he remembered a newspaper story he had seen once.

He waited for Johnson among those objects of Johnson's and tried to piece together . . . for lack of anything better to do . . . a story. He opened the drawers and searched for anything he might have written down. And as he got to know Johnson, he got to know that he was such a man that would know that the only way to pervert Reubenlike men was to leave them alone, and simply make the drug available. Not openly, but hidden in those places where they would be looking for something else. Let us not call heroin an escape: no one believes that . . . it's a pretense either for too much knowledge or too little, the way someone will say "time is the fourth dimension" in order to simplify the issue or to make it sound like he knows more than he does. Let us not talk about it directly at all. That way if you have been at one time intimate with the disease then you will not be insulted by seeing it simplified, sort of made available to the mass media; on the other hand if you know nothing about it then you can continue on — no one gets hurt.

He looked for Johnson at the warehouse, and asked the clown people where he could be found. They did not know and were afraid. He knew that he must be with Mary, but did not know how to find his way there. He was anxious. The ice wagon stopped in front of the warehouse and Reuben waited for it twice. Then he did not wait any longer and only drank the water that he had found.

He has done this on purpose, he thought, leaving me here; he wants what is happening to me.

By the time that Johnson came back Reuben was dependent.

He had used the heroin in the apartment and had even gone to the warehouse and brought back another package, though he did not write down his name on the paper or look at the date.

"You knew this would happen," accused Reuben.

"I thought it would," said Johnson, sitting down. "I didn't know; you might have surprised me."

There was a knock at the door. J.J. opened it and a frightened young man, nearly in tears, pleaded with him from the outside. Their voices were indistinct, but Reuben understood from enough that this unfortunate's wife or girlfriend had disappeared from their hidden attic room and he wanted J.J. to ask the iceman, and the others, if they had seen her and what, if any, hope could be given. Johnson talked calmly from the top of the stairs, looking down, promising that he would check — that he would have an answer in a week — but that there was no hope whatever, and if she were alive, she would be mad. The young man, crying intermittently now, complained of a hateful midget who had come in and propositioned her some three weeks before, offering her money and finally escape if she would do what he asked, whenever he asked. "I know him," said Johnson. "She isn't there." Then the young man went away. Johnson shut the door on him.

"And you knew this would happen," accused Reuben. "You knew that I wouldn't leave."

"I knew that. Because you think I know how to get to the monuments."

"You don't, do you?"

"Yes, I do, but what difference does it make now?"

"Nothing's changed."

"How long do you think you could last, outside, even if you could get out — which you can't?"

"I don't care what you think. You promised to take me to the monuments. You will!"

"Don't threaten me. I could've had you killed at any time after you came in. I've known everywhere you've been. I control this City. You stay alive only because it pleases me. If anything happens to me the iceman will take vengeance. No one touches me with impunity."

"That's good. You've probably fooled a lot of people with that; women and children and old men, but I know all about you."

"You know nothing about me — only what Mary told you."

"And what I remembered, from before . . . and what I put together in this apartment."

"Bullshit," Johnson said, but he was not so sure.

"Do you know how to get to the monuments?"

"Yes. But I'll never show you."

"You will."

"Why should I . . . I'll simply have you killed."

"Don't be stupid. You'll tell me because for all your pomp there's something you are afraid of."

"Come on. I've had enough of this."

"Memories. The memory of your sniveling perverted life outside."

"It wasn't what you say, and you don't know anything about it."

"Ropes," said Reuben, and Johnson Johnson sat back in his chair as though the word had struck him across the face.

"The way I see it," began Reuben, "you had two possibilities after graduating from the University of Iowa; one was to teach English in a high school in Cedar Rapids — where you grew up — the other was to do the same thing in Des Moines. The choice would be — you believed at the time — inconsequential. Either way your somniferous life would go on. You chose Des Moines, thinking that Cedar Rapids was the lowest place in the world, the first of many actions that might have been better. But of course you had no way of knowing, then."

Johnson remained silent.

"You moved into an apartment that the high school had arranged for you to look at, not liking it but not wanting to look for one yourself. Any romantic ideas you had concerning teaching (which is doubtful in itself) were soon swept away and your students — as you felt — despised and ridiculed you behind your back. Nothing you could say would make any impression on them, or even direct their attention from the walls and windows. They chewed their pencils and indicated to you in intricate subtle ways that you were just as dreary as you imagined yourself to be. You assigned work, which was not turned in."

"That's not true," said Johnson.

"It's close enough . . . the other teachers shunned you and rather than decide it was because of an age difference — you were younger — you felt it was because of your unworldliness . . . a bland personality that bored even your students to the point of revulsion.

"So you began going to taverns, dimly lit taverns where you could sit in a corner and drink beer until when drunk you could with some conviction think it was all not true. You bought popular records, and despite the disapproval of the superintendent, who said several times that the purpose of education was to structure young minds not cater to unformulated whims, played them to your classes, hoping in this way to revive them. You introduced movies of car races and gang bangs. Nothing worked and your ideas ran out. You felt that they, the students, were secretly seeing through you, and laughing at your pathetic attempts to communicate."

"That's exaggerated."

Reuben tied the necktie around his arm and injected some heroin into his arm, with as much ceremony as squashing a bug. "Only for the sake of clarity," he said, "so there can be no misunderstanding. . . .

"Driven further to overcome your unworldliness you frequented those places you noticed your students going to . . . meeting them in root beer stands and sitting down with them, trying to be casual, buying them pop.

"However you managed this next thing I don't know; but at twenty-four you married a nineteen-year-old girl named Rona who worked in a drugstore selling candy and peanuts from behind a glass display case; not that that is so bizarre in itself, but that you thought it would help you . . . that you actually believed it had."

"You're leaving out a lot," said Johnson.

"It's not important. There's no one you can blame for what happened later on."

"Her father," Johnson said, "drove down from Mason City in an old Buick, and stood around in a jacket with ripped lapels during the wedding and didn't say anything. He eyed the ring suspiciously, but I knew he couldn't tell the difference. I gave him money for gas and oil back home, plus twenty dollars, which was cheap I gathered from the way he was eyeing my two-year-old Chevrolet, a car he said of the kind every man should own."

"That's not important," Reuben said, and regained his narrative. "You considered yourself well-adjusted then and changed in your attitude toward your students from intimidation to contempt, indiscriminately lowering grade points for being inattentive in class. You took Rona to bars with you and fed her beer although she was underage.

"And then, one year later; the ropes."

"You're bluffing," said Johnson. "There's no way you could know."

"At first," continued Reuben, "you approached her as though it was a game to you . . . probably wrestling. But gradually it became impossible to hide the serious effect the game had on you and you began making demands — forcing Rona to dress in black underclothes and high heels while you tied her hand and foot with ropes. The pleasure of seeing her squirming on the floor or bed, her muscles twitching, so far exceeded lovemaking that you abandoned it altogether, even as afterplay, and devised more intensely erotic situations, such as tying her loosely so that she might escape momentarily, only to be rebound, or taking pictures of her with a flashbulb. How you loved it!"

"It's not true," muttered J.J., a gloom setting into him and sinking him down further into the chair.

"But it gets worse, doesn't it? Rona read an article in a magazine while you were at school once, an article written by a member of a women's organization that said women — wives — did not have to do anything they didn't want to, and when you came home she confronted you with it and refused to be tied up. You were infuriated and stripped her and tied her up and made her lie for over an hour before letting her up, making her promise to never deny you again. She did; and in the morning the police came and took you to Independence."

"Stop."

"And you only stayed two weeks. But it must have seemed like a year, because even the other patients called you a deviant . . . and you were so terrified of ever going back there again that you did not dare vindicate yourself. When you went home you found Rona's father had moved into the house and threatened to sue you for misusing his daughter — a threat that cost you your automobile and forty-two hundred dollars, which he said was 'getting off easy.'"

"It was only a hundred dollars."

"It's not important . . . you kept the scandal hidden, sent her father back to Mason City, and imagined that everything was better between you and your wife, who now knew she was not helpless and began attending meetings of the WLF. Schoolteaching was not going well. No work was being turned in. Rona, taunting you, asked only once if you would like to tie her up . . . and you did. Later that week you did again (with her permission). Soon you became demanding and were taken off to Independence, ushered out of your house by two state patrolmen under the smiling, bitter gaze of Rona and three of her friends from the WLF whom she had invited over to watch.

"You stayed for a month; and this time it was worse. The orderlies left pictures from crime magazines of bound victims stuck to your door. The psychiatrists left short pieces of rope on your night table. The patients called you a pervert and made puns like 'Can you teach us the ropes, Johnson?' Finally they let you out and you were terrified of your wife . . . that she would send you there again. Life must have been awful then. . . . Rona brings her friends home, where they sit three and four abreast on the couch looking at you, saying things between them like 'They're all alike,' and Rona would explain how they weren't, how you were worse than most. You were afraid of losing your job. The superintendent knew you were in Independence, and had called up to find out what was the matter; and though they did not tell him — classified information — he learned enough to know that the reason you had given him for going (prostate trouble) was not true. It was spring and many of your students even stopped coming to class altogether."

"I didn't tell him it was prostate trouble."

"It doesn't make any difference. You had what you thought was a brain buster of an idea, and went to see the superintendent, Mr. Walpole."

"Wallpolie," said Johnson.

". . . so you went to him and began:

"'Well, as you know, I had two minor hospitalizations not too long ago and to be completely honest with you I didn't tell you the truth about why I was there.'

"He smiled at you and said that whatever had happened was none of his business, but if it would make you feel better, go ahead. 'You know, Johnson, you have been a considerable asset to this school since you have come.'

"'I'd like to think so, Sir,' you said. 'I still have a lot to learn . . . about teaching and students, I mean.'

" 'We all do, really. We all do. Now what did you want to tell me?'

" 'Well, as you know, I was married not over two years ago, and to a girl I think the world of. But though I didn't know it at the time I later found out that she had been a prostitute before I married her.'

" 'A prostitute!'

" 'Yes, a p-r-o-s-t-i-t-u-t-e. And as you might imagine when I found this out I nearly went out of my mind. With jealousy and anger, I mean.'

" 'I can imagine,' he said.

" 'Sometimes I would be so angry and hurt that I would call her names . . . to her face.'

" 'What kind of names?' he asked. You had him.

"You pretended that you were shy. 'Slut, whore, and fucking bitch,' you said. 'That would hurt her so much that she cried and would threaten to do away with herself. She was on the point of suicide, John. I was filled with remorse, told her I was sorry and begged for forgiveness. Nothing helped. She cried constantly and one day I found her sitting in the bath scratching at her wrists with a razor blade. I knew then that I needed help and went to Independence for a week to talk with the doctors and nurses about treatment, and commitment papers. I left her with her father while I was gone and when I returned she had settled down and I thought everything was all right.'

" 'But it wasn't?'

" 'No, it wasn't. I learned several weeks from then that during the time I was away she had gone back to her old ways, telling her father she was going out to visit friends in the country.'

" 'My God, what did you do?'

" 'I'm getting to that. Naturally I was upset, but realized that to vent my anger might kill my wife. I love my wife, honestly I do. She is a kind, gentle person, and has had a very difficult time changing her life-style . . . she's been living on her own since the age of thirteen.'

"'Thirteen!'

"'Yes. So I went to Independence again to ask for help, counseling, I mean, with my problem. They were very understanding there and recommended that I be patient with her and give her all the freedom she demanded. Also they said that prostitution is more a nervous disorder than anything else and prescribed a local tranquilizer for me to give to her. I did, and I am happy to say that we are getting along well now.'

"'A tranquilizer.' The superintendent sat silently for a long time. Then he confessed that he had had misgivings about you and he wanted that you should overlook those 'petty shortsightednesses' and that after what you had been through you needed all the moral support you could get.

"You thanked him and as you were leaving the office turned back to his desk: 'Oh, John, concerning the students' poor performance of late, I think I have a suggestion.'

"'Let's hear it.'

"'Tie them up with ropes if they refuse to work.'

"'Tie them up.'

"'Just an experiment. It would be better than the paddle, because they can take a couple swats and it's all over. By tying them up, after school I mean, they would have plenty of time to think about it. It would also be very frustrating for them.' (You hid the word 'frustrating' from him by cleverly disguising it in monotone.)

"'I'm skeptical, but if you think it will work, go ahead. I'm beginning to lose my patience with them, too.'

"And you went home, feeling not only elated, but belligerent, even to the point of calling Rona's friends dikes and dildo worshipers, locking yourself in the bathroom and ignoring them."

"How could you know?" Johnson asked.

"Rona wrote a book."

"She couldn't."

"She had help from her friends . . . published as pornographic true-story propaganda."

"You're joking," said Johnson, pathetically.

"The next morning was possibly the happiest of your life . . . surely the day itself was. You carried short pieces of rope to school in your jacket pockets. Four pieces. In anticipation you nearly forgot a Western Civilization class. At one-thirty you walked into your American Literature class and spent the hour choosing. Then, after the bell, you asked three of the girls to remain. To your wonderful luck, not only had all of these girls not been preparing for class lately, but one of them, Marsha Fields, was chewing gum. Your hands shook and you could hardly control yourself. You asked her to come see you after school. How slowly the rest of the day passed!

"After school you rushed upstairs from the study hall, spilling a cup of coffee on the stairs and over yourself because you didn't want to take the time to set it down. 'A little preoccupied today, Johnson,' said a typing teacher, coming downstairs. 'Yes,' you answered, 'a little preoccupied.'

"You felt in your jacket pockets. Yes, they were still there, and you burst into the room. Marsha was startled and sprang from her standing position next to the window, her eyes wide and fearful. You took out your ropes and placed them on the table, struggling to keep your voice box from quivering.

"'What are you going to do with those ropes?' she asked, her eyes tearing slightly.

"'What are ropes usually used for, Marsha?'

"'You aren't going to beat my fanny, are you, Mr. Johnson?' Her hands were shaking as much as your own. 'You aren't going to, are you, Mr. Johnson?'

"'Are you afraid that I might? Are you afraid of that, Marsha?' Oh how you were enjoying yourself.

"'Yes, Mr. Johnson. My father whips my fanny sometimes — for no reason at all sometimes. It hurts something awful. Once he beat my fanny until it bled. You aren't going to do that, are you, Mr. Johnson?' She was almost crying now.

" 'No, I'm not, Marsha. Come here.' She came up to the front of the room and you asked her to sit down on the floor, watching as her young leg muscles flexed in her calves. You pulled her thin arms behind her and with your right hand pulled her over onto her stomach, revealing her undershorts and smooth thighs. You tied her ankles together and fastened that rope to her wrists. You had one piece left so you tied it snugly around her hips. Then you stood back and looked at her as she struggled against her confinement, trying to look back at you, bewildered and afraid.

" 'What are you going to do, Mr. Johnson?' she asked.

"What am I going to do, you thought. The simple fool doesn't know that it has already been done . . . that you could barely speak for excitement, and felt a warm deposit of sperm spurt out under your belt, unprompted by anything other than the pressure of the clothes. Then you began to compose and relax and gained your speech back.

" 'Let this be a lesson to you, Marsha. From now on I want you to do the work that is assigned. All the work, and no gum chewing,' you said and untied her. She got up from the floor.

" 'You can go now, Marsha.'

" 'Yes, Mr. Johnson,' she said, hesitated for a moment, and walked slowly from the room, looking back several times at you in disbelief. You returned home and made love to Rona despite her protests, holding in your mind's eye the picture of Marsha bound hand and foot on the floor of the classroom.

"That was the first of many after-school encounters with your students. You became greedy with your newfound happiness and would bring as many as six students into the classroom to be tied up . . . six young, squirming bodies on the floor. It was wonderful. But as I said, you became greedy and forgetful because of it, letting your tying up sessions go longer than you rationally could justify . . . keeping them until after their dinner time. Needless to say you soon became trapped by your own invention and did not notice that Parents' Day had arrived. Rona had come with several of her friends, and with five squirming, bound students on the cement floor, and you babbling uncontrollably in the corner, the door opened and Rona, her friends, the parents, and the school board walked into the classroom. Rona gasped and screamed out, 'Pervert, he's a pervert! He's done this before. He's done this to me! Somebody call the police.' The students' parents were swarming around the room untying their children. Several of the fathers advanced toward you. Though they were bewildered by the whole scene, they nevertheless were sure that a sexual transgression had taken place on their innocent, stupid children. Pushed onward by the shouting from Rona and her friends, who kept muttering, 'Let them fight it out. Let them fight it out.' The superintendent fled into his office, dialing for the police, calling, 'Vice Squad, quickly, quickly . . . Vice Squad. We have a sodomist here.'"

"And so I came down here," said Johnson. "But that's all over. I've changed. That's in the past."

"And now," said Reuben, "how would you like to be tied up?" and he took two lengths of rope out from under one of the cushions on the sofa and held them up in front of Johnson's face.

"No," he screamed, and ran to the other side of the room. "Put them back. I only keep them to remind me. I'll take you to the monuments." He sat down again, this time on the floor. "Give me another hit," he said . . . , "for the road. It makes it easier."

"Sure," said Reuben, and handed him the syringe and waited.

"Yes," said Johnson, "that's it. O.K. Let's go."

"Bring the stuff," said Reuben, "in case it takes longer than . . ."

And they left, clinging almost to each other, Reuben a little behind, creeping down the street — looking around corners and standing for long periods in the darker areas, searching for signs of danger.

"I thought you knew this place," whispered Reuben.

"I do. Shut up. Just have to be careful, that's all. We're going into iceman territory."

"A friend of yours, I hope," he whispered.

"Of course; but in the dark, I mean, he might not recognize me."

"Us," Reuben demanded.

"I thought you didn't know him," whispered Johnson. "Just keep moving."

And in this manner they inched their way out of the lighted area of the City. The screaming diminished. Soon they were accompanied only by the minute sounds of their own whispering and were forced to feel their way along the buildings.

"How far?" whispered Reuben.

"A long ways," answered Johnson, and found a corner with his hands.

"Are you sure you know where you're going?"

"Yes. Shut up. Go right here."

And they went on, and on, and on. The darkness did not let up.

"We're going in circles," whispered Reuben. "Quiet, keep walking."

Later he said again: "We're going in circles."

"No."

"Then why are we still walking downhill? Shouldn't we be going up?"

"That's just a trick the fog plays on you. Keep walking —"

"Give me a hit, Johnson," he said, and they stopped.

"I can't find it," said Reuben.

"Under your tongue," whispered Johnson.

"What!" said Reuben.

"An old trick to hide tracks," said Johnson.

After a while Reuben said, "It works. You want some?" Johnson took the bag and syringe.

"Let's go," said Johnson, and they set off again, sneaking through the darkness, listening for noises. Then Johnson sat down on the street, and didn't move.

"Get up," said Reuben. "For God's sake get up!"

"Too much," said Johnson, "I think I must have taken too much. Can't go on." Then he went into a nod.

"Get up!" Reuben shouted. "Get up. . . . Get Up . . . Get Up . . . Get Up."

He lit a cigarette. I should probably give up smoking, he thought, and sank down onto the street in desperation. He tried to reason with himself, with his situation, but knew that whatever process was going on in his head, it was not that.

Facts. He remembered the facts. Collect information, get to the monuments, think of a way out. It had seemed so simple. He shook Johnson, making no impression. Tricked.

And then, for the third time, he heard the sound of a giant boulder dropping several feet into a grass-lined pocket of earth. The mockery, he thought. We are so far away. Perhaps I will never get out of here. Perhaps there are no facts. No, there are always facts.

Corn. He remembered that. He remembered how it grew ten feet in a couple of months. The green. How insufferably hot it was inside a field of corn; walking through it. The leaves like cat tongues scratching his arms; pollen falling down your neck. The green. Everywhere green. The smell. Fields and fields, as far as he could see, corn growing up to the horizon, the sun setting over the tassels.

"You don't know how to get to the monuments," Reuben said. "You never did."

"Yes I do," said Johnson. "It's just harder than I thought it would be."

"You don't know," said Reuben.

"It's just a little more difficult than one would think. . . . I think we should head back now, and try again later." They were still sitting down.

"Go ahead," said Reuben.

"You come too."

"No. Go ahead, and if you ever tie up my sister, I'll kill you."

"I'm not like that anymore. I changed. Once I was — now I'm not."

"Nobody changes; just don't do it, that's all."

"Things change."

"No they don't. Go back. Leave me alone."

"You come too. What happens when you need a hit?"

"I won't."

"Nobody gets off."

"Do you know how to get back?" asked Reuben.

"Yes, it's only four —" then he stopped.

"Get out of here, you disgust me."

"You'll be lost, and crashing. Have you ever seen a heroin fit?"

"I'd rather be lost by myself than know where I am with you. Besides, what does it matter?"

"You know, you can never get out of here."

"Then I'd just as soon be dead. Leave me alone . . . and take these with you, tie yourself up." Reuben threw him the lengths of rope he had in his pocket.

"No, I've changed."

"Get out of here."

Johnson Johnson walked into the darkness and from a distance Reuben judged was a little more than a block, he stopped and began shouting, telling Reuben that he would have him cut up and put in the wagon, and that there was no place in the City where he could go that he, Johnson, wouldn't know about. Nothing could save him — when his body started to convulse he, Reuben, would be back.

I wonder, thought Reuben, how well he sleeps? He had heard that cowards and priests did not sleep well; but he suspected that it was not true. How could what you were make any difference in your sleeping — as though when one fell asleep he became somebody else who then remembered his former self with repugnance. Reuben used these thoughts to keep from worrying, and lay flat out on the street. Then, the thoughts became more difficult to sustain, and he fell off into sleep with the intention and design of a speared fish in three inches of water.

He slept for a long time, but not well. His clothes were completely wet and he felt a corner of the sickness begin in him. He was cold. Well then, let it come on, he said to himself, and wandered away from where he was. He tried to laugh at the idea that someone could change, but couldn't. Nothing of Johnson had been of any use to him.

Well then let it come on.

And this might have been the end of Reuben — alone, without food, lost, crashing, and without hope — had not something happened to him (Reuben, it might be remembered, was not so healthy when left alone).

He heard the clamor of the ice wagon. It doesn't come here, he thought, it's supposed to stay in the lighted parts of the City; But then he remembered who had told him that and knew it might not be a fact. He also wasn't sure his withdrawal wasn't playing tricks on him, and racked with pain he sank down to the bricks, in an alleyway among milk crates. The noise became louder. He crawled out of the alleyway and onto the street, where he could see a flickering light, about twenty-five yards down from him, and heard a voice, a sound that he should have remembered because he had heard it before. The wagon came closer and the talking was more distinct — someone talking to the albino, gently, as though using the animal for company. Still he did not remember, yet now he was beginning to think, I should know that voice. The light was coming from a torch and after another twenty yards he saw a face, illuminated by the yellow flame.

"Walt!" he cried, and tears ran out of his eyes. "Walt . . . help me." His brother stopped and then began running toward him, casting the torch to his side because he could not run so fast carrying it, as though he might toss aside one of his limbs or an army of men should it stand between him and where he was going. He gathered Reuben up and held him against his body.

"Walt, get me some junk," said Reuben.

"I'm sorry," said Walt, the sound of his voice driving some of the cold out of Reuben's body.

"It's bad," said Reuben. "Walt, it's bad." And his brother began to cry. And Reuben thought he must be dreaming, dreaming that Walt was kneeling beside him on the street, holding his head in his hands, crying.

"Why," said Walt. "Why did you ever come here? You should never have come here, Reuben."

"Don't do that, Walt," he said, and soon after passed into full-blown delirium. Walt laid him down on the street and went back for the torch, which he recovered by moving on his hands and knees. Once found, he relit and fixed it into the harness so that it shone down in front of the horse, yet was out of the animal's direct sight. He then picked up Reuben and carried him, walking beside the albino down the dark streets and finally into a small, scantily furnished room and laid him down on a shallow bedding of hay. He then returned outside and loosed the horse from the wagon and dragged a bale of hay out of the building next door and set it in the street. Back again in the room he sat on the floor next to Reuben and like a mother over her first-born kept vigil . . . until when for the fourth time Reuben woke and saw him he said quietly, "There will be dying. I must go. I will be back." And when Reuben woke again Walt was there, and gave him some meat. He swallowed and vomited.

□□□

"You're the iceman," said Reuben.

"Yes," said Walt.

"Why?" asked Reuben.

"God has wanted it done, and I carry it out."

"They say you kill people, if—"

"They say that because they are afraid to find out. There are always enough dead here. There always will be."

"But will there always be someone to do what you do?"

"There are always those too. God provides."

"But God couldn't want . . . this."

"Not in the beginning. But after He saw how things were — how we were, then it was necessary."

"Why do you live here? — there are better places than this — in the lighted part."

"It's better I live here — so that the others do not see me."

"Walt, how can I — we —"

"First, tell me about Nellie."

"Nellie's fine. Nellie will always be fine. But, you — you're . . . you're different."

"Why did you come here, Reuben? Did you come here to find—" and his words trailed off. Reuben looked at him in the torchlight and thought, how strange, how odd, that Walt should be like this.

"I wondered where you had gone, Walt. No one knew."

"And you came for me," said Walt, and Reuben was silent. Then Walt began to cry again.

"Don't do that." Reuben thought, this is not good — how Walt is now.

"Walt, did you know what they did to Nellie?"

Walt looked up — "You said she was fine."

"She is, now; but you know what they did to her?"

"Don't tell me."

"Listen," Reuben said. "Listen. They whipped her, Walt. They whipped her until she bled and was screaming. . . ." (Shouting now.) "After you left they whipped her and she was screaming and couldn't see and they raped her and burned her with cigarette butts."

But Walt's eyes did not change, and he stared down at his hands.

"Say it, Walt. Say it. Those 'son-of-a-bitches.' Say it!" But Walt sat and looked at his hands.

"But now," he said quietly. "But now, she's fine; I mean Paul looks after her."

"She was," Reuben said. "But they may come again and take her out in the street and with whips and—"

"Don't," Walt said. "Don't." And Reuben didn't, and soon fell asleep.

When he woke Walt was not in the room. Not even a chair, thought Reuben, as he looked around the room. Why would anyone live without a chair . . . no one would, unless: Madness. No, he knew that wasn't right. Whatever could happen to Walt might have happened, but he could never be mad. He might change, but he could never be like that—I must not think these things, he said to himself, lying on the bed, watching as though down a long tunnel, his ancient fear of madness coming toward him. A small shape scurried across the floor of the room. Rats, thought Reuben—multiply by one thousand for the total population of rats. My God, he thought, I must not lose it here; I could never recover—to everyone else it would make no difference, and he thought about his one comfort: escape; thinking about it desperately, making himself believe that there was a direct correspondence between the word and how he thought about it.

Then he went for the last submergence into delirium, and in order to keep that painful, long experience intact, let us leave it alone, and say nothing other than that he went on and was still alive after he had passed through it.

"You know," he said, "that the inhabitants are afraid of you, and that by cooking this stuff it would make it not spoil, and that they could sit with it by a monument until it opens and it's only because of their fear of you that they don't do it."

"Then it's a good thing," said Walt. "Because once God leads you here He wants you to stay; and it is not good to forget what you are eating."

"How could God want you to stay? How could He want this to go on?"

"If He didn't want you here you couldn't have come — but even here God provides. . . . It won't be so bad here, together. If He didn't want the City here He would have torn it down."

"Perhaps," said Reuben, "He didn't have anything to do with it."

"He has something to do with everything," said Walt.

"You wouldn't have said that before, when we were at home," said Reuben. "You would have said that it wasn't necessarily so — that things would go on one way or another."

"There has to be a reason, for all this," said Walt, and Reuben closed his eyes. He could not argue against that, not so much because of the steel-bound logic of it, but because he knew that Walt *believed* it; and more than that, that he did too — when all the covering was torn away. It was just a matter of finding the facts — those things with feminine characteristics that beliefs can be woven around.

"Tell me," said Reuben, "about the City. Tell me how it was built — why — by whom. Tell me what you know. Tell me the facts and I will tell you how to look at them — how we can get out — " Walt began to speak. "Without going against God," added Reuben.

Walt stirred the dirt floor with his foot, and like a child in a moment of confession, said, "I don't know for sure."

Compassion overran Reuben. But he hid it. "Tell me how it must have been. Let God do His own work." Strange, thought Reuben, that I should talk like that, when all I really care about is the comic, is escape.

"The City was built by farmers. But the idea for it was not pure. They got it from watching the ground and thinking about themselves and putting the two together."

"The Indians could have done that—they were here first."

"They were first, true. But the conception, the concentration necessary to build it . . . they were simply too busy doing other things. No, the blame, I fear, is ours. I've thought about it every way I could, but it always comes out the same: the Indian was first insofar as he noticed that when a particular seed was put down in the ground a certain plant would grow up, and that the plant could be predicted from the shape and color of the seed. It was, I admit, a terrible thing—but they realized that and consequently never really settled down onto one place of ground, afraid of the earth revolting and swallowing them. No, evil is in many cases a matter of magnitude and they were instrumental in it only as much as they showed us what they had noticed."

"But there's no difference between them and us," said Reuben.

"I hoped that was true too. But I'm afraid the way it seems is that they knew that living could be easier by planting. This was enough to frighten them, and they never went any further; but there's a big difference between that and *using* the land, and the idea of the City wasn't started, as such, until then."

"I don't know if you expect me to be getting all this; but if you do, you're wrong."

"It's not too difficult. You brought up the Indian and he's not really that important—without him it would have happened anyway. He merely observed that his life might be easier if instead of depending entirely on foraging he might also plant corn and squash; and because no other animals he knew had it easy, and because his religion was inextricably bound up in his being a part of everything else he knew, it frightened him, and so he kept moving around for fear something would crack open.

"But when we got ahold of this information some interesting

changes occurred. Because this was the promised land to begin with, living an easier life was taken for granted. Who would expect a man to live in any other but the easiest way—it didn't make sense. And just next door to this were thousands upon thousands of giant monocultures, where everything that wasn't monetarily negotiable was called a *weed* and exterminated."

"Wait a minute," said Reuben. "If I'm going to find us a way out of here from this, you're going to have to do better than that. Pay more attention to details. Please." He smiled.

"Well . . . long before it is now, when woods and prairie grass and wildlife ran rampant, the small farmer would occasionally have a moment in which he took time to imagine. And what he imagined amounted to the disappearance of woods, prairie grass and wildlife, and in its place monocultures. But of course they could never have even imagined that it would be the way it is now. Each successive generation could imagine a little more into what it is now—extend the borders of their fences a little farther. They were implementing their imaginations, so to say. In other words, they could not conceive of what it would really be like until the whole phenomenon began unfolding around them, until they had experienced that a man could grow more than enough for himself and his family, and that the excess could be traded, and then sold, and that this would allow other men to spend their time making things to exchange for food . . . things that he could buy that would allow him to grow even more food. (It also provided for other things, like insurance and pool halls, but that's not important.)"

"But there are always prophets . . . men with vision," said Reuben.

"That's right," said Walt. "But it wasn't necessary for more than one of the group to be one . . . all the people that built the City did not have the vision. They only accepted it from someone. They were fanatics."

"Wait a minute," said Reuben. "The details."

"The guilt. The irresponsible use/misuse of God's country. Moral corruption! Spiritual debility! Emotional wastelands! Pillage and Rape! Filling His ground with pink and white and green chemical fertilizers, dusting up behind the machines; pesticides which kill bugs and birds and animals and get into the plants; chemicals stuffed into cattle and sheep, making them go insane and eat towards incredible sizes. Farmers do not relax during the winter, sit in their homes and eat popcorn, they furiously feed cattle and hogs and wander in the snow, hating, unaware that it isn't the snow, the government and the land they hate, but themselves. The small farmers have fled in horror to the cities where they believed they could be safe from the certain destruction that the land was preparing for those mindless, power-hungry dirt farmers that go raping across the topsoil."

"Farmers aren't really that bad," ventured Reuben.

"Not compared to bankers, politicians, and other out-and-out warlocks. But they, the farmers, are not growing food . . . to eat; that is they don't think of it that way. They do it for money."

"But the way the world—"

"No one makes them care for nothing but money."

"Maybe not."

"But all this was foreseen by a group, not more than a hundred, of religious fanatics; religious because all farmers are religious, intensely Protestant, especially the women and children, who must clean up after the husband; fanatics because their religion, their vision, was not ignored or token but was so important that it forced its way into their active lives. And they built a symbol for that vision, a place through which God could take vengeance, a place where some people could live and suffer in order that the rest could go on. And so in the area that ironically became called Des Moines, City of the Monks, the fanatics began working, always at night, on the terrible structure. No one knew how the pieces would fit together, or ever saw the entire conception at once . . . only one old, childless, bitter man, who wrote it down and handed out seven sections of the plan. The children worked, and the children's children worked, and after maybe a hundred and fifty years it was completed, built from concrete and giant stone from the fields and streams, carried at night by horses and tractors down into the hole. God must have helped them — such concentration is unnatural."

"That doesn't explain the monuments. Surely they didn't have the technology to make the monuments work."

"They didn't need technology. There is something frighteningly organic about this place. They merely put it together and when they had set the last stone the monuments worked as they do. They didn't even know that it would happen. They were inspired. Many things are like that, synergetic, impossible to predict the way a whole thing will work by looking at its separate parts; impossible to know what would happen when a nucleus of an atom is overloaded; impossible to know how a negatively charged particle would react to another one, by examining the two separately; no way to know for sure that a hydrogen bomb wouldn't cause a giant chain reaction."

"But the heroin . . . the movie theaters."

"I'm not sure about those. It could have been two ways. On one hand they might have thought that wretched people should be left to wretched ways. That's one reason. Another is that they had a certain degree of compassion for those people God would lead in."

"And cannibalism."

"That just happened."

"And the hay?"

"I don't know about that. I just found it."

"And the horse."

"That animal, as you may have noticed, was burned badly, and being an old horse and so being as a member of the family, as they say, whoever owned him could not bear to shoot him . . . and so here he is. God provides."

"I know how to get out of here." Walt was quiet, then said, "We shouldn't try . . . or He wouldn't have sent us here. He wants us to suffer. But even in that He provides. He brought us together. It will not be so bad, together."

So strange, thought Reuben, that he could have changed, like that.

"Listen. It might have been a trick. This place. I was tricked into coming in here; someone tricked me. I didn't feel compelled to come."

"No one gets tricked into here . . . it's impossible. No one could be that stupid." He thought and spoke again. "My work. All the others would starve."

Let them, Reuben began to say, but didn't. "Like you said, 'God provides.' "

"But He doesn't want us out. He wants us to stay."

"Then He won't let us out. It won't hurt to try."

"It won't work," Walt said. "How?"

"A tractor!"

"A tractor."

"Yes. Think about it . . . tractors rape the land; tractors carry stones that build hellish Cities. We'll get a tractor and pull down a monument. Then everyone can get out. No one has to starve. We can just walk out of here. Just walk out of here and up that hill, into the warm sunshine."

"Well, I don't know."

"If we can't get out . . . then that means that we were not supposed to. There are tractors down here. I've seen them."

"I don't know."

"Look, we can work on it just a half day at a time: that way we can keep the people fed. I'll help you."

"It won't work."

"Maybe not. But what harm will it do to try?"

"We shouldn't try to escape."

"Why?"

"If we weren't supposed to be here, then we wouldn't be here."

"With the same reasoning then, if the monument comes down then that means that it was supposed to . . . that it should."

"Not necessarily."

"Are you ready to start looking for a tractor? Help me."

"You mean right now — this minute?"

"Why not!"

"I guess it wouldn't hurt . . . at half a day at a time. What kind of tractor? Would that make any difference?"

"Yes. We have to get one of those old ones with metal wheels and wide front wheelbases; none of those rubber-tire, dual-headlight, radio, streamlined, blue-and-orange new ones. We need a tractor they would have used . . . one that they might have left behind."

"There's not many of those around."

"We'll find one. We have to make an honest try to do things right."

And so Reuben and his brother went out into the City looking for an old tractor, leaving Mildew behind with the hay. They were not at first lucky and over a period of five days (the word "day" here is used as a convention — one day = one entire waking period) found only three tractors in various states of dilapidation. Walt insisted that they settle for one, but Reuben would not give up, not wanting to sacrifice any of the plan to laziness. They looked more, asking the inhabitants if they had seen any. But most of these people were either too one way or another to offer any help. Finally one man who called himself Fats Domino told them that he had seen one at one time somewhere in Locust Street, and thought it was an old one. They looked, and found a Waterloo Boy. They stood looking at it.

"We can never fix that," said Walt.

"Sure we can."

"It doesn't even have front wheels." They walked up to it. "And the steering cam is rusted tight."

"We can do it," said Reuben.

They began combing the City, looking for tools. Those cars that had carried their mother, father, and older brother down, along with Reuben's "fast car," were by no means the only ones in the City. And in the trunks and glove compartments, under the seats, they found tools; a screwdriver in one, a wrench in another, pliers, a pipe wrench, and a sledgehammer which reminded the young men of how when they were children they had been teased because of their odd name — Sledgehammer being the usual pun on it. They laughed and traded stories that ten years before they would have been embarrassed to tell . . . like the first day at school when the teacher would call out the name, sounding as though she were talking about a ton of coal, and the rest of the kids would break up. They were overjoyed when in the trunk of one was a five-gallon can half filled with clean oil. Walt told a story. "Once a friend of mine went to New York. Someone asked her where she was from and when she said Iowa the man told her that people from the East pronounced it 'Ohio.'"

"What luck!" said Reuben. "We don't have to drain a crankcase."

"Say," Walt said in a slow, meditative voice, "if God didn't want us to escape . . . we couldn't have even got the idea, the plan, I mean. It wouldn't have occurred to us. It would have been blanked out."

Reuben smiled, and they carried the tools back to the tractor, dropping them hard onto the brick, filling the street with echoes.

"Let them hear it," said Reuben, almost laughing.

"Don't talk about them like that," said Walt, but the next load of tools he carried back he threw down too, and smiled. "I've been sneaking around for so long," he said, and then went back to fetch Mildew and fill the wagon; Reuben, keeping his word, abandoned the tractor and in the lighted areas went searching for cadavers, secretly hoping he might not chance upon one. And this first time he didn't, and when he rejoined Walt at the tractor had nothing to report.

"I looked, though," he said.

"I know," said Walt. "It's important to know where to look. Some places are better than others, and you don't know the City well enough. I can do it from now on alone."

"Bats," said Reuben. "I said I'll help and I will. Give me your knife and lead me to them."

"It's taken care of, today," Walt said, feeling a definite elation from using the word . . . because he and Reuben were now using watches in order to divide the day equally, and could therefore talk about todays and tonights. It was like a convict, upon his release from prison, telling his wife . . . "I think I'll go downtown and get a drink." Simple things can be symbols for freedom.

With the oil and tools they worked on the head bolts and finally removed them, uncovering a large piston and several tight-rusted valves. They took wheels off another tractor and put them on the Waterloo Boy, using automobile jacks. Reuben thought it would be all right to have rubber tires — on the front.

Each day Walt and Reuben would quit working at three and go off together into the unlit parts of the City, carrying torches. Reuben was given a knife and he cut into those day- or two-old bodies, first with revulsion and later with dexterity . . . and filled the ice wagon. They freed one of the valves and Walt had begun working on the other. "Which are the best parts to eat?" asked Reuben.

"It makes no difference."

"Did you know that Mary was here?" asked Reuben, cautiously.

"Johnson's Mary? The one in the plant house . . . with the empty head?"

". . . that's her. Did you ever think that she might be our sister?"

"No."

"You know the one, the one that —"

"I know. But it couldn't be her."

"And did you ever wonder that maybe that dress she wears was actually one of our sheets and she had by some —"

"No. That's impossible. I'd never believe that."

"Good; I mean I don't believe it either."

"Why?" asked Walt.

"I don't know — Hey, stop hammering on that valve or you'll break it. Use a little ingenuity." They laughed.

The second valve came free. Three o'clock came and Walt said that there was plenty of time, and that they could do it the next day. In this way they began skipping days and after some weeks Walt was no longer filling the wagon at all and they parked the wagon next to the tractor and ate out of it. At night they returned to Walt's room and slept on the hay.

Reuben was learning his way around the City, and this gave him a comfortable feeling . . . something he did not think would ever be possible. He was no longer afraid.

"When we go, maybe we could take somebody with us."

"Like who?"

"Mary."

"Why?"

"Well . . . because she thinks that she's our sister."

"What gave her that idea?"

"I did."

"Why? I don't think we should bring her."

"Walt!" said Reuben, "how could you say that? Besides, I sort of figured out that because she couldn't remember being outside and —"

"She couldn't remember if it happened last week. She's too stupid to retain anything so complex as a memory."

"You sound uncharitable."

"I'm sorry. Sure, bring her along . . . after we're ready to go . . . we better fill the wagon."

"Let them feed themselves."

"Don't talk like that. Don't let escaping do that to you. It's wrong, to be like that."

Reuben and Walt filled the ice wagon. The ice, Walt explained, he took a piece at a time from a very large block of it left in a locker.

"Those fanatics did a lot of work," said Reuben.

"I guess they wanted it to be just like outside, in every way, except that you couldn't get out."

"Must have been," said Reuben. "You don't think they could have been building themselves a home, a place to live, do you?"

"Like this?" said Walt, and Reuben agreed. No one would do that.

"What did you do after I left?"

"I worked for a farmer," Reuben confessed. "Then I had an accident and was in the hospital and had blackouts." They walked along.

"Nothing serious, I hope."

"Not as long as you're sure you're there," laughed Reuben. "Then the doctor said that I might have dysphasia, and become autistic."

"Oh," said Walt.

"How did you happen to come here?" asked Reuben.

"I just did. I just came walking down here."

"I mean why did you do it?"

"No reason, I guess. I never thought about it. Just one day I decided to come down here. Maybe it was the weather."

"Was it Father?" They were back at the tractor.

"Maybe that had something to do with it too. I just don't know."

How odd, thought Reuben, that something like that should happen. And he didn't believe it. "There must have been a reason," he said. "You said before . . . that things have reasons. There must have been a reason that you had something to do with . . . not just a reason understood by God, like when someone dies and we say there is a reason for it, just because we can't see any ourselves."

"I guess I did," said Walt, and smiled. "But maybe it's a fact. I mean maybe coming down here was reason in itself for doing it."

"You're just trying to confuse me," said Reuben, smashing his finger knuckles when the pair of pliers he was using slipped.

"No. I'm trying to be honest with myself. I was brought here. No one forced me. Nothing frightened me. I was in complete control of my senses and mind."

"That's not true," said Reuben. "No one could be all those things and come here. Maybe it was Father's death that brought you here. Remember what Nellie said to you — that she hated you? After that you were gone."

"It couldn't have been that," said Walt.

They worked. Walt had worn away the nut he was laboring on into a circle and still tried to keep hold of it and twist it. He thought to himself: There's no reason why if a monument got pulled down — why we couldn't just walk over it, out into the outside. There's really no real reason to stay, if there's clearly a way out. And if we have a way out, then He provided it.

"After all," said Reuben, giving up momentarily on the cotter pin, "wasn't Christ supposed to have gone flat out and suffered and died and particularly rose from the dead in order that we could live, despite the guilt, and not have to have places like this?"

"Yes. But no one believes that. No one believed that. It was too hard to picture ourselves as masters of the world without forgetting that we had been paid for. We resurrected the guilt in order to see ourselves as more important."

"Maybe you're right," said Reuben, "but it shouldn't be like that, on either side."

"Stop trying to confuse me," said Walt, and they both laughed and later did not even bother to return to the dark part of the City, but slept near the tractor in the street.

"Say, Walt, if we took some of that heroin with us . . . we could be rich," said Reuben.

Walt laid the crankshaft down on the street. He was troubling. "Have you met a waterhead that lives here?"

"The squid? Yes. Why?"

"What did he tell you about this place?"

"Nothing."

"No. He told you something. He always tells the same story."

"You mean about the land in between?"

"Yes. And how you might get out upside down."

"I remember."

"Well think about it. Sometimes I wonder if you shouldn't stay here . . . with ideas like that."

"Ideas don't hurt anything."

"Ideas trap you. If you have too many of them. Like John Charles, like Will, like Father, like — "

"You," said Reuben, and Walt was silent and picked up the crankshaft, then said, "It's different."

"It's all the same," said Reuben, "it's the same thing . . . something that you can't see to the end of; any idea that's so large that it doesn't look like an idea anymore and becomes a fact, a feminine fact, to you."

"Why do you call facts feminine?"

"Because they both start with 'f.'"

"Call them frogs."

Reuben put the magneto back in place. "Because they deceive," he said.

Finally the tractor was finished. The two had been neglecting to fill the wagon and decided, before they left, to load it one more time, send it around and leave it in front of the warehouse. The albino Walt wanted to take with him. Many had died while they had been working on the tractor.

"Do you think this was a Romantic?" asked Reuben, gutting a carcass.

"Maybe. What difference does it make now?"

"I don't know," said Reuben, thinking, This is odd, that I should be like this.

"It's unnecessary, our doing this," Reuben said. "After we pull the monument down everyone can leave."

"No," said Walt. "Most of them won't leave . . . they'll stay here."

"Even if they know they can get out?"

"Even then."

"You've got to be wrong this time. That's insane."

"Maybe so. But it's true. For instance. The people have always known that the government cheats them and . . ."

"Don't talk like that," said Reuben. "That's political."

"So?"

"So during the second world war . . . in the prisoner of war camps the old men . . . the survivors . . . used to line up when they brought a new group of prisoners in; and standing behind them would call out as they came through the wire gate, 'yes' or 'no.' They could tell, by looking, which would survive and which couldn't. Things can get that bad. But when they do I don't want to be here. Surviving is important unless the world becomes so drastically unlike the way you want it that . . . well, what's the use then? Politics are like that."

"Since you brought it up. In those same camps . . . when the prisoners were finally rescued and had the gates opened; many of them were afraid of their rescuers and had to be dragged out of their barrack cells."

"That's hard to believe," said Reuben.

"Exactly," said Walt. "But there is no reason why we can't just walk right out of here. God will provide for those that stay behind."

They shut the doors on the ice wagon and sent the albino on his way back into the lighted area of the City. Then they set out to find Mary, who was at a theater. At first she did not want to come, but was interested in seeing a tractor — something she had never seen before. The three left the movie theater and walked by the warehouse, where they waited and took Mildew out of his harness and led him behind them to the tractor.

"The chain," said Reuben. "Do you have the chain?"

"In the toolbox," said Walt, and they turned the huge fly-wheel around.

"Turn on the gas," said Walt, and Reuben climbed up and opened the valve. They turned it again and a backfire hoomed out across the street and echoed throughout the City. Another try and nothing. On the fourth pull the tractor backfired, coughed, and then caught hold, its single piston banging back and forth inside the cylinder. Walt and Reuben began to laugh. Mary climbed up on the seat, and holding the steering wheel began shouting to begin the drive to the monument. Mildew was afraid of the noise but Walt calmed him and tied him behind the tractor.

Walt and Reuben had suspected that their progress in fixing the tractor had been of some interest to others. But now, from out of windows and alleys and doors came inhabitants, afraid but still venturing out into the street.

Walt lit four or five torches he had made from the hay and handed them to some of these men and women. For many it was the first time since they had been in the City that they had seen fire, and so there were three or four of them running back into the darker areas, to follow at a safer distance. Some of them left for good. Walt climbed up and put Mary beside him on the fender, not looking at her. Reuben sat on top of the motor, on the heavy casing around it, behind the mufflerless stack.

Walt put it into gear and let the clutch out slowly. We should have practiced this first, he must have thought, but decided it made no difference.

The Waterloo Boy lurched forward, spraying bricks back at the albino from its metal lugs. Reuben jumped from the tractor and went back to unloose the horse. Walt had stopped moving, but still the motor roared. The machine started up again and inched forward. Reuben stayed behind with the albino and old people. Most of the other inhabitants were in front carrying the poor torches, listening to Walt shouting directions to them. Stone furrows, thought Reuben, as he watched the metal wheels tear out strips of bricks. These streets were not made so well. Mary bounced up and down on the fender, laughing and talking as though the only reason she had ever wanted to stay in the City was because no one had told her about tractors, asking Walt (whom she already talked to like a brother) if they, she and he, could drive the tractor everyday outside . . . if she could drive it. Walt ignored her. How fine, thought Reuben, he looks sitting up there, driving into the light cones and into darker areas, the streets filling with the noise. So easy, thought Reuben, when you know the facts. Some of the infirm were carried.

The procession cleared the lighted area of the City and crossed over into the unmarked, dark area surrounding the center. Walt and Reuben lost one out of five of their followers then, running out of the crowd and back, farther into the City. They moved more slowly now, the torches cutting less than ten feet into the fog. Above the noise of the tractor Walt talked to the front men, directing them, keeping them together.

Walt, thought Reuben; how good it is . . . what you are now. Mary continued laughing and talking, calling names back at

the people who two at a time were dropping behind and running in to the lighted area. Reuben led the horse, feeding it
as he followed from an unlit torch. One old woman fell back
beside him.

"I can't keep up," she said. Reuben lifted her onto the albino's back.

"We're going to get out, aren't we," she exclaimed, holding
onto the white mane.

"Yes," said Reuben, "we're going to get out." Sounding to
himself like a doctor. "Watch where you put your feet. This animal has been burned."

They went on, even more slowly. Of the people that had
begun the trip, only half remained.

"Why do they do that?" asked Reuben.

"They are afraid," said the old woman, "of the iceman. He
lives here in these darker parts."

"Maybe he's here — somewhere among us."

"I hope so," she said. "I hope so. God I hope so; because
when we get out of here we can find him and burn him at the
stake and take his heart out and feed it to the snakes."

"How will you know him?" asked Reuben, thinking, what
grand fun this is, and feeling something entirely different,
more like horror.

"By his cloven feet," she said.

"How do you know that?"

"It's his fault, this place. If it wasn't for him we would all be
dead. That would have been better, far better than living the
way we do. It's him. And I know what I know."

Walt was the first to know when they had reached the monument: Second Avenue Monument, being more familiar with
the behavior of light and sound near it. The rest of the group
noticed that the light from the torches could no longer penetrate the darkness and that the sound of the tractor was
softer by almost three quarters. In fact the monument was not

discovered until the men in the lead were less than two feet from it. "Hold up," one shouted, seeing that it was not that the light could not penetrate into the fog but that it was being absorbed by the six-inch covering of fungi at the base of the monument. These dark, dark green fungi also acted like black cotton to the sound of the tractor, reducing its throbbing and banging to a near murmur.

They lost another half of the remaining inhabitants then and later, after they had built a fire and looked up at the three ghastly, pale faces looming above them from thirty feet in the air, gazing through the fog and out into the City, another three turned and ran. Even Mary was silent then and looked out across the group for Johnson. But of course he was not there.

"Walt," called Reuben, "more gas." Walt looked back and waved, and opened up the throttle further, hoping to boost the spirits of the inhabitants. Several more fled: Reuben abandoned the old woman seated on Mildew and went to help Walt with the chain, fashioned from any piece of metal that they could find that would link together with another piece. "We've come this far," whispered Walt. Reuben smiled, and together with four other men from the group of now eight or nine they, with much effort, swung the chain around and threw it up toward the heads. It clattered against the side and fell down. Three more inhabitants ran back into the City. On the second attempt the hook, made from a piece of tractor frame bent into a curve by the use of unbelievable leverage, fastened around the middle neck. The six or so inhabitants wandered back around the old woman on the horse, and Walt fastened the other end to the tractor.

"Get off, please," he said to Mary, who gladly ran back to join the others. He turned the tractor around, facing away from the monument, and eased slowly forward, not wanting to snap the chain.

He crept forward until the slack was taken up, put in the

clutch and opened the throttle to full. The ground shook from the noise.

The neck might break, thought Reuben, and then decided that if it did they would pull it down in pieces. He stood back to the side. The noise, he thought, should be louder; I guess this makes it more subtle. Quiet Power. Silent Strength. The inhabitants huddled together, talking quietly, but fast. Walt let the clutch out and the tractor lurched forward, spraying brick back onto the base of the monument. The front wheels lifted up, and then as though the entire machine had collapsed, fell to the ground like a piece of trash. The motor smoked, rattled once, and was quiet. The inhabitants turned and walked back farther into the City, leading the albino. They were not talking, except for the old woman, who talked to them of how it was the iceman who made things the way they were. Mary lingered for a moment longer than the rest, then turned and ran to catch them, who though ignorant of the way back, did not care — just wanting to be away from the monument, which as a symbol seemed not only to stand for everything the City was — represent it — but also be worse.

Reuben walked over to Walt, who still sat without moving on the seat of the tractor.

"Look, Walt, with two tractors, or three," he began, but then was quiet. He looked back at the monument. No . . . maybe if there had been just the smallest sign that it had given.

No, this was the end. Walt climbed down to the street and put a pair of gloves he had been wearing into his back pocket. He started to say something to Reuben, but turned aside and walked back into the darkness.

There is always help, thought Reuben. He did not think that this was the end; he was trying not to think at all. He walked over to the chain, which hung without tension in a sad droop between the tractor and the middle neck. He reached up to a place where a section of link, a horseshoe, had stretched open, and though still holding together the piece before it and after it, more resembled its original shape. Reuben pulled it loose and the chain separated, one falling with a clatter onto the street, the other falling back silently into the layer of fungi where it hung waist high, waiting to be covered with the green mold. "It wouldn't have held anyway," mumbled Reuben to himself, and there were no echoes from that. He was alone. The fire was nearly out and there was nothing more to feed it with.

And then he did think something. Looking at the chain he thought, The mockery. If I were strong I could climb up that chain, refasten it and climb down the other side. But of course I am not strong enough — no one here is. It would be suicide. Only someone healthy — someone who had just come in could maybe turn around and climb up. It would be possible, he thought . . . but it would never happen. The fire went completely out and he could no longer see the chain, the tractor . . . anything. It's better this way, thought Reuben . . . in the dark . . . like a dog. He sat down and leaned back against the base of the monument — the wet fungi. He shuddered once more and let the cold begin to numb his body, only now he didn't care, thinking, I will look like a Romantic. What mockery.

But this was not the end. Such things are inexhaustible; and in the total silence he heard a very peculiar noise, more like a moan than a scream, and more like a sigh than that, very faint. What can be worse, he thought, and stood up, cautiously stepping out into the utter darkness, following the sound, his feet never leaving the ground — sliding them along in front of him.

In this slow manner he continued on, stopping frequently because the noise, though increasingly louder, was infrequent. Just as he would be ready to give up the search he would hear it again, and this would propel him another eight or ten steps, where he would wait again for it to return.

He inched ahead, and after a very good distance Reuben sensed that the sound, though still very faint, was somewhere close around him. Yet it had an echo — a reverberation of its own, and as though inspired he fell down on all fours, moving ahead with his hands, thinking that whatever it was might be in a hole. And as with inspirations, he was right, and soon was feeling the edge of what seemed to be like some sort of well, built from street bricks. The sound was coming up from this hole, easily, as though whatever was making it was unaware of his listening. In his jacket pocket he could find nothing — only a dead horse (empty cigarette package, colloq.), and matches, which were not heavy enough. So he took off his belt and wound it into a spiral and dropped it down. After what he ascertained to be just over fifteen feet he heard it strike water. Silence then, momentarily; then up from the well came a real, honest scream and thrashing sounds from the water. There's something down there, Reuben decided, finally sure that there was in fact something alive, perhaps human, down in the pit, and not just meaningless noises coming up from somewhere, tricking him. He stood up.

Although walking for the most part faster back toward the monument, he found it a very long distance. Surely I'm not going the right way, he thought — the well couldn't have been this far away. But his sense of direction was uncanny and he walked straight into the wet fungi covering the base. Then on hands and knees he groped for that part of the chain connected to the tractor; found it, followed it to where it was fastened, flung the pin that held it aside, and began dragging it back to the well.

The second time was easier. The sounds were louder than before, and he knew what to expect. Finally close enough, he judged. He got down on his hands and knees, dragging the chain in jerking motionings with his right hand. Finding the edge of the hole, he began lowering the chain, slowing, thinking if he should call down something like, Grab hold of this, I'll pull you up. But he did not. He took off his shirt, which when lit smoldered more than burned, but gave some light.

After a while of continuous lowering, he began letting the

chain down in stages—four or five inches down and a little tug upward. He continued this until the thing in the well had taken hold and offered some resistance to the tugs upward. At this time it stopped screaming and Reuben stood up and began to pull, slowly, thinking that the creature would be bracing itself against the sides of the hole, and like a fly walking upward.

And Reuben then began to imagine: What could this be on the other end of the chain? Garbled, snarled sounds were coming up, heavy vowel noises that went on and on. Reuben became slightly afraid; then became terrified and pulled more slowly than before. What if he were letting loose some monster, some Grendel that had for years ravaged through the City; and that after several decades had been outwitted at great personal sacrifice to the people and trapped and thrown into the well, where for generations he had been unable to vindicate himself. He had heard no one speak of such a monster, however, but perhaps he had been imprisoned for so long that no one could remember him and his awful deeds; not even Mary.

He pulled up more slowly and the noises became more clear, Reuben recognized a design: the garbled sounds were attempts at pronouncing words. The phrasing and intonation guaranteed this. It was human—a woman, he thought—at least having feminine characteristics.

Still the sounds were unclear. Perhaps, he thought, in these times spent conversing with the walls of the well she had found a new language partially composed of her old one, and partially of the sound of echoes . . . and now she was trying to remember, and translate. He felt a new terror rise in him. Living in a well with several feet of water—how would she sleep, would she stand up all the time, letting the water eat into the skin in her legs and feet? Did the fear of dissolving drive her mad?

Surely she must be mad, he thought. She may try to kill me, to avenge herself on the one who would let her out. Mad people think like that. What would she look like when she came out?

Would she be grayish-white? Who would she expect to take care of her — keep her?

He pulled up slowly, more slowly than before. The words were becoming more clear and Reuben could make out two of them clearly . . . "I can. . . ." The rest was not intelligible. Then he saw her head; bald, though not necessarily from age but because of the water somehow making the hair come off. He lifted her — it was a woman — partially out of the well as she braced her swollen feet against the edge of the circular wall. Her face was in a hideous laugh, trying to thank him in this way . . . insanely from her joy; her legs and hips were swollen like an elephantiasis victim from the water, her eyes wide and crazy in the firelight. "I can tell you —" she clearly said and a deep sickness crept through Reuben. He let go of the chain. Her eyes flashed, and shrieking she fell back into the well.

He stood listening, and after the initial splash, heard nothing. He kicked down the smoldering shirt and the darkness returned.

Reuben walked back to the monument. He was walking uphill! How can this be, he thought. There is no reason for it. It must be a trick of perception. He sat down where he had been before he had heard the noise. This is the end, he thought; I have no hope of ever leaving.

Of course it is not to be inferred from this that Reuben did no longer care about escaping — that he did no longer want to; what it means is that Reuben had no hope of leaving . . . the way a farmer may dream — plan — and talk for hours about a cabin he is going to buy in the woods next to a clearbluewater lake, tell his friends about the fishing gear he intends to use to catch the smallmouth bass and how to find the big ones — at different times of the day. He could tell just what the forest would look like in the morning, before the dew was melted and was just beginning to bead, when the sun was red and outlined by a stretched amoeba-shaped area of light pink, then turquoise, exploding finally into the deep navy blue that covered all the rest. He would tell how in the middle of his pond you could look down and down and see the fish and turtles . . . how you could drop in a marble and watch it sink down for fifteen feet where not because of muck but because of the overbearing blues and reds (from the underside of water plants, or in the fall the reflection of silent floating leaves) between it and your eyes, it would sink out of sight. Though maybe having only been there once as a child, or never, he could tell how the sounds of his wife wading in the water, scaring frogs back into the pond and talking to their dog running along the bank, would come to him where he sat on the opposite side, and how the sound would be different with the weight of squirrel barking and chattering and at night loons, evening thrushes, and copper-throated warblers. His friends would come to visit him and sometimes they would hunt coon, with flashlights, but usually they would sit together on the porch, munching on handfuls of fresh radishes and popcorn, talking and telling stories that are half true and half more wonderful than things could ever be in actual living. He could tell you of the ice over the pond and how after a winter rain the wind blows the ice-coated branches together and his forest sounds like a million-stringed wind chime. He could tell you about talking to God there. And he would throttle anyone who would tell him that he would never get there . . . that it was all a fantasy. And yet with all this, still he might have no hope of ever leaving, or ever being able to keep from growing old and finally having his children set him in a brick house in town where he would not need to be watched after so closely. Reuben thought these things.

He felt cold. The darkness was so complete that he could not even see his hand pressed to touching his face. Looking down at his legs he could not tell where the black fog left off and he began. The cold was beginning to numb his senses, which finally amounted to his not being able to feel where he left off and the fog began. I'm dissolving, he thought with no consternation, and I have nothing left. If this is the end, then well, let it come on.

Silently, without even the tearing sound of the fungus being pulled apart from itself, the monument broke open and the two halves fell back aside. Faint traces of light crept in from outside. Reuben turned and looked and down through the thin wraithlike strands of fog that hovered around directly in front of the opening, came walking a man, older than Reuben, dressed in overalls and a gray hooded sweatshirt soiled on the sides by his hard hands having many times pulled it up around his face to shroud it from the winter. The turns of fog clung to his pant legs as he came straight into the opening. Reuben stood up and ran to him. "Wait," he shouted. "Don't go in there!"

This man looked at him but said nothing, his eyes gray, absolutely clear, as though they had always been outside watching and working, never having seen through glass; and he had always been so close to the world that even while he worked he could imagine nothing else, nothing better, nothing worse. He took a step forward.

"You stupid farmer. Don't go in there. Do you think anybody gives a good goddamn?" The man looked at Reuben and his face, filled with lines and hollows, was calm, and Reuben imagined that maybe his father had never looked like that, not even asleep, and that Reuben himself, in a lifetime could never look like that.

"Wait!" said Reuben. "I mean if you go in there . . . whatever you do . . . I'm going out. How could you expect me to do anything else?" But he knew when he asked. Nothing was expected of him. Nothing was asked. Reuben reached out to touch him, but didn't.

"But why would you do it? For me? . . . I mean if you think that I'll come back, you're crazy. Never! But why? Why? . . . There are so many better than me. I have a brother. I have a sister — I have a whole family that was that is, so much in the presence of God that they are like His fingers. Of His hands!" Reuben shouted, beginning to cry. "You stupid plow pusher. Don't go in there."

This man, shrouded by his sweatshirt, looked at Reuben and he, Reuben, believed he saw a smile, though his mouth did not move. He went then and walked into the City. Reuben walked out, turned and watched him disappear in the dark fog, stepping lightly on the bricks, the heavy air sucking around him, taking him in.

Walking up the incline he listened to the sound of a giant boulder being dropped several feet into a grass-lined pocket of earth, a terrible sound. Inside, he knew there would be echoes. He wondered if he would realize that he had been tricked. No, he thought, there are more kinds of things in this world than I could ever know . . . better things. And as if on the end car of that thought he walked out onto the street and the sun shone on him and he could see maybe three miles through the clean air to his house.

Epilogue

....

I AM ADJUSTING. I AM LEARNING HOW TO LIVE, HERE, THOUGH without a doubt it makes no difference, one way or another. This is not easy, and some days I am sure that I have it together, only to glance once too quickly to the side of me, and lose it . . . the thin balance between being so much myself that nothing matters but my own vision, and being nothing . . . so much of everything that it all, good and bad, passes through me without comment or concern. It is inevitable that I should have arrived here, at this finished, unfinished position. What next?

I looked for Tabor and found her by following a path laid out by a succession of forwarding addresses . . . following my own letter, so to say, in an apartment building with a private swimming pool that had been put in when the manager (or former manager) had imagined that he would have enough money for its upkeep (finally investing in a piece of blue-green plastic that perhaps from a blimp would look like water, which was put on top). I did not attempt to explain to her what it had been like. I was more transfixed on her boots, which didn't even look like leather and were red.

"Why did you buy those?" I asked.

"I don't know," she said, and I felt happy because of that . . . because what reason could there be for buying a pair of red, unleather boots; I mean that she could tell me.

"Do you want to get married?" I asked.

"I don't know. I'm not sure," she answered.

And so by more or less brute force we were married and I took her home with me to live with Nellie and Paul. I watch her. She seems restless and sometimes I think that she will leave us soon. I should pay more attention to her, if there is time. But if she leaves it will not be by train. They have closed them down. Tickie is dead and they have boarded up the station.

What next?

Whatever happens now will have to come here. It will of course; but it will have passed through many more places before it reaches Des Moines — though no one will believe that it is really happening . . . and then how long will it take to stretch out and devour the small towns?

There are small towns in Iowa. Gravel and broken blacktop highways spiral into these places, occupying in total somewhere near three hundred acres; a main street with one continually blinking yellow light that can be turned red by pushing a button on the pole at the level of a fourth-grader's shoulder . . . one-aisle drugstores that have cardboard boxes of used 45 rpm records for sale for twenty-five cents or obtainable through trade. Beside this is a restaurant that has also pool tables with leather pockets, pinball machines, a back room where old men play cards for pennies and nickels, calendars from the two-window bank across the street, gum-ball vendors, a display of combs, cigarette lighters, key chains with colored rabbits' feet, postcards, candy, and booths of red plastic and linoleum-covered tables. Next to the bank a Bible supplies store, a hardware store, and a things shop where you can buy plaster-of-paris praying hands that glow in the dark, pictures of children with very large eyes, and a choice of three hollow figurettes to set in your yard . . . a black midget in a monkey suit extending an invitation, plastic fawns, or models of chickens. One Ford auto and implement lot. Three gas stations and three taverns with salt pork rinds on the bar. All of this scattered down Main Street. (I must think of a way to get Walt out of there.)

From the front porch of any one of the houses in any one of these towns, in the summer, notice the insufferable wet heat curling up from the streets. Watch a fifteen-year-old girl walk toward the restaurant, wrapped in a towel, her hair dripping. Large, overfed, loud twelve-year-olds rush around her and careen into the door and up to the counter, clutching in their fingers pieces of sweating money. A bright orange automobile with chrome wheels comes meandering down Main Street with two youths in it. They stop and the fifteen-year-old walks up to it and they talk as though in secret in the middle of the street. Then they leave and roar down another several blocks and turn up to drive by the school — only to return again to Main Street, where for the most part they drive back and forth all day long, along with another dozen or so cars that do the same thing. At night more cars (and riders) join them, and at every intersection along the town they sit, lights off, motors running. Occasionally one will turn on his lights and race off into the country and return fifteen minutes later and take his place in the line.

From your porch you could watch a man, possibly your neighbor, walk across your lawn to enter his own: yellow, stovepipe western boots, a socket inside his mouth where he keeps a deposit of tobacco. Faded denim pants. Two cats indignantly get out of his way. He passes between two plastic fawns, past a large white house that has been abandoned because of the water pipes exploding while the owner, a retired farmer, spent his winter in Florida, past an empty doghouse, the occupant dead now two weeks, the covered space not yet filled by one of the many half-starving ancient dogs that ravage and bark in back of the Star Grocery Store, up to a blue trailer with dark rotting hay sagging at all places between its bottom and the ground — put up in the fall to protect against the wind and save money on heat, not taken away in the spring and now dark and foul. He walks inside and fetches a beer from the refrigerator and sits in the kitchen. His wife is small, thin and fierce, her curly red hair short, wearing bell-bottom pants, hard ironical speech with long sneering vowels.

"That Wilson kid shot Billy with an arrow today," she says.

"What am I suppose to do about it?"

"Nothin'. Bill!" she screams. Billy comes in the kitchen and stands as close to the door as he can and still be considered in the room. "Show Daddy," she shouts. Billy holds out his arm.

"Go over where he can see it, stupid," she commands. Billy walks.

"How'd you get that?"

"I told you," she answers for him. "That Wilson kid shot him." No one speaks and Billy leaves the room.

"I'm going to the stock car races tonight, in Newton," he says, and gets another beer.

"Well, Betty and I are going bowling."

He goes into the living room where his four children sit — the two younger ones in their underwear — and watch television, eating soggy potato chips.

These people do not sleep well — he better than she — for three or four hours a night. They are afraid of the police.

We, Paul and I, sit on the one remaining bench in the depot and wait . . . wait

I envision an Inquisition held by all the maimed, hungry, and desperate people of the earth. It will happen. They will rise up and group together. They will come into Des Moines. They will come from everywhere and they will reach out everywhere. No one will escape. They will carry us out of our homes and drag us down the streets, up winding staircases, and one at a time into tremendous stone rooms where they will sit in circular balconies looking down, their eyes gleaming, as we stand in the middle of the floor, alone. They will be very silent and then one, perhaps all, of them will cry down at us with one question: "What did you do to help?"

There will be many answers to this question and many tortures to fit the answers. Only several thousand of us will be left alive when they have finished cutting at us with piano wires and white-hot knives. Many of us will say "What could I do?" or "If only I'd . . ." or "Because of the way the world works, it . . ." or "In my own small way I . . ." or "One time when I was in my early twenties I . . ." or "I always cared, but . . ."

They will scream down to the guards to carry us away and instruct them to draw our deaths out until the pain becomes so terrible that by freeing one of our hands we will tear open our eyes and rip out our throats to end it.

I will say none of those things. They know now what I will tell them, and they are preparing for me. They are working night and day to devise a torture horrible enough for me, painful enough for me. I have one chance, however. I may escape if only Nellie is there to judge me. . . . If when I tell them that I made the world a little more beautiful Nellie is there among them.

When they come for me I will be hiding in the City. They will know I am there, of course; but they will believe me, Nellie, when I tell them that I have written this for you.

As a young man, **David Rhodes** worked in fields, hospitals, and factories across Iowa, nurturing his love of reading along the way. After receiving an MFA from the Iowa Writers' Workshop in 1971, he published three novels in rapid succession: *The Last Fair Deal Going Down* (Atlantic/Little, Brown, 1972), *The Easter House* (Harper & Row, 1974), and *Rock Island Line* (Harper & Row, 1975). A motorcycle accident in 1976 left him paralyzed from the chest down, which brought a temporary halt to his publishing career. In 2008, he returned to publication with *Driftless*, which has been heralded as a critical success and the "best work of fiction to come out of the Midwest in many years" *(Chicago Tribune)*. He lives with his wife, Edna, in rural Wisconsin.

More Fiction from David Rhodes

To order books, or for more information,
visit Milkweed Editions at www.milkweed.org,
or call (800) 520-6455.

Driftless

"Rhodes's fourth, and, I have to shout it out, finest book yet. *Driftless* is the best work of fiction to come out of the Midwest in many years." —*Chicago Tribune*

"*Driftless* is a fast-moving story about small town life with characters that seem to have walked off the pages of Edgar Lee Masters's *Spoon River Anthology*." —*Wall Street Journal*

Rock Island Line

"Wildly imaginative." —*Saturday Review*

"A kind of dark but luminous *Candide*, *Rock Island Line* is beautiful and haunting in a way you have not encountered before." —Jonathan Carroll, author of *The Ghost of Love*

The Easter House

"Murder, secrecy, even the names—C, Cell, The Associate— lend a surreal and peculiar air to bucolic Ontario. Rhodes' ultra-real hand painting of a tilted, mercurial world makes this novel a success." —*Star Tribune*

"I wouldn't trade a word of *The Easter House* for anything." —*New York Times Book Review*

Milkweed Editions

Founded in 1979, Milkweed Editions is one of the largest independent, nonprofit literary publishers in the United States. Milkweed publishes with the intention of making a humane impact on society, in the belief that good writing can transform the human heart and spirit.

Join Us

Milkweed depends on the generosity of foundations and individuals like you, in addition to the sales of its books. In an increasingly consolidated and bottom-line-driven publishing world, your support allows us to select and publish books on the basis of their literary quality and the depth of their message. Please visit our Web site (www.milkweed.org) or contact us at (800) 520-6455 to learn more about our donor program.

Milkweed Editions, a nonprofit publisher, gratefully acknowledges sustaining support from Emilie and Henry Buchwald; the Patrick and Aimee Butler Foundation; the Dougherty Family Foundation; the Ecolab Foundation; the General Mills Foundation; John and Joanne Gordon; William and Jeanne Grandy; the Jerome Foundation; Robert and Stephanie Karon; the Lerner Foundation; Sally Macut; Sanders and Tasha Marvin; the McKnight Foundation; Mid-Continent Engineering; the Minnesota State Arts Board, through an appropriation by the Minnesota State Legislature, a grant from the Wells Fargo Foundation Minnesota, and a grant from the National Endowment for the Arts; Kelly Morrison and John Willoughby; the National Endowment for the Arts, and the American Reinvestment and Recovery Act; the Navarre Corporation; Ann and Doug Ness; Jörg and Angie Pierach; the RBC Foundation USA; Ellen Sturgis; the Target Foundation; the James R. Thorpe Foundation; the Travelers Foundation; Moira and John Turner; and Edward and Jenny Wahl.

Interior design by Wendy Holdman
Typeset in Chaparral Pro
by BookMobile Design and Publishing Services
Printed on acid-free 100% post consumer waste paper
by Friesens Corporation

ENVIRONMENTAL BENEFITS STATEMENT

Milkweed Editions saved the following resources by printing the pages of this book on chlorine free paper made with 100% post-consumer waste.

TREES	WATER	SOLID WASTE	GREENHOUSE GASES
33	15,235	925	3,163
FULLY GROWN	GALLONS	POUNDS	POUNDS

Calculations based on research by Environmental Defense and the Paper Task Force.
Manufactured at Friesens Corporation